MERIDIAN

MERIDIAN

AMBER KIZER

delacorte press

Copyright © 2009 by Amber Kizer
All rights reserved. Published in the United States by Delacorte Press, an imprint of Random House Children's Books, a division of Random House, Inc., New York.

Delacorte Press is a registered trademark and the colophon is a trademark of Random House, Inc.

Visit us on the Web! www.randomhouse.com/teens
Educators and librarians, for a variety of teaching tools, visit us at
www.randomhouse.com/teachers

Library of Congress Cataloging-in-Publication Data
Kizer, Amber.
Meridian / Amber Kizer.
p.   cm.
Summary: On her sixteenth birthday, Meridian is whisked off to her great-aunt's home in Revelation, Colorado, where she learns that she is a Fenestra, the half-human, half-angel link between the living and the dead, and must learn to help human souls to the afterlife before the dark forces reach them.
ISBN 978-0-385-73668-8 (hardcover)—ISBN 978-0-385-90621-0 (lib. bdg.)—
ISBN 978-0-375-89263-9 (e-book)
[1. Angels—Fiction.   2. Supernatural—Fiction.   3. Death—Fiction.   4. Great-aunts—
Fiction.   5. Good and evil—Fiction.   6. Colorado—Fiction.]   I. Title.
PZ7.K6745Mer 2009
[Fic]—dc22
2008035666

The text of this book is set in 12.5-point Apollo MT.
Book design by Angela Carlino.
Printed in the United States of America

10   9   8   7   6   5   4   3
First Edition

To Miss Tara Kelly, a modern "Irish" blessing
for one of my best friends:

MAY THE ROAD ALWAYS BE ACCOMPANIED
BY MOVING SIDEWALKS.

MAY THE WIND NEVER KNOCK OUT THE POWER
OR RUIN YOUR UMBRELLA.

MAY THE SUN SHINE WARM UPON YOUR FACE,
BUT NOT SO WARM IT MAKES YOU CRISPY, AND MAY CURRENCY
IN ANY FORM FALL SOFT UPON YOUR BACKYARD.

MAY YOUR LIFE BE FULL OF KIND LAUGHTER
AND OF BOUNTIFUL LOVE.

MAY DIVO NEVER FAIL YOU DURING SWEEPS.

AND UNTIL WE MEET AGAIN,

MAY GOD TEASE SOMEONE ELSE
MORE DESERVING OF "ADVENTURE."

acknowledgments

For the friends and family who made the first book tour so special, thank you. Lynne Vasiliades, Kathy and Alyssa Wick, thank you for the laughs, the champagne, and the memories. "OnStar, anyone?" Lynda and Mike Marazzini, who braved Texas-sized traffic. Chris Rasmussen, who slogged through the wind and rain on a business trip to show up at a signing. Karla and Andy Gilbert, who risked ridicule carrying a Hello Kitty basket to a karaoke birthday party. To the friends of friends who came to support a stranger, your kindness exceeds my ability to express thanks: Jan Witsoe's friends, Megan, Gracyn, and Linda. Caren Kamlet and teens, Tammy Green, and the Johnsons from Houston. The Humphreys, the Giannis, Georgia and Mike Donnelly, Bonnie. Sue Owen. Liz Gallagher. JR, Linda, and Walker. Sarah LaMar. Barney Wick. Lynn and Katie James. Molly Malecki and David Waterman. Thank you all. Special thanks to: Gail LaForest, Computer MD; Lynne Malecki; Sue Wiant—congrats on your own, *Between the Bylines: A Father's Legacy*. To Greg Edson, Charles "Chaz" Foreman, Lizbely Rivera, Tyler Alder Breeze, Joshua Turner—and all our military men and women who make my job possible—my deepest and eternal gratitude to you all. To my boundaries advisor— thanks for the best two lines ever. Mom, thank you feels so inadequate—I love you.

In the economy of Nature nothing is ever lost.
I cannot believe that the soul of man
shall prove the one exception.

—Gene Stratton-Porter,
Afterword from *Jesus of the Emerald,* 1923

MERIDIAN

PROLOGUE

The first creatures to seek me were the insects; my parents cleaned the bassinet free of dead ants the morning after they brought me home from the hospital. My first word was "dead."

After age four, when I stepped out of bed one day and popped a giant toad like a water balloon, I never again turned any lights off.

For all of my sixth year, I slept sitting up, thinking I'd spot the dying coming toward me.

There were times when it felt like my insides were

full of broken glass, times when the souls of the animals passing through me felt too big, too much. I'd open my eyes in the morning and peer into the glassy gaze of a mouse on my pillow. Death never became my comfortable companion.

I didn't have nightmares about monsters; I wasn't afraid of a thing in my closet. In fact, there were many times when I wished they, the dying, would hide under my bed instead of burrowing into the pile of stuffed animals by my head.

My mother hugged me, told me I was special. I'd like to think my parents weren't revolted by me. But I'll never forget the feelings apparent in the glances they exchanged over my head. Worry. Fear. Repulsion. Concern.

My first chore was to clean up the carcasses. My second was to make the bed. I'd don rubber gloves and pick the dead up. My hands grew calloused from digging so many graves. We ran out of room in the backyard by my fourteenth birthday. When I was too ill to do it, my dad stepped in and removed them, always with thinly veiled disgust.

I trembled my way through the days, constantly sleep-deprived, chronically ill. My stomach always hurt. Low-grade headaches constantly thumped a slow tempo. Doctors labeled me a hypochondriac, or worse; still, they never found causes for the symptoms. The pain was real, the cause a mystery. They suggested shrinks. Perhaps I was one of those children who required lots of attention. I'd catch my mom staring at me—she often started conversations, only to break off and leave the room.

With each moon phase, each month that passed, the animals got bigger. Soon, they came not only at night but during the day as well. At school, kids whispered my nicknames: Reaper, Grave Digger, Witch. Other names I pretended not to hear. Adults ostracized me too. It hurt.

As I got older and stopped trying to bond, I came to the same conclusion as everyone else: I was weird. A freak. A sideshow act.

When my brother, Sam, was born, I kept a vigil in his room. Intent on cleaning up the dead things before he woke. I focused on making him feel like he wasn't alone, that I understood how scary this world could be. I wouldn't let him suffer my fears; he'd be normal in my eyes. By the time he was a month old and the only dead venturing near him came because of me, I retreated.

My parents pretended it didn't matter. That nothing ever died around me. That our backyard wasn't a cemetary. If anything, they acted like I had a talent. A gift.

If we had any extended family, I didn't know them. The exception was my namesake, a great-aunt who sent me a birthday quilt every year. My world was, and is, me and death. It's a lonely place to live, but I thought things were getting better.

My name is Meridian Sozu, and I was wrong.

CHAPTER I

I got up the morning of December twenty-first anticipating a four-day weekend for the Christmas holiday. I went to a snotty private prep school that took breaks the way most people went to the dentist—only when they really, really had to.

Which was why I had school on the twenty-first, my sixteenth birthday. My parents refused to let me skip. It was a typical, normal day. For me "normal" meant that my stomach churned so much I swallowed Tums by the roll, and never went anywhere without Advil. I used

Visine to keep my eyes clear; without it, looking in the mirror meant seeing the eyes of a lifetime alcoholic. I kept a stash of Ace bandages and braces in my locker at school.

I coped. I studied. I kept up the facade, but I desperately needed a break. Time to sleep late. Time to eat too much and catch up on painting my nails with glitter. Time to stop faking it and be myself, even if no one noticed. Time to dye my hair again—currently it was the obnoxious red of tomato juice. I figured black would be a nice way to start the New Year. It fit my mood. There were also a bunch of new DVDs I wanted to watch. Movies about girls my age having crushes and friends and being absolutely, completely normal.

I tucked my requisite white cotton blouse into my perfectly pleated tartan skirt. I applied thick black eyeliner and three coats of mascara, as if I could make the bruises beneath my eyes an accessory, then painted on clear lip gloss. I tugged at the opaque tights I wore, pushing our dress code to the limit. I didn't mind uniforms. At least I was part of a group for once in my life. But I hated looking like a little Lolita. I stared at my reflection, hoping to see answers. Wishing I saw the solution to my life.

The phone shrilled: once, twice. I tossed my toothbrush into the sink and grabbed the hallway extension. The phone never rang for me, but I always answered it, hoping.

"Hello?"

Silence. Breathing. Murmuring.

"Hello?" I repeated.

Mom appeared at the top of the stairs. "Who is it?" Concern deepened the lines on her face, aging her.

I shrugged at her, shook my head. "Hello?"

She yanked the phone cord out of the wall, breathing fast, suddenly wild-eyed and pale.

Dad raced up the stairs, clearly just as upset. "Another one?"

Mom's fist clenched the cord and she fiercely wrenched me into her arms. What the hell?

"What's going on?" I let her hold me as she caught her breath. My dad kept petting my hair. For the last five years, they hadn't touched me except for accidents or un-avoidables. Now they didn't seem to want to let go.

"It's started." Dad was the first to step away.

"What's started?" I pushed away as the downstairs phone rang.

"We'll talk more after school. You have a big test today." I recognized the stubborn expression on Mom's face.

Dad pressed her shoulders, rubbed her neck like he always did when she was upset. "I think we should—"

"No, not yet. Not yet," Mom chanted.

"What is going on?" I felt fear sizzle in my spine.

"Rosie—" Dad cradled Mom's cheek with one hand and reached for me.

"After school," Mom said firmly. "Be careful today, extra careful."

"Why don't you tell me why?" I asked. "Is this about turning sixteen? I can wait to get my license for a few months. I mean, I'd like to drive, but if you're this scared we can talk about it."

Mom smoothed my hair, shaking her head. "After school."

I shrugged and looked to my father for guidance. His expression told me he wouldn't break rank. "Is it boys? I'm not dating; it's not like there's a guy—"

Mom cut me off. "Do you want pancakes?"

I never eat breakfast. "No, that's okay. I should catch the bus or I'll be late." *What else can there be? My grades are excellent.*

"Mer-D!" Sammy launched himself at me. As a toddler he'd given me a nickname that stuck, so even now that he was six, I was still his Mer-D. "Happy birthday! I got you a presie. I got you a presie. Wanna know? Wanna know?" He danced with a maple syrup–covered fork, Jackson Pollocking every surface with stickiness.

"Later, Sammy. After school, okay? With cake?" I adored him. Loved him with the unconditional love I'd never received, except from him. He wasn't afraid of me. He'd pretend to blow up the dead things with his Lego men or pose them in little forts, like caricatures of life.

"Cake, cake, makey-cakey." He pranced around, his face split in a grin.

Turning back to my mom, "Why are you so freaked?" I dropped my voice so Sammy wouldn't hear me.

Dad answered for her. "There is something we need to discuss when you get home, but it can wait."

"Are you sure?" I pressed. I hadn't ever seen either of them this anxious.

"You don't want to miss your bus." Mom hovered. She'd been swinging from overprotective to distant for the past few months. There was an almost tangible distance between us. I'd catch her scrutinizing me, like she was trying to memorize my DNA.

"You have everything you need?" She stared at me, patted my hair, and tucked an errant curl behind my ear. She always made me want to shake my head and mess up my curls even more. Mom gave me a pathetic, sad smile. She didn't say anything else.

"Fine. Yep." I shrugged her off, marching out of the kitchen feeling like a kid at an adults-only party, pissed that they wouldn't just tell me what was going on. Secrets made me feel small and insignificant. There was a vibe I couldn't place. I slid my backpack on.

Dad strode out from the kitchen. "Meridian, wait." He drew me to him, hugging me so tight that breathing was a challenge.

"Dad?" I leaned away, confused.

At least Sammy wasn't acting strange. He was playing with the Lego set he'd opened the day before, on his birthday. My mom, brother, and I were all born within a day or two of one another.

I heard the bus clank down the street and I set off at a limping gallop without glancing back. The bus made a distinct chugging sound that made me want to hurry even when I was already waiting at the bus stop. *So*

Pavlov. My right knee felt stiff and swollen. I reached the stop as the doors opened; other prep kids got on in front of me. None of us spoke—or more accurately, everyone ignored me. Another day, another eye roll.

I passed my bio test. Turned in my English term paper about graphic novels as a new, Dickensian serial, listed two hundred countries and their capitals for a pop quiz in world history, and skipped lunch per usual since the cafeteria was a realm I avoided at all costs. When I wanted to evade the rest of humanity, I typically hung out backstage, in the costume room. Besides, that made it easier to hide the carcasses creeping in around me.

The bus rolled back to my stop at four-thirty. My mind raced. Four days off. I wanted to start doing nothing immediately. First order of business, dumping this utility uniform and boots. Kids poured off the bus behind me, all chatting incessantly. I almost broke into a flat-out bunny hop up the block to my house. A blue Mustang full of senior guys slowed as they hung out the windows and flirted with my bus mates. I felt invisible, but I listened with one ear as my house came into view.

A white SUV with tinted windows roared around the corner ahead. The driver had to see the Mustang and the group of teens in the middle of the road. I'd swear he sped up, accelerating as he raced toward me. I dropped my backpack, frozen with shock.

Mom must have been watching for me out the window. She ran out of the house yelling and waving her arms. Chills vibrated up my spine. Her voice broke my trance and I leapt out of the SUV's way, into some bushes, but the group of kids behind me was not so lucky.

I heard the impact of metal against metal. Glass cracking and breaking. Screams. I felt as if my arm were ripped out of its socket, as if there were no more oxygen left in my lungs.

The accident only lasted seconds, but the world around me slowed to a crawl. The SUV went into reverse and sped away, leaving the driver of the Mustang half inside the vehicle and half out. Crumpled metal littered the road like scattered tissue paper. A girl from my bio class lay motionless on the ground with others I didn't recognize. Lots of limbs lay at unnatural angles. Moans and groans from more victims meant they were alive. I moved toward the carnage to help when pain doubled me over. It felt like hot pokers piercing my eyes. Breathing became almost impossible. I fell to the road, tears streaking my cheeks as flashes of each person's life played like disjointed movie trailers in my mind.

Mom lifted and dragged me farther and farther away. Her words were jumbled, her tone frantic. Another spasm hit me. What was happening to me? Then, Dad was there too, placing me on the backseat of the family sedan. I held my stomach, my eyes tightly shut against the pain, bathed in sweat.

"Get her out of here. We're packed. Sam and I will meet you," Mom ordered my father, the car already moving. She yelled to me, "I love you, Meridian. Don't forget that!" Dad hit the gas.

He kept talking to me. Nonsense words. Assurances. Prayers. But I was in so much pain I barely heard him.

The farther we drove from the house and the wreck, the less tortured I felt. My breath came back; the pain receded like a tide going out. Finally, I was able to sit up and wipe my cheeks with a tissue Dad passed back.

"Better?" he asked, glancing at me in the rearview mirror.

I nodded, giving myself a moment to find my voice. "What's going on?"

"We've run out of time. Mom should have told you sooner. She should have explained. But she wanted you safe. Believe me, she wanted you to stay safe. And happy. To be a kid, for as long as possible."

He wasn't making sense. "What are you talking about?" I asked when he paused to catch a breath. It wasn't as if I'd ever been a safe, happy, normal kid.

"You're not human. Not *completely* human. You're special. That pain you felt was a human soul, I think. It's complicated."

Huh? I swallowed. "Dad, are you okay?"

"You have to leave, Meridian. You have to go to Auntie's house and learn how to do this thing."

"*What* thing?"

He blew out a frustrated huff of air. "I don't *know.* Your mother was supposed to explain it to you. I've never seen it before. All those years she knew the pain was real and never told me why until Thanksgiving when the calls started—"

I raised my voice to stop him. "She's not here! *You* are! What do you mean, I'm not human?"

We made eye contact in the rearview mirror. "You're an angel being called a Fenestra."

Clearly, I'd fallen asleep on the bus and this was a terribly odd nightmare. "Of course."

"I'm not insane, young lady." Dad gave me his best stern face and voice.

We drove into the Costco parking lot.

"Can you walk?" he asked me.

I felt sturdier, but the aches, like those of a tenacious influenza, still cramped my muscles.

Dad helped me to my feet and half-carried, half-hauled me through the long aisles of bulk goods. He kept glancing over his shoulder as if he expected to be followed. Luggage hung off his shoulders and bumped displays as we struggled to the back.

As we pushed through an exit marked Employees Only, a brisk wind ruffled my hair and chafed my cheeks. "Dad?"

A taxi was parked right outside the door. A scruffy skater type not much older than me got out and started transferring luggage, without a word, from Dad's hands to the taxi.

Dad's eyes were those of a trapped animal. "I have to get back to your mother and brother. Don't come home. We won't be there. Maybe someday we'll see you again. You will never be alone, Meridian. Never. We will love you always, but the rest of this journey you must take by yourself."

"What's happening? What's going on?" Tears threatened to choke off my voice.

Dad pointed at the cabdriver. "This is Gabe. He's going to drive you to the bus station. You need to get to Auntie."

"I'm going to Colorado?"

He nodded. "She'll be able to help you. But you must be very careful. Very, very careful. Stay away from people who are sick or dying, do you hear me? Run the other way from them until you get to Auntie's." His hands bruised my upper arms.

Nothing made sense.

"Promise me, Meridian, promise you'll stay away from the dying until you get to Auntie's." He shook me. "Promise!" I'd never witnessed such intensity on my father's face. He scared me.

"I—I—p-promise." I stuttered out the words.

"They've arrived." Gabe's scratchy smoker's voice broke the spell of my father's gaze.

"You have to go now. There's a letter for you in your coat."

I glanced into the back of the taxi and, blinking, finally recognized my duffle bag and camping backpack. "I don't want to go—"

"Trust me. You have to go." Dad kissed my forehead and pressed me into the back of the taxi. "Keep your head down. This will be over soon, I promise."

Before I could respond, he'd shut the door and disappeared back into the warehouse. "Dad? Daddy!" I yelled.

"You'd best be silent and lie down back there, or they'll see you," Gabe said, his eyes shifting in the rearview mirror.

"Who?"

"For lack of a better explanation, the bad guys."

"Bad guys?"

"You know what that makes you?" He gave me a feeble smile.

"Nuts?"

"Nope, one of the good ones." The taxi rumbled out of the parking lot and I rested my head in my hands. This had to be a dream. Didn't it?

CHAPTER 2

"Hey, kid, we're here." Gabe slowed and braked the taxi.

"Here?" I asked, not recognizing this part of town.

"The bus station. They'll probably be watching the airports. Put this on to cover your hair." He handed me a Portland Trail Blazers baseball cap. "There's money in the backpack, plus your ticket."

"Ticket?" I barely mimicked his words correctly. Try as I might, I couldn't quite wrap my mind around this.

"To wherever you're going." He unloaded stuff as I crawled from the taxi. I hurt. My mouth was parched.

"Where?" I asked. Had Dad said Colorado?

"I don't know. I don't want to know. Plausible denia-bility. I'm only doing a favor for a friend."

"Huh?"

"All I know is you help people get to heaven. Other than that, you need someone better informed."

I help people get to heaven? Is he a loon?

"There's a letter from your mom. Keep your head down, kid." He slammed the trunk closed and leveled a stare at me. "Get inside the station. Get on the bus. Pay at-tention. Got it?" Then he revved the engine and sped away, leaving me in the parking lot.

My arms screamed at the weight of my duffel and backpack, so I paused every few steps to catch my breath on the way into the terminal. I scanned the empty lobby and picked the far corner to camp in. I kept my back to the wall. *Whom am I watching for? Will I know them? Who is after me? And why?*

I rifled through the coat's pockets. It was a heavy win-ter coat I'd never seen before. If Mom hadn't written my name on the tag inside, I'd have assumed it belonged to a stranger.

The letter I found in my search of the pockets was written by my mom in her lyrical script. I loved her hand-writing. So fluid, so graceful. A pang of longing struck me as I began to read.

December Twenty-first
My Baby's Sixteenth Birthday

Dearest Meridian,

As hard as it is to write this letter, I know it is harder still for you to hold it, to read it. I know the sorrow in my heart is matched only by yours. I wish I could tell you not to be afraid. I've protected you all these years, and now I wonder if I didn't make your destiny more difficult, if my need to hang on to you as long as possible has placed you in great peril. There was never a good time. I kept thinking you'd ask me, demand to know more, but you simply accepted your life as normal. I know this is scary and unexpected. I hoped to travel with you to Auntie's this summer. To be with you. To help you. But we ran out of time and I hope someday you will forgive us. My darling girl, you are a woman now, and it's time you take your place as a Fenestra, a title I know you are unfamiliar with.

You are special, Meridian. You have always known this. And so have I. I knew the moment your cry sounded on midnight this day sixteen years ago that you were remarkable. A blood Fenestra, with Creator-given gifts and blessed talents. But with these comes immense responsibility, for true greatness demands great sacrifice.

The Creators will keep you safe on your journey. I do not know in what form they will appear, but I do know they will help you reach Auntie's. Know that we will see you again. If not in this lifetime, then on the other side. Know that you will be protected. Know that your journey is necessary and that others have felt what you are feeling. Though some aren't strong enough, I know you have the strength of a perfect diamond and the courage born of indelible compassion.

Learn everything you can from Auntie. Be kind to yourself. Listen to your inner voice. Know that we love you, always. We, too, have to flee to safety. Under no circumstances come home. It is empty.

You are going to Great-aunt Merry's home, in Revelation, Colorado. Get on the seven a.m. bus. Get off at the second stop after Walsenburg and watch for the green Land Rover. You'll know it when you see it. I have enclosed extra money in case you run into trouble or get hungry on the trip. I packed everything I think you'll want. Please forgive me if I overlooked a beloved token of your childhood. I did my best. Your father sends his love. Sam will miss you more than the rest of us combined, I fear. You are one of the Chosen, Meridian. For that I am both grateful and sorrowful. It means you must navigate your path without us, but know that I am always in your heart and you will always be in mine.

Your mother in this life,
Mom

I hugged my bags to me and read the letter over and over again. I memorized it, casting furtive glances at anyone who entered the dingy space. They all appeared normal and completely uninterested in me. Twelve hours to kill. When my stomach growled, I checked out the vending machines.

I plugged a dollar bill in and pressed the button for knockoff Hostess cupcakes. I leaned against the glass. The twirly thing caught on the edge of the packet before it could drop. *Figures.* Nothing was easy.

I slammed the side of my fist against the glass. "Come on!" I shouted and pounded again. Finally, the cupcakes fell into the well and I fished them out.

I tried to hum a few bars of "Happy Birthday," but I couldn't get past the first notes before tears clogged my throat and I was unable to breathe. *Useless.*

"Happy super sixteenth birthday, Meridian," I said, biting into the stale, waxy cupcake. I chewed and swallowed by rote, leaning back in the hard plastic chair and letting my head roll back. I studied the water stains on the ceiling high above me. They were the patina and sepia tones of ancient continental maps.

When I was little, Sam's age maybe, I studied the single photograph of Great-aunt Merry we had in the house. It was snapped during her days as a nurse during World War II. I used to study it to see if I looked like her. My namesake. But Mom hadn't acted like Great-aunt Merry was a real person, more like she was a fairy tale or a myth.

In my family, most of our birthdays were within three

days of one another's, except for Dad's. But I shared the same day with Auntie. I'd never met her, and frankly, it was creepy being named after someone alive. Like they're paying attention, making sure you live up to whatever it is they think *they* are.

Auntie left me alone except on my—our—birthday. She usually sent a quilt. They grew in size with me over the years. Created from intricately stitched, brightly colored tiny pieces of fabric, some were like impressionist paintings, others like photographs of places, people, and events I didn't recognize.

Each time I touched them, they seemed to tell a story. Like a tuning fork being struck, a hum vibrated up my arm. So I put them in the hall closet, and tried not to come into contact with them. There was nothing comforting about the stack of quilts; it made the little hairs on my body stand up as though an electrical storm hovered over me.

I jerked upright. Nothing had come this year. No package for me to open first thing in the morning. *She knows I'm coming? Is this part of a plan?* I resisted the urge to call my parents and ask. I inhaled ample breaths and tried to relax. Was my family really not home anymore?

The bus station smelled of sweaty dollar bills and despair. It reeked of loneliness and solitary travel. Hyped on adrenaline and not just a little fear, I resisted tumbling toward the edge of sleep.

I kept swiveling my head, thinking that if I could see

the threat coming I could do something brave and heroic, like get the hell out of the way. There were so few people in the station that I began to relax. Just a little.

Finally, the sun lit the edge of the horizon. The rapid-fire click of high heels broke the silence. The woman's raven hair, a color I could never find in a box, was tugged back into a tight bun. Her lips were bright fuchsia and her suit would have been a power suit in the fifties. It was well cared for, but the light blue fabric had faded to gray. She had a regal bearing, but it rang false to me as I studied the woven bag slung over her shoulder. She could carry the world in that bag.

The woman raced to the counter. Her hands did as much talking as her mouth, yet the bored ticket seller barely flicked his eyes away from the muted television with a grainy screen on the counter beside him.

The woman slapped the counter and stomped her heels, but her hodgepodge of Spanish and English didn't elicit much of a response from the clerk. Or maybe he chose not to understand her. I closed my eyes, leaned my head against my bags, and tried to tune out somebody else's problem.

What had Mom packed for me? How could she know what I needed in this situation?

The conversation at the counter escalated and the woman's gesticulations became more desperate. I didn't want to interfere. I'd studied five languages, but never actually used any of them. The clerk's voice went up an octave. The woman started to get hysterical. She didn't have enough money for the ticket.

Fine. I lumbered to a standing position. Let the blood drain south and bring the feet back online. I dragged my bags behind me, hoping if I walked slow enough the confrontation would be over by the time I'd shuffled those ten feet to the counter.

No dice. I asked if I could help.

The clerk's face bloomed with near-comic relief. "She insists on going to some place in Colorado, but she's forty bucks short. I can't sell her a ticket."

I explained this to the woman in my rudimentary Spanish. Her face lit up as if someone finally heard her. I listened as she poured out a river of story way too fast for me to catch. Her daughter was having babies—twins. She had no other money. Something about work and losing her job. She kept smiling at me, as if I could make it better.

This could be a trick. A story to sucker me. But I dug into my coat pockets.

Her name was Marcela Portalso. Forty bucks was everything to her. Surely Mom had given me more than two twenties for emergencies. I pushed the money under the glass partition.

"No, no," Señora Portalso protested.

"Por favor." Please.

She didn't want charity. A hard worker. No handouts.

I reached into my Spanish vocabulary and put together the words for *present* and *baby*. I have no idea if I said them in the right order.

The clerk shoved the ticket beneath the window. A

beautiful smile decorated the señora's face and she clutched the ticket like it was a gift from God.

Standing there, it was all I could do not to start crying for my own mother.

Señora Portalso insisted she would pay me back in Colorado City, or Denver, or Podunk. I wandered back to my corner. The minutes clicked by until finally they called our bus number. I stashed my duffel and backpack under the bus, inhaling exhaust as it idled. Ten other people crowded around, like a swarm of gnats, trying to be the first on. I hung back, feeling the need to keep my distance. I prayed they wouldn't talk to me. I didn't see any bad guys or speeding SUVs.

I didn't want to get on the bus at all. I wasn't a big traveler; my parents only tried a family vacation once and it ended horribly.

Señora Portalso patted the seat next to her with obvious enthusiasm when she saw me. As I settled into the cramped space, she tapped my hand. *"Muy linda,"* she kept saying. *"Luz! Luz!"*

Very pretty. Light. Light.

I stopped thanking her after the tenth time. I didn't have much to say. I was full of questions, but she couldn't answer any of them.

I slept fitfully as the winter sun rose high in the sky, then drifted behind storm clouds. The lights of the interstate flashed in bursts as we passed truck stops and rest areas. The inside of the bus was a dingier, more claustrophobic dark than that of any room I'd ever slept in. I kept my knees tucked up tight against the seat in front of me so my feet stayed off the floor.

Bits of conversation drifted through the darkened interior. "A job . . . family . . . never been to Colorado . . . heading to Disney World . . . nothing better to do . . ." They all had a reason, even if it wasn't a good one, to be heading out. And what was mine? *What happens if I stay on the bus? Go on to New York City or Miami? Will anyone notice? Will anyone care?*

We stopped at a couple of diners for pee breaks and to grab a quick snack. I came out of the bathroom at one place and heard a voice that sounded like my father's asking for more coffee. I whipped my head around, but it wasn't him. I kept an eye out for anyone following me; my father's ominous instructions to be careful echoed in my head.

In the early morning light, I split a sandwich with the señora, who gave me a mealy apple and several crumbly homemade cookies in return. The cookies reminded me of my mother. I swiped at tears that leaked from the corners of my eyes. What were my parents doing now? Were they okay? Was Sam more scared than me?

Oregon disappeared in the distance; Nevada and Utah came and went. Finally, we crossed the Colorado state line. In Durango, I ate a Milky Way. Mom wasn't here to tell me not to. Monte Vista was unremarkable; the snow picked up speed in Alamosa. In Walsenburg, we turned north, heading to Pueblo, but I watched for my stopas instructed. My heartbeat sped up. I watched the miles crawl by, barely seeing more than a thick cottony white.

What I could see were lighted, flashing billboards proclaiming, FIND SALVATION IN REVELATION and FAITH IS A LIFESTYLE FOR ETERNITY. They popped up every few miles. *Weird*. It felt a little like the Vegas Strip.

We drove into Revelation a full day after I'd gotten on the bus. Revelation, Colorado? Someone's idea of a joke, right? My school uniform was wrinkled and smudged with God knows what. My legs hurt from sitting all that time. I wanted a shower. Real sleep. Someone to tell me this was a mistake. *Ha-ha! Anyone?*

We climbed down off the bus as fat white snowflakes fell with an icy hush. They covered my hair and stuck in my eyelashes.

"Worst snowstorm in a century. Good thing we got here when we did; they're grounding the fleet until this blows over. Some fools are going to be spending Christmas in small towns they never wanted to see." The third driver of this trip cackled with mirth as he unloaded our bags. I wondered how he could find pleasure in other people's misery. I didn't ask.

I collected my bags; hefting them, I wondered how they had gained so much weight riding under the bus.

I was supposed to look for a green Land Rover. One I'd know when I saw it. With the flakes falling smaller but faster, I could barely make out the shapes of buses in the lot. White swirled everywhere. No sign of green anything.

Already my fingers and nose had that stiff, unreal

feeling of numbness. *I'll recognize* what *when I see it? A person? The Land Rover? Aunt Merry herself?*

"Better get inside before you freeze." The driver slapped the luggage bin closed and hocked spit onto a snowdrift before hustling on his way.

All the passengers raced inside, seeking light and heat. I stood alone. As always.

CHAPTER 3

Standing in the bleak alone of Revelation's bus terminal parking lot, I saw no answers, felt no epiphany.

I trudged into the overflowing terminal. Grumpy stranded travelers seemed surprised that it snowed in Colorado right before Christmas. An elderly man in a wheelchair fiddled with the oxygen tube in his nose, and the hair on the back of my neck suddenly stood up. I was swamped with the feeling of holding my breath too long underwater, as if every moment without an inhalation was one closer to full-out panic.

I'd felt this way at the car accident two days ago. My father's voice shouted in my head: "Promise you'll run. Run, Meridian, go!"

I had to get away. I needed to create distance between me and the dying man. Someone, some person was dying, and they'd hurt me. I turned in circles, searching for a safe place, but there was nothing. I wheezed, choking on my breath.

The old guy turned and stared in my direction. But not at me, past me, as if I weren't really standing there. His eyes widened and his hands reached toward me.

A sharp pain shot through my head and rippled down my arm. I started stumbling toward the exit. The man's family bustled around, a toddler threw a tantrum, and still the old man's gaze locked on me until he smiled.

The doors whooshed open and I tripped out into the snow. But I could breathe. The pull lessened and I kept going, backing away one step at a time. When I'd made it several blocks, I knelt and vomited in a curbside garbage can. I tasted blood. I grabbed a handful of what I hoped was clean snow and let it melt in my mouth until I could spit out the taste. Sweat beaded along my face and arms.

Placing one foot in front of the other, I pushed on until I found a bench in an ATM booth. I sat to gather my strength, closing my eyes against the waves of nausea and pain. An ambulance raced past me with its lights flashing. It stopped at the bus station. I waited until they'd loaded a stretcher into it and then I ambled back to the station. I didn't have another option.

"Meridian. Meridian." Hearing my name being yelled, I turned.

A heavily pregnant woman toddled behind Señora Portalso, waving her hands. I stopped. I'd forgotten the señora.

"I'm Dr. Portalso-Marquez. Thank you so much for helping my mother." She shook my hand and kissed my cheek.

"You're welcome." I cleared my throat, uncomfortable with the señora's scrutiny.

"She wants you to have this." Dr. Portalso-Marquez gestured to the señora, who nodded and handed me a fifty-dollar bill.

"I only gave her forty bucks," I said, trying to give the money back.

"Yes, but you shared your food and she wants to make sure you have enough to eat tonight. Are you okay? You don't look well."

What must they think of me? What must they assume? "Oh, I'm fine, thanks. I can't—"

"Please. Keep it. We have to get to the hospital—my contractions have started, I think." That explained the pain etched around her mouth and eyes. "Here's my card. If you need anything, please call me. My mother simply didn't receive the wire transfer before she left. She refuses to learn English." With a wave of her hand and a sigh, Dr. Portalso-Marquez turned to her mother.

"Thank you." I put the business card in my pocket along with the money. "I'm meeting someone." I needed to explain that I wasn't alone.

Señora Portalso leaned into her daughter and spoke rapidly. The young woman turned back to me and translated. "She wants you to know that she'll see you again." She shrugged, hesitating. "If you're sure you're okay?"

"*Bella, bella luz.*" Beautiful, beautiful light. The Señora tapped my cheek and the two women moved toward the wall of doors.

I wanted to ask what she knew about light. What did she see? But I kept my mouth shut and watched them walk away.

I stayed behind a post as people shook the snow from their coats and stomped their feet. No one surveyed the bus station like they were searching for a sixteen-year-old they'd never met. Evidently, no one expected me.

I sat for hours, eating Milky Ways and drinking ginger ale. I dredged out the paper Mom had written Auntie's address on:

EastMeetsWest
115 North South Road

I was torn between wanting to follow Mom's directions and thinking there was no way with this snow that a centurion was going to make it, even in a Land Rover.

An imposing black man marched toward me. I studied my bags, refusing to make eye contact. His vibe was dangerous—contained, in a way that felt protective and intimidating.

"You be needin' a cab, missy?" His thick African accent blew through me with power.

"Huh?" I asked, my gaze snapping to his.

"You be goin' someplace?" he said.

I peered up at the clock. Five hours, eight Milky Ways, ten packages of Doritos, and three ginger ales. I shifted against the pillar I'd been holding up with my back.

"Maybe." I didn't know if he was the "you'll know it," as in, you'll be asked point-blank, or if this was fate giving my tush a little push. *I can sit here and wait, or I can get myself to Auntie's house and demand answers.*

He scratched his chin and reached into his coat pocket but didn't take his spellbinding eyes off my face. "I make six trips to and from this place. You be sittin' here that whole time." He held out a photograph and shoved it under my nose. "My daughter Sofi. She's in Boston. Stuck in big nor'easter. I hope she not alone like you. I'm Josiah. Where your family? Where you need to go?"

What a question. Where is *my family?*

I'd never learned to trust my instincts. Did I even *possess* instincts? I didn't know if I could trust this man with midnight skin and golden eyes.

I wanted a bed, a shower, and broccoli, a weird thing to crave. I scrounged in my pocket for the paper. Worst-case scenario, he was a serial killer who preyed on stranded travelers with the help of blizzards. At least my death would end this.

"Okay. Sure. One Fifteen North South."

"The big place off Sixty-nine?" he asked.

"I guess."

His brow wrinkled, "You got family there?"

"My aunt." I swallowed.

"I drive you to the turnout, but snow too heavy out there for this little car to make it up the hill."

"You don't drive a Land Rover?" I asked, sure this man was my "you'll know."

His boundless laughter rolled over me as he bent and lifted my bags. "No, missy. An ol' Subaru. With older chains."

"Oh." I followed him. He was very talkative. He told me about his family, his daughter studying immigration law in Boston. I sat back and listened. I nodded and grunted when it was appropriate. He didn't ask many questions, but his voice seemed to chase the darkness away. We rolled by mounds of snow and plows passed us in both directions. I couldn't have said where we were if my life depended on it. And I was too tired to truly care.

"Here we go." He slowed the car to a stop and popped the trunk.

In the far distance, if I used my imagination, I could almost see the glow of lights. The driveway was covered in snowdrifts and icy patches.

"You sure?" I asked, reluctant to leave the heat of the car.

"I'm sure." He climbed out.

I tucked my scarf around my mouth and shoved my hands into my gloves. I glanced down at my very cute boots and wished I'd known to wear ski clothes. Not that I actually owned any. I wasn't dressed for a long hike in the snow. *Don't have a lot of choice, now, do I?*

Josiah hesitated at the trunk. "You certain? I can drop

you at a motel in town and you can phone your auntie." He seemed reluctant to strand me in the wilderness, in the obscurity of the unknown.

I put on a brave smile. "I'll be okay. Thank you." I held out the fifty dollars the señora had given me.

"Too much. A gift." He gave me a little bow and didn't touch the money.

"Thank you, but please take it," I insisted. "Send it to your daughter for a cab ride. She might need it."

" 'Kay." He scribbled on a scrap of paper and pressed it into my hand. "You need 'elp, you call me."

"Thank you." I pushed his makeshift card into my pocket and started up the driveway.

I couldn't see a house. There was nothing to make me think this was a good idea. I listened to the gears engage on the old, rusted Subaru and felt more than saw its taillights fade away. There was no point in glancing back. But my God, it required everything I had not to run after him and beg him to drive me all the way home.

CHAPTER 4

I slogged for ages. A lifetime. Until I finally had to rest, or collapse where I stood.

No stars lit the sky, and there was not enough ambient light to see beyond the fuzziest of shapes in front of me. Was this what blindness felt like? This powerless, sluggish nothingness?

"Aaaaaa-ooowwww." A wolf howled in my ear.

I leapt up, throwing snow every which way, my heart rattling and my breathing labored. Adrenaline pumped through me.

"Great, Meridian. Fall asleep in the snow. All you need is a damn book of matches and you're a fairy tale with a bad ending." I started walking again, towing my bags behind me.

The snow stopped and my visibility improved.

"You did not actually hear a wolf. You're tired. Delirious. And freezing to death. But you did not hear a wolf howl." I trudged on, lifting my knees to my chest, my lungs burning with the exertion.

The intermittent sound of running water forced me to pay attention to my feet. A stone bridge loomed ahead of me. It rose, curving above the earth as if it hovered above the influence of gravity. A brook tried to run through the icicles and ice-slicked rocks. Just a bit of water flowed without freezing.

I imagined this place lush and green, with birds and chipmunks in the trees around me. My stomach growled and the sound jerked me back. I shook it off, but then I heard the growl again, and it wasn't my stomach.

I turned in circles, trying to see the growling animal. "I'm not the only one hungry, am I?" I whispered, swallowing hard.

"Arrrrwwwllll."

The sound was terrible and ferocious, so beastly it shook me, vibrating down my spine. I was the rabbit for the wolf. I was the modern Little Red Riding Hood.

I grabbed my bags, hoping they might shield me from an attack, and stumbled up the road. Behind me the bushes rustled.

My legs refused to hold me up, they were so petrified. I fell, throwing my hands out in front of me. My knee hit the frozen ground and scraped across rocks hidden by the snow. I felt warmth trickle down my leg and saw the shadow of blood ooze from a gash.

"Ggggrrrrreeeeerrrr."

I peered into the night, unable to spot the growler. I hauled myself to my feet, abandoning my duffel. I ran, a half stumble, half lurch. I paused, heaving. My hands on my knees, I tried to hear above the rasping of my breath. Footsteps crunched. Closer.

I raised my head. In the distance, I saw the twinkle of lights. I heard voices floating on the wind. As I moved closer, shadows and shapes became things: a woodpile, a cart, a house and outbuildings.

The house was monstrous, with turrets and gables and massive chimneys. Light poured from the porch and the downstairs windows, turning the snow to butter. A green Land Rover languished by the side of the house.

"Help!" I shouted, sounding like a mouse with laryngitis.

"She's been waiting for hours—"

"If you'd let me keep four spares, rather than having to repair these—"

"Who keeps four spares?" The lilting notes of a flute-like voice came from behind the SUV.

A low rumble answered it. "Someone who's been getting their tires slashed a lot should think about it."

"They'd simply slash the new ones, too. But you're

right. Get spares as soon as possible. What must she be thinking?"

I turned the corner of the Land Rover and slumped against its side. "Excu—" I couldn't get the words out, so I tried to knock on the side of the vehicle to attract their attention. What little energy I had left seeped through my feet into the snow. My eyes wouldn't stay open for longer than nanoseconds.

They didn't hear me. Then a crashing came through the woods behind me, and I turned to see a giant wolf launch itself at me. I screamed, I think. I'm not sure.

The wolf grabbed a boot attached to a twill-clad leg that protruded from under the SUV, and began tugging.

A body pushed itself out from under the car. A boy unfolded to a height of over six feet. I glimpsed inky black hair, cheekbones like razors, hands the size of dinner plates. He was so tall my neck complained.

"See, I told you she'd show up." His low baritone grumbled almost like the wolf's growl.

I held on tighter to the side of the Rover. "I—"

"Dear me, she's half-frozen." Bright colors fluttered toward me.

"She could have put more clothes on. You said her mom was going to pack bags with what she needed. Where are they?"

I swallowed, tried to point behind me as the world tilted, and darkened at the edges. I opened my mouth to speak, but the world went black.

CHAPTER 5

I dreamed in detail so real that I smelled, tasted, and touched. My parents sat in a full amphitheater watching me with thousands of others. I was center stage, spotlighted with too-bright lights. If I squinted hard enough, I saw the outlines of individual people in the audience. I felt their collective breath held tight as they waited to see my performance. But I didn't know what I was supposed to do.

I held a harp, then a needle, then a gun. With every blink, the contents in my hands changed.

Someone tried to push me off the stage. I didn't want to go. I fought. Then I heard applause and fell into the orchestra pit, kept falling. I fell through space so infinite and black and so full of nothing that it felt heavy like liquid steel.

I gasped and opened my eyes. I stared up at a canopy of luxurious blue silk, my breath ragged like I'd been sprinting from the devil himself.

"Easy, little one." Bright blue eyes and platinum hair filled my vision. "I'm your auntie. You're going to be all right."

I blinked and tried to find myself under the stacks of blankets. My skin tingled and itched.

"Unless we have to amputate your left foot because of frostbite." The lanky giant carried in a tray. He seemed standoffish. Not that I blamed him—we didn't know each other. Yet somehow he felt familiar to me. The aroma of fresh chicken soup with parsley and celery filled the small space.

Panic must have shown on my face, because Auntie scolded, "Tens, don't tease her." She brushed her hand over my leg. "Your foot is simply a little bitten."

He snorted, not the least bit concerned. "She deserves it, hiking two miles in the snow in a miniskirt."

I didn't realize I gripped the wolf's fur in my right hand until it pushed against my arm. I jerked my hand away.

"Don't worry, dear, she's adopted you. Picky one, our Custos; she doesn't usually like strangers."

"Eats them for breakfast usually. Good thing you got

here so late." Only the barest hint of a smile appeared on Tens's lips. His sense of humor definitely needed work.

"Tens!" Auntie admonished him as I pushed myself up to a sitting position. "Custos won't bite you," she told me. "Probably." Auntie fluffed the pillows behind my head, creating a cloud of musty, damp air.

A fire roared in the hearth, its snap and crackle making me feel like I'd been sucked into a time warp. Auntie drew up a chair and motioned Tens closer. "This is Tens, Meridian, my guy Friday and a stand-up comic on the weekends."

He disconcerted me, made me want to stammer and stutter. He put the tray in my lap and moved away like I was contagious. "Here. Eat."

I realized then that I was only dressed in a T-shirt— not even one I recognized. The thought that this hot guy, who couldn't seem to stand me, might have seen me naked sent the blood rushing to my cheeks. My hand shook and I put the spoon down before I spilled any soup. "What am I doing here?"

Custos whined and sidled closer to the bed, as if she wanted permission to join me. I felt safer with her than I did with Tens.

"She doesn't bite me." He smirked as he bent down to pat Custos, causing my embarrassment to run even wilder.

"What?" I asked.

"Custos. She doesn't bite people she likes." Turning his back to me, he poked at the fire.

"Great. But what is going on?"

"She seems to like you." He said it in such a way that it made me think he didn't agree with the wolf, or with anyone else for that matter.

"Thanks. I get it. Will you answer me?" I gave up and lifted the spoon with nary a rattle.

Auntie clucked and cooed. "Tens, stop teasing her. Don't mind him, little one. Eat your soup before it gets as cold as you were. Then you can tell us about your adventure. I'm sorry we weren't there to pick you up. I wanted to be."

Tens grunted. He muttered something under his breath that sounded suspiciously like "suicide attempt."

"Tens," Auntie admonished him again, iron lacing her words. This time he sprang to his feet and stalked from the room, slamming the door behind him. He startled me so that I sloshed the soup down the front of my shirt.

"Crap," I said as Auntie mopped at me. She handed me another shirt I didn't recognize to change into. How long since I'd eaten real food? Days? "Why weren't you there? What am I?"

She ignored my questions and kept up a steady stream of chatter about nothing and everything, as if I'd pressed play on my iPod. I didn't catch most of it because I was too busy trying not to spill more soup. I'd never tasted anything as delicious as that soup, but as much as I wanted seconds I didn't ask. "What's a Fenestra? Where are my parents?" I gave up asking questions after she blithely sidestepped them.

It was hard to stay irritated, because I felt a calming,

almost hypnotic peace in her presence. She only needed occasional grunts from me to keep talking. Soon, I fell back into that black oblivion.

I woke with the feeling that I'd slept too long and missed an important event. The fire burned low in the grate, but it was bright enough that I saw two piles of clothes stacked on a chair. I gazed around the room. The floral wallpaper could have come straight from George Washington's house. The hearth and mantel were glossy white. Antique furniture in varying shades of brown was scattered around the room. The huge four-poster bed felt like a lake. Velvets and brocades hung about the room, and a stale, seldom-used smell clung to the sheets. I stretched, languid and content, until I spotted my favorite childhood stuffed rabbit propped against the pillows. And several framed family photos perched on the nightstand next to me.

My mother's smiling face brought reality crashing back. I wanted to huddle under the covers and hope this was all a bad dream, but it wasn't my style to hide—I hoped. Did I even *have* a style?

I recognized my clothes in the piles and realized I'd have to thank Tens for yet another rescue. I couldn't imagine Auntie slogging through the snow for my stuff. I didn't want to owe him anything. I slid to a standing position and wiggled my toes. They were sore and bruised, like I'd sprained them.

I dressed in panties and my comfiest bra, my favorite pair of jeans, a thermal henley, and the red cashmere sweater my parents gave me last Christmas. Not the most stylish outfit. I'm unusually tiny for my age—unlike the rest of my tall, sturdy family, I could pass for an elf. Or a third grader with boobs. For a minute I considered changing, until I caught myself thinking about impressing Tens and shuddered. *Great. A crush on a man who hates me. That's self-inflicted pain.* If he didn't like what he saw . . . well, I already knew he didn't like what he saw. He probably liked exceptionally tall, athletic blondes with fabulous tans.

There was no clock in the room, and my watch wasn't on my wrist. I tugged back the heavy curtains to see if the sun was out, but the pitch-black outside sucked the light from the fire behind me. A shiver danced along my spine. How long had I slept?

Scratching at the bedroom door interrupted my thoughts.

I cracked open the door, my legs wobbly. The snorting snout of the wolf pressed into the opening, wedging it further so she could get into the room. She leapt onto the bed and wagged her tail. Her face bloomed with an almost human smile and she peered at me with questioning eyes.

"I'm not getting back into bed," I said to her.

She sat down, planting her butt right on my pillow.

"Nice, thanks." I grabbed a pair of thick woolly socks and jerked them onto my feet. I paused, not sure if I was allowed to leave the room, not sure what prompted me to wonder why I shouldn't.

The silence in the house was a physical presence. As if a thousand stories were being whispered too quietly to make out the individual words. But I felt the emotion of them. A thousand individual conversations just out of reach. I shivered.

"Are you coming or not?" I pointed to the door and moved ahead of Custos, not glancing back, knowing she saw more than I wanted anyone to see.

CHAPTER 6

The sconces in the hallway were dim. My skin crawled like it was trying to get away from the shadows. A thick, well-worn flowered carpet stretched down the center of the hallway, drawing me along. I tiptoed for no good reason, creeping like an intruder. Feeling as if I was being studied, I kept checking behind me.

Gloomy wood hid corners and paneled the walls. Quilts of all shapes and sizes hung along the corridor. Spiders danced in the creases and dust darkened the molding in drifts. There were no clocks. Paintings graced the walls, partially covered by quilts, as though the subjects felt the wintertime cold.

I kept seeing movement in my peripheral vision, a shadow that spun one way and then another—I was unable to catch it square on. Whatever it was, I couldn't make myself turn my head fast enough to get a good look. Maybe I was losing my mind.

Custos padded along next to me, silent and watchful. She no longer scared me. Her thick caramel fur was dusted with black tips, and a stripe of black painting her in halves ran down her back from her nose to the tip of her tail. She wore a black mask like a bandit and had golden eyes that seemed to glow. Her tongue had a spot of black in the middle, like she'd sucked on a pen.

The farther down the hallway I trooped, the more quilts I passed. Stacks of them, as well as pillow covers and chairs with quilted seats. I felt as if I were moving through one of those glass-beaded kaleidoscopes I'd had as a kid.

I found myself at the top of a massive curving staircase. Lights from below flickered through the banisters, creating leaping deer and round-eyed owls along the walls.

Custos nudged me and flitted down the stairs. I followed, happy enough to let a wolf make this decision.

I peeked around a corner into a spacious living room. The only quilts here were folded along the back of an antique horsehair sofa. Vibrant emerald velvet wing chairs sat on either side of a marble fireplace. An enormous fir tree was lit with real candles and ancient glass bulbs in every color of the rainbow. Was it Christmas already?

"Well, if it isn't Sleeping Beauty."

I swallowed, feeling Tens's dislike of me pulse through the room. I wish I knew what I'd done to make him hate me. "I guess that makes you the beast, huh?"

"Funny. You hungry?" He turned and headed down a hallway. Custos trotted along beside him.

"Traitor," I muttered.

I trailed behind. The scents of cinnamon, vanilla, and fresh-baked bread made my stomach growl.

"She's hungry, at least," Tens said, as we entered the kitchen. "Hope she likes to eat Bambi." He extracted a jug of orange juice from the refrigerator and gulped from it greedily as I leaned against the doorframe.

"That's enough." Auntie's voice held a lilt of age and steel. "Hello, little one. Are you feeling more like yourself?" She briskly took my face in her hands, peering up into my eyes. I hadn't noticed how short she was earlier.

"I guess." I hadn't the first clue how to answer that question.

"You'll be hungry. Sit."

My mind turned to the candles burning unattended on the tree in the parlor. My mother was adamant that candles were for emergencies only, never to be left unattended. I couldn't handle fire casually because I didn't know anyone who did. "Are you sure we shouldn't blow out the candles?"

"Pooh, that's a fresh tree. They won't be burning

down this house tonight. It's Christmas Eve, child. It's tradition." Auntie grinned and brushed my hair back.

"Oh." Christmas Eve. How fast things changed. I wondered where my parents were and what Sam was doing tonight. He used to sneak into my room to try to stay awake to see Santa. What would he do tonight? Would he try to stay up? Would he miss me? I didn't know what he'd asked Santa for. Had he not told me or had I simply not listened?

Auntie shooed me to a seat at an old mahogany farm table and placed a thick slab of bread in front of me. She slathered on the butter as if I were an invalid. "I can do it." I reached for the knife.

She handed it to me. "Of course, of course. You gave us such a fright."

"Sorry." I felt like the apology was expected.

"You have questions, I know." Auntie spooned thick brown stew into a crockery bowl.

"Yep, she looks like a war refugee," Tens piped up from the background.

Great, I look that bad? Why did I care? I shot him a glare I hoped he felt like a slap.

"There'll be Christmas cookies for dessert if you like. Dig in. We ate earlier. Tens, pour me tea, please, and grab a grape soda for Meridian."

I glanced up with a questioning look. How did she know I liked grape soda?

"We all do, dear." She patted my hand and stirred four heaping spoonfuls of sugar into a mug that held a concotion that appeared more like licorice pudding than tea. "Tens, sit with us."

He straddled a chair backward as if he wanted to put the back of the chair between us.

I shoveled stew into my mouth, refusing to contemplate Tens's comment about Bambi. I chased it with a large bite of the best-tasting bread I'd ever had in my life. I was nearly finished lapping up the last of the broth when I realized they were both gawking at me like they'd never seen anyone eat. I couldn't remember the last time I'd been that hungry, nor that mannerless. "Sorry." I abruptly stopped and inhaled.

"I'm glad it tasted good to you. You've had a long journey, one that'll be longer yet." Auntie sipped her tea, but didn't offer any explanation.

I couldn't hold back any longer. "What am I doing here? Who are you? I mean, I know you're my great-aunt, my namesake, but I've never met you. What is happening to me? Why did my parents toss me in a cab and make me trek across the country to some godforsaken castle in the middle of freakin' nowhere and then you"—I paused long enough to point a finger at Tens—"make nasty comments and stare at me all woogy eyed and smirky and you"—swinging my attention back to Auntie—"act like I'm just here visiting on holiday and you"—focusing on Custos, who had been asleep on the floor by the kitchen sink—"nearly kill me in the blizzard and then decide we're friends. We're not friends."

CHAPTER 7

I continued, unable to stave off the flow of questions, "Where are my parents and when do I get to see them again? And what the hell is a Fenestra? I don't want to be one. I don't want to have anything to do with it." I pushed back my chair and leaned against the table, then swung back to Tens. "And if you're not nicer to me I'll just wiggle my eyebrows or purse my lips or whatever the hell I do to kill everything around me and then you'll be dead. And then we'll see who gets the last laugh." I deflated, flopping back down into my chair, exhausted and not just a little mortified.

Tens had the audacity to smile at me like I'd made him the prince of Egypt. I growled. I actually growled like a damn dog. "I told you I should have gone to Portland to get her," he said to Auntie. "We teens don't do what we're told anymore—we expect an explanation."

Auntie nodded at him, unruffled. "Perhaps. Well, I see we've got work to do. I do so love this time of year. Tens, get Meridian some of that cocoa and bring another cup of tea for me into the parlor, please. It'll be a long night. Come along, dear child, and let's see if I can't unravel some of that thread that's knotted in your brain."

Auntie had a surprisingly strong grip as she tugged on my elbow.

Custos scratched at the kitchen door and Auntie opened it for her absently while she muttered, "Where to start, where to start? Send her to me completely unaware? What in Gabriel's legacy were they thinking? Have they told you nothing? This is the information age, for Creator's sake."

She positioned me by the fire and tucked one of the numberless quilts around my shoulders. The food kicked in; I finally felt more like a human being and less like a bitchy zombie.

"Where do I start? I've never done this before. Never had to." She seemed frail. For a moment it was as if all the life left in her diminished into that one question.

I wasn't feeling nice, but I was tired of being angry. "Why don't you start at the beginning?"

Auntie lowered herself into a rocking chair and set a

soothing, slow rhythm with her feet. "What do you know of your history? Religion? Politics?"

What a question. School? What does school have to do with this? "I'm a good student. I've paid attention, I guess. I get As."

"Hmmm. And did you never wonder why dead things accumulated in your presence?"

"She just thought she was a freak." Tens handed me a mug. He was too perceptive for comfort. "Right?"

I scooted deeper into the couch and quilt. "Don't I . . ." I swallowed, but forced out the question. ". . . kill them?"

"No! No!" Auntie leapt up, almost spilling her drink. "Your mother, I could spank her. How could she let you think that?"

"I never asked." But yeah, I'd wondered that too. Weren't my deathly skills a rather huge elephant to ignore?

"Do you know the law of conservation of energy?" she asked.

"Energy cannot be created or destroyed, but can change its form?"

"Exactly." I had pleased her with my answer. "Do you understand that hot air rises and cool air sinks?"

"I guess." Color me crazy, but this sounded a hell of a lot like a couple of science lectures I'd already heard.

She pursed her lips, "Have you ever examined a dead thing?"

"I've seen plenty."

"Yes, but have you studied them? Really examined

them? The thing that makes life, that breathes substance into a form is energy. When that body—be it animal or human—when that shell, that carcass dies, the energy in it rises like heat."

She paused as if waiting for me to make an acknowledgment.

"You are *not* death. You do *not* bring death, you do *not* control it, you *cannot* change the destiny of that fate. You could administer lifesaving measures like CPR, but if that soul is ready to rise, then nothing you, or I, can do will stop it."

"If I'm not death, than what am I?"

"You're a Fenestra, a window. An open attic window, in the tallest of houses, for the transition of life energy into the purest, best world possible."

"You're a door to paradise—the afterlife—Supergirl." Tens tossed a handful of mixed nuts into his mouth and chomped down. I hated how calm he appeared.

"Right." Thinking he was messing with me, I let sarcasm color my tone.

Auntie smiled at me. "You don't believe."

I shrugged. "It's the best definition I've gotten yet, but I mean really, would *you* believe you?" ·

"Probably not." Tens shrugged.

"Why haven't I heard about Fenestras?" I asked.

"Because people don't live to talk about them?" Tens grabbed another handful of nuts.

I rolled my eyes at him.

Auntie picked through the nuts and collected a

handful of cashews. "We're protected. By the Creators. By a special group called Protectors."

"Uh-huh, and am I human, or from Mars?"

Auntie giggled like a schoolgirl. "Mars?"

"You're from Venus, Supergirl, or haven't you heard?" Tens tossed out.

"Shut up," I snapped. "Just stop teasing me."

He quirked a brow at me, but fell silent.

"Life all started in the same place, with the same Creator."

"God?"

Auntie smiled at me. "There are many names, from many cultures and traditions. Though the names are almost infinite in number, none of them truly call the Creator or Creators by their full being."

I rubbed my temples. "Now you're sounding like a fortune cookie."

"Religion isn't what we're about. It's bigger than the human idea of rituals. We're created to help souls move on to what Buddhists call enlightenment, what Christians call heaven, and so on."

"Everything is about religion." This I knew from world history. Wars, genocides—they all led back to beliefs and man's intolerance for his own organized religion.

"That may be, but Fenestras are not affiliated with a specific branch of belief. Neither are the Protectors, though human aids are often very spiritual people. Nor are the Aternocti, for that matter, but they come from the Destroyers' side."

"But people will hate you anyway," Tens said with a scowl.

I wanted to ask what he meant, but his face was so closed, so shuttered I didn't dare. "Where did they come from?"

"*We* came from a blending of angel and human DNA," Auntie said.

"Huh?"

"Sangre angels used to do the work, used to be there for every transition, but as the population of humans grew there weren't enough of them to keep up. Plus, they were needed for other things—to keep the balance."

"But you said energy doesn't change."

"It changes forms, but never disappears or appears. If a being dies without a Fenestra or an Aternocti present, it circles again."

"Reincarnation?"

"Yes."

"What are the Aterwhats?" I was beginning to feel as if I were trapped in a *Star Wars* movie.

"That's another discussion, but they carry souls into the lightless place."

"Hell," Tens tossed at me.

Auntie shrugged in agreement. "To a transitional soul, you appear as light. A bright white tunnel."

"Don't tell me the 'go to the light' thing someone always says to dying people in movies is accurate." I was trapped in a Lifetime special.

"In a way. To the living world, you appear human.

Except for a few little things, we live our lives as most of humanity lives theirs."

"What little things?"

"You'll begin to see your light out of your peripheral vision, and there are humans who can see it as well."

"Now I'm a glowworm?" I shook my head. "What else?"

"Do you have any photographs from your childhood?" Even though Auntie had asked the question, she clearly already knew the answer.

I thought about it. I didn't. Something always happened to the film, or we had plans when class photos were being taken. I couldn't think of a single photograph I was present in. "No."

"That's one of the little things."

"Speaking of family photos, why the cloak-and-dagger journey to the middle of nowhere? Where are my parents?" I glanced between Auntie and Tens, their faces a study of secrets and stubbornness.

The silence stretched.

I repeated my question. "Where is my family? Who is after us?"

"They're not after your parents," Tens replied. "Just you. The Aternocti hunt Fenestras before they've reached their full power. Did you move a lot as a kid?"

"Yeah, Dad kept changing jobs."

Tens shook his head. "Maybe, but it was mainly so they'd keep you alive until you turned sixteen."

"Are you kidding me?"

"No, sorry. They moved again right after you left the house. That car crash wasn't an accident, Meridian. The best way to kill a Fenestra is to make a human soul try to pass through her before she's ready."

Did the teenagers in the crash die because of me? "What happens?" *Did I want to know?*

Auntie jumped in. "There are things you must know. Methods of coping that you can only learn from another Fenestra. When you turned sixteen, the window opened fully—at that moment human souls needing to pass over began to sense you. Before then, your window was only a crack that insects and small animals squeezed through."

"What if I don't want to be one?" I asked.

"You *are* one."

"But what if I close the window or put a sign out that says 'Go somewhere else'?"

"You'll die."

"Excuse me?"

"You'll die. It's really quite simple. Either you learn to do what you were born for or you'll be sucked through when the right soul passes through you. There's a third option. . . ."

I stopped breathing for a stuttering second. I couldn't possibly have heard correctly. "Die?"

"Auntie." Tens's voice was sharp and commanding.

"What's the third option?" I asked.

Auntie let Tens answer. "You figure out how to be a Fenestra or you'll be towed through." He stared me down.

"Yes, dear, it's rather simple." Auntie patted my hand

like she'd just told me I couldn't have more candy. "I'm quite sleepy all of a sudden."

Tens jumped up, rushing to cover Auntie with one of her quilts and raise her feet to an ottoman. The concern on his face seemed disproportionate to an old lady's feeling tired.

"Shoo." She batted his hands away. "Take Meridian and give her a tour. Go for a walk. I'll be fine, Tens. It's not time yet."

"Time?" I asked, but no one answered me. I couldn't quite get past "you'll die."

CHAPTER 8

Tens was about as talkative as dirt as we walked around the drafty rooms. I peeked at him from beneath my eyelashes, trying to figure out his deal. "So . . . ," I said, trying to fill the awkward space. "Are you—"

"Nope."

I nodded. "A cousin?"

"Nope."

"And she's not insane?"

"Nope."

"Do you have something against me?"

"No—"

"—ope," I finished for him, grabbing his forearm to stop him. I gazed at Tens, trying to decipher whether he was friend or foe. Then a thought wiggled behind my eyes. "How did you know about the car crash that happened right before I came here? Did my parents call?"

He sighed. "I could tell you that your parents called to say you were on your way."

"But?" My instincts screamed I might not like the answer, but I needed to know it.

"How strong are you, Supergirl?"

Not very. "Enough," I answered.

"I know things. Before they happen. Even when they happen somewhere far away. I just know them."

"How?"

He licked his lips and crossed his arms. I could tell he was trying to decide how much to say.

"Do you read minds? Do you know what I'm thinking?" Heat stole across my face.

He smiled at me. "It'd be fun to tell you I could, but no. It's not like that."

I let a huge wave of relief sweep over me. "Oh. So then, what?"

"Dreams. Feelings." He opened French doors and pointed down a long hallway. "This wing is unused. We usually keep these doors closed because of the heating. There are probably critters living in it. I'd stay out."

"Okay. What about your—" I had to jog to keep up

61

with his long-legged sprint. Clearly, he wanted to get this over with as quickly as possible.

"Up this staircase is another bunch of rooms. Again, don't go up there—"

"You're not going to fully answer me, are you?"

"In here is the gallery; that's the library/study. Back here is the kitchen." He went upstairs and downstairs and through hallways so quickly, I spent more time watching my feet than thinking about his evasion. "Up that staircase and down the hallway is your bedroom. Auntie's is almost directly below yours on the second floor. Mine is back there." He pointed in a general direction as if he didn't want me to know where to find him.

"So then, what—"

Abruptly, we were back in the kitchen. Sweat beaded my forehead and my legs ached.

Tens turned away from me. "There's a ton of stuff I have to do, okay?"

"I'll help." I wanted to drag an explanation out of him.

"You wash dishes?"

"Sure." I thought maybe I'd wash and he'd dry and we'd have time to talk things through. But less than ten minutes later I found myself alone, wearing yellow rubber gloves, staring at a pile of food-caked pots and pans.

Custos whined at my elbow.

"I don't think he wants to talk, do you?" I asked her as she sat and leaned into me. By the time the kitchen was clean, my back ached and my head throbbed. I got a bowl of cookies and a glass of milk to carry up to my room. I tossed a cookie to Custos, and she caught it in midair with a smile. Despite the tour, I got lost trying to find the bedroom I'd slept in. When I finally found it, I picked at the piles of clothes, feeling homesick, missing my family. I held a sweater to my nose and inhaled, but I couldn't even smell home anymore.

What the hell was happening to me?

How would I ever find them again?

Was I allowed to?

* * *

I slept without dreaming for the first time in ages. "Merry Christmas. Where's Auntie?" I yawned, wandering back into the kitchen. I finally felt human. Although, *was* I human?

"Sleep okay, Supergirl? You're chipper for a Christmas without Santa." Tens used tongs to flip over the bacon sizzling on the stove. He looked domestic. I expected him to think cooking was beneath him, but he seemed very much at home.

"So, where is Auntie?" I asked.

"Out."

I sat at the table and studied him. He paid no attention to me. I could have been invisible.

"Do you like it here?"

"It's fine," he muttered.

I let silence expand between us until I couldn't tolerate it anymore. "Why don't you look at me?"

"Ego much?" he asked, not turning.

"I don't mean I'm gorgeous, but you avoid me. It's not contagious." I stopped, temporarily flummoxed by the idea. "Oh my God, is it contagious?" The shock in my voice most have distressed Tens, because he came and sat next to me.

He hesitated, as if he didn't know how to comfort me. In the end, he didn't touch me. "You're born, not infected," he said. "I have my reasons. None of which are because you're a Fenestra. Drink some OJ, it's fresh-squeezed." He scrambled away from me to pour a glass.

I snorted. "Fresh? What man squeezes fresh OJ?"

"Don't tell me you buy that crap stereotype that guys eat cold beans out of a can?"

"Only the straight ones." I grinned, but it came off more like teeth-baring. He didn't respond. "Fresh-squeezed, huh?" I sipped. "Good."

Tens dished up scrambled eggs, an English muffin, a couple of sausage links, and bacon. "Eat up. Auntie left you lesson number one."

The smell of food made my stomach turn. "I don't want breakfast."

"You need to eat."

"I never eat breakfast. Seriously, never. If I eat it I'll probably just puke all over you." Even if I was hungry, his I-know-what's-best-for-you tone made me want to be ornery.

I saw a flash of hurt cross his face. He ran water in the sink and started scrubbing the frying pan.

I closed my eyes, wondering when I'd morphed into a total harpy. "Look, I'm sorry."

"I get it," he grunted.

"You do? Because I don't. I'm not a mean person, but you make me mad."

He kept scrubbing the pan. It had to be clean by now. "You're cornered. I haven't exactly cut you a lot of slack either."

I swallowed more juice, enjoying its sweetness and its bite. "No, you haven't. Why don't you like me?"

He paused, but continued to stare out the window instead of at me. "I don't dislike you."

"Riiiight."

"Listen, I—" He broke off and gulped a deep breath. "I-if you can't . . . If you don't . . ."

I waited. I barely inhaled, afraid I'd scare him into keeping his mouth shut.

Tens shook his head as if losing an argument with himself. "I won't force you to eat. When you're finished with the juice, I have something Auntie asked me to give you. It's not a present or anything."

"Whatever."

A loud clanging erupted, like the Tin Man had fallen into a pile of pots and pans. I leapt to my feet. "What is that?"

Tens chuckled, already moving into the hallway. "The phone. Auntie asked me to tweak it so she could hear it anywhere in the house."

"I think they heard it in Alaska." I followed him.

"Hello?" Tension jerked his body tight as he held the receiver against his ear. I could almost see his wiry muscles coiling to attack. "Answer me!" He dropped his voice to a whisper, so I moved closer. "Listen up, you piece of shit. Knock it off." Tens slammed the phone into the cradle and rubbed his hands over his face.

"What was that?"

"A telemarketer."

"Hmm . . . really?"

He exhaled. "No. Auntie's been getting hang-up calls and weird breathing on the line. Sometimes a robotic voice recites Bible verses. The calls are coming more often."

"It's probably kids."

"Maybe."

"You don't think so?"

"No, I don't."

"Oh." I hadn't expected him to actually answer the question. "Then what is it?"

"What is it? It's time for you to work on lesson number one."

"Where is Auntie anyway?"

"She went into town for groceries and thread before the stores close until after the first of the year."

"Why didn't we go with her? Why didn't *you* go? The weather can't be much better for driving than it was when I got here."

"She instructed me to stay here. With you."

An unspoken statement lingered just behind his words.

I nodded.

He sighed. "Listen, there are things you don't know."

"So tell me." I pleaded.

"I made a promise that I wouldn't tell you anything until Auntie thinks you're ready. But I think you should be prepared."

"Prepared? You make it sound like we're going to war."

"Things have been escalating the past several months with a local cult that masquerades as a legitimate evangelical congregation. There's a minister who is really good at convincing people to do things. He has it in for anybody who doesn't see the world his way." Tens paused and frowned. "Or it could be something else entirely."

"What else?"

"When you were home, did you get any phone calls?" He asked like he already knew the answer.

"No—oh my God. Yes. Lots in the weeks before my birthday. My mom freaked out completely." It felt like a lifetime ago.

"The Aternocti are hunting you. They know where Auntie is."

"So they know where I am." I closed my eyes.

"That's what I'm thinking. And I don't have the first fucking clue how to keep them from hurting us."

"Oh."

He rubbed his hands through his hair. "Don't tell her I told you. Be careful, okay? Keep your eyes open."

A church cult. The devil's minions. "Anyone else?" I asked, only half kidding.

He didn't smile. "I don't know for sure." He held my gaze and I felt an odd shimmy in my stomach. I didn't want to glance away, but I knew I wasn't the least bit invisible to Tens. He seemed to see all of me, and that knowledge made me nervous.

The Land Rover drove into the yard.

"She's back," I said.

Tens shoved his arms into a down coat and slammed out the door to help Auntie. I wondered if he ever did anything quietly. I unpacked groceries as Tens brought them in, three or four bags at a time.

"Just leave the jerky and dried fruit in a bag or two, okay?" he said.

"Okay." Whatever. I wasn't going to steal dried venison or banana chips in the middle of the night.

"Hello, little one. Did you sleep okay?" Auntie brushed my cheek with her lips and I caught a whiff of fresh-cut grass and apple blossoms.

"Yes, thanks."

She turned to Tens. "I heard Peggy and Ruth talking. Winnie, she's a neighbor, has pneumonia. I'm going to go visit her, see if there's anything I can do for the family. It's so hard on the living when the dying pick holidays."

"Okay." Tens studied her for a minute. I couldn't decipher his silence.

Auntie shook her head carefully as if calling off a pitch. "Did you find what I asked you to?"

"Yep, they're ready for you." He leaned against the counter and crossed his arms. Apprehension radiated from him.

"My timing is perfect, then. Come." She patted my cheek and tugged me along to the parlor.

CHAPTER 9

"You have to practice consciously opening your window. Visualization is your biggest tool for coping. If you believe the soul can easily flow through you, then odds are it will. You have to live mindfully. Sit," Auntie commanded as she motioned to a wingback chair.

I perched on the edge of the seat, nervous about this first lesson. *What if I'm not good at it?* "Don't animals die around me all the time? What's the problem?"

"You're sick because they pushed through and tangled in your energy. You have to give the soul the exit, or they'll keep hurting you. It's about giving them the right-of-way, of yielding. Now that you've turned sixteen, all souls, of every size, can sense you—humans especially. And until you're able to control your own energy, to open and close the window for yourself, you're in danger." Auntie brushed at my curls.

Tens lingered in the doorway, watching.

"Close your eyes. Which is your favorite season?" she asked.

"Summer."

"Okay, I want you to visualize an open window. A breeze is blowing, it feels cool against the heat of the sun. You want to feel the breeze so the energy disperses as quickly as possible. Okay? What color are the curtains?" Auntie asked.

"Curtains?" I cracked an eye open.

"Put curtains on the window. It makes it more real. Reality is in the details. Remember that." She put her hand over my eyes.

"Okay. They're white lace."

"Good. The curtains are rustling in the breeze. It's a big window. With a view of?" She let the question dangle.

"Oh. A sunset?"

"A sunset it is. Picture yourself in the room with the window, but you've moved far enough back from the window that you don't feel the breeze. You love this room, you're content in this room, you never want to leave this room. What's on the other side of the window, the view, will be determined by the soul passing through you. Just go with whatever you see when that happens. Don't fight it."

I pictured my bedroom at home. I felt safe there. "Okay."

"Now you're going to focus on the window and staying on this side, right? There's plenty of room to go through it—it's a big window—but you like seeing the sunset from here."

This all felt very Sci Fi Channel to me. "Okay."

"Now, keep that up until Tens tells you to stop. I can't stay here or my own power will interfere with you using yours. I need to go pay my respects to my neighbor. Winnie was a good friend for many years. She won't be alive tomorrow."

"Can I come with you?" I opened one eye again only to have her put my own hands over them.

"No, you're not ready yet. We need to start you small. I think Winnie might grab hold of you and keep going. I'll be back by dinner. Keep watching that window until Tens thinks—"

"I'm good." I had a feeling I'd be sitting here until she came back if I listened to him.

I heard the Land Rover start up and spin off. I counted to ten. Then to ten again. I opened my eyes and found Tens watching me. The expression in his eyes made blood rush to my face and brightened the tips of my ears with heat. "Okay, I'm done." I stood up and stretched my aching muscles.

"You sure?"

"Am I sure I'm done visualizing a window? Yes, I'm finished."

"Okay then, wait here."

"What?"

"There's more to do. I'll be right back."

I wandered off, listening to him grumble and head outside.

I was sitting on the couch flipping through an old photo album when he returned holding a pile of rags. "What's that?"

"Lesson number two. Baby bunnies. Help them transition." He said this so matter-of-factly that I wondered if I'd misheard him.

"What?" I stiffened.

"Custos found them this morning. Their mother was already frozen."

"And you want me to . . ." He had to be playing an elaborate joke on me. No way had Auntie suggested he hand me orphaned bunnies to kill.

"Visualize the window."

I inched back into the far corner of the couch. The stink of rabbit urine and feces began wafting around the room. "You're serious, aren't you? There really are bunnies in there."

"What about this made you think I was kidding?" He peeled back a few layers of cloth to reveal four perfectly formed brown baby bunnies with white paws and white blazes down their foreheads.

My heart broke. They looked like my favorite stuffed animal. "You're sick. I'm not doing it." I leapt up, wanting space between us.

Tens laid the bundle of rags in front of me. "You don't have to do anything."

"I have to let them die. I won't. Not so I can practice." Why didn't this bother him more?

"Animals die around you all the time. They're going to die anyway."

"Not if I can help it. I don't stand by and watch. I don't *help* them die." I tore down the hallway to the kitchen with Tens hot on my tail.

"What are you doing?"

"I'm searching for milk. Condensed milk, or cream, or *something*." I threw open cabinets and shoved cans around.

"Meridian. Stop." Tens paused in the doorway, keeping his distance as if I were rabid.

"No. I'm not going to just stand there and watch them die." I found a can of condensed milk in the far reaches of a cupboard and ripped off the lid. I grabbed a spoon.

"It won't matter."

"You don't know that. You don't!"

He stood in my way, blocking the doorway. "I do."

"Get out of my way!" I tried to push past him but tears blurred my vision.

He grabbed my shoulders. It was the first time he'd voluntarily touched me since the night I arrived. "Meridian." His voice broke, and for a moment it sounded as if he was going to cry too.

"What?" I knew I sounded like a petulant toddler, but I couldn't help it.

"You need a medicine dropper. Second drawer down, by the stove." He whispered this, gently turning me around. I don't know what made him stop fighting me, but I wasn't going to argue.

I snatched up the dropper and ducked under his arm. In the living room, I tried unsuccessfully to pick up the bundle while carrying the open can of milk and the dropper.

Tens was right beside me. "Where do you want them?"

"By the fire."

I noticed how gently he cradled the baby rabbits, lovingly setting them on the carpet in front of the fire. I sank to the floor and lifted one up. Its bitty body made my hand seem enormous. A tiny bundle of fur and the faintest heartbeat. "Come on, baby, eat. You have to eat." I placed a dropperful of milk against its mouth, but it wouldn't open. Tears pooled in my eyes and ran down my cheeks.

I kept trying to force milk into the closed mouth. I knelt on the floor, hovering over it, as if by positioning myself I could convince the little bunny to live.

Tens sat down behind me and leaned against a chair. Then he tugged me to lean back against him. "They were out there too long, Meridian. Their mom was cold. They haven't been weaned yet."

I closed my eyes as I sat and stroked the babies, hoping they could feel my desire for them to live. But my gut told me none of them would eat.

Tens was solid and warm. The fire heated my face and made my cheeks glow. With each breath I inhaled the pine, earth, and manly spice that made up Tens's aroma. If I paid attention, I could even smell Custos tangled up in his scent.

The fire died down. The flames got smaller and the coals glowed. But Tens didn't shift or suggest I'd tried long enough.

I felt the faintest shiver, the smallest energy change. I did as Auntie instructed, opening a window in my mind and picturing myself on this earthly side of it. I sat there holding the baby until it was cold, then I picked up the next one, and the next. Eventually, they were all cold.

"They're gone." Tens brushed my hair out of my eyes. "I'm sorry."

I put them down, nestled them into the bundle of rags. "Why are you being so nice to me?"

I felt him shrug. "I know what's it like to fight something you can't win."

"What?"

He didn't answer. Instead he asked, "Do you feel sick? Headache? Nausea?"

I closed my eyes and tried to breathe as bile rose in the back of my throat. Lying, I said, "I'm okay. Sad, I guess, but okay."

"Are you sure? You're a little green. Paler than normal and definitely green."

"No, I'm fine." My gag reflex threatened.

He heaved a sigh as if my answer was vitally important. "That's good, then. Right?"

I was about to throw up. I didn't want to puke. I *really* didn't want to puke. I tried to inhale past it.

Tens continued, accepting my answer at face value. "Don't you get sick? Have pain and stuff? That's what Auntie said."

There was a connection between the pain, the illness, and being a Fenestra. I wasn't simply a walking malady. I stood, quickly, trying to make it to the bathroom in time.

"Meri—"

I raced to a huge vase and leaned over it, puking up last night's cookies. I heaved until there was nothing left.

"Here." Tens helped me lie down and returned from the bathroom with a cool cloth for my face. "I guess we've got practicing to do, huh?" He slid a wingback chair next to the sofa and perched on it.

All I felt at the moment was a sensation like when the elevator drops out, that weightless free falling for a second or less.

"I'm okay," I said, feeling him study me.

"That's what you said before."

"I know, but I need space."

"Okay." Tens began gathering the bunnies up.

"Where are you going?" I asked.

"I'm going to bury them. Call for Custos. Then I have the next lesson for you."

"What?"

"Custos's dinner tonight is chicken. I'm going to butcher the hens, you'll help them cross, Custos'll eat them."

"No way—"

"Are you a vegetarian?"

That sounded more and more appealing. "No, but—"

"Neither is she. You need the practice with animals, Meridian. Before—"

"I know, but—"

"Meet me outside in a minute, okay?"

I knew he was right. I ate chicken. The least I should be able to do was watch him kill one. "How?"

"How what?"

"How are you going to, you know . . ."

"Break the neck. It's quick, so you'll have to be on your toes."

I nodded. "Give me a few minutes, okay?"

"Don't be long. This needs to be easy."

Easy? Was he kidding?

CHAPTER 10

Tens cleaned up outside while Custos munched on the chickens. Nothing was wasted, and I'd actually done it. Barely. I was tired, but I didn't puke this time and my neck didn't hurt, which was an improvement over the bunnies. And the two hens were now safely in a lovely meadow across the way.

Auntie was still at the neighbors' and I was anxious to report my progress to her. Custos needing fresh meat was entirely different from baby-anything. After grabbing a glass of juice, I wandered around the house.

The terrible clanging of the phone made me jump out of my skin. I ignored it, hoping Tens would return soon. It stopped.

I picked up a heavy silver frame with a photograph of Auntie and a man I didn't recognize, both smiling.

The phone rang again. Fifteen times. I counted each ring while I watched out the window for Tens. It finally stopped.

Five minutes passed before it started up again. "Crap." By the twelfth ring, I couldn't stand it and went to stand in front of the phone.

The ringing stopped. I turned to walk away and it started again.

I inhaled and picked up the phone. "Hello?"

"Meridian."

I didn't recognize the tinny electronic voice. *A man's?*

"Who is this?" I felt fear choke my throat.

"We're watching you. Tick tock."

"Who is this?"

"We're waiting for you in the darkness. Tickety—"

I slammed down the phone, trying to calm my heartbeat and my breathing.

Tens walked in and dropped his gloves and coat on the floor as he hurried to reach my side. "What happened?"

"The phone."

"Who called?"

"I don't know." I was still answering Tens's questions when Auntie got home. "I don't know," I kept repeating.

Auntie rubbed my hands between hers as Tens filled

her in. She nodded. "I see. That fits with gossip Winnie's daughter passed along. Meridian, you've come during a very volatile time in this community. This church—"

"It's a cult," Tens interrupted. "It's not a church."

Auntie fluttered her hands. "The leader, Reverend Perimo, is very charismatic and convincing. He calls it the Church of Forging Purity. He uses the Old Testament to turn back the clock on progress and to help people find blame for their dire circumstances."

"Sounds peachy," I said.

"Did you see the billboards coming into town?"

"That's him?" I asked. "He's all movie-star-meets-plastic-surgery. He's a pastor?"

Tens scowled. "Using the term loosely, yeah."

Auntie sighed. "His sermon for Christmas was about cleaning up the town. He predicted God's wrath visited on outsiders and nonbelievers. He spoke of getting rid of the unrighteous, the unclean by Epiphany. He's told people the end days will start in Revelation; he's backed his claim up with signs that he mysteriously predicts ahead of time. Epiphany is the newest date he's received from above."

"What is that, January sixth? That's not far away. Are they serious?"

Auntie sat down and picked up her sewing. She started talking, disregarding me, her fingers stitching as though they belonged to a robot. "January sixth is the supposed baptism of Christ—combine that with the New Year and it's a powerful time. The Hansons' cattle were poisoned last week. They lost half the herd, and that's only the most recent event. Perimo has instituted a prayer list of people whose souls are in the most danger. Guess who's at the top of the list for pagan practices and witchcraft?"

"He didn't." Tens stabbed his knife into the floor.

"You?" I asked.

She nodded. "There are many who want us dead. Human and not."

"Are we evil?"

"Heavens no, child. But people fear death, and loved ones often see us at the bedsides of the dying. It's easy in grief to give explanation to the wrong things."

"Blame by association?" I asked.

"Especially at this time in history. There was a time when death was longed for and celebrated."

"Why?" Who wanted death? Who longs for an ending?

"Life was harder. People grew weary or pained. The old called open their own windows with a purpose. The sick cast about till they, too, found a way. The soul was ready and willing to rest, to try again later. Death was merely a new beginning. But now . . ." She trailed off.

"Now?" I prompted her.

"Now there are those who fear death more than anything. Other souls have everything they want right here. Plenty to eat. Health. Wealth. They get greedy. There are those who think if they get rid of us, they'll get rid of death itself."

"But could they really get rid of death?" I asked.

Auntie shook her head. "No, of course not. Death isn't

us. We aren't bringers of it, nor do we hasten it. We are the pillows, the blankets, the hugs that accompany the sleep of death. Yes, that's it, we are the comfort. Our presence helps a soul find eternal peace." She paused. "Then there are those who work not for the Creators but for the Destroyers, trying to tip the balance away from the light."

"The Aternocti are hunting us, aren't they?" I asked.

She nodded. "Tens?"

I blanched. "Sorry," I muttered to him.

Tens snorted, but didn't glance up from whittling pieces of wood.

"Tens, how much have you told her?" Auntie asked in an ominous tone.

He set down his tools and stilled, staring first at me, then at Auntie. He shook his head. "Not all of it."

"There's more?" I asked, my head already reeling.

Auntie nodded. "Yes, death isn't the only choice you're faced with."

Tens sprang to his feet and began pacing. "It's not viable. You shouldn't even tell her."

Auntie put down her sewing and calmly said, "It's not up to you. You can't force Meridian—"

He growled in frustration. "I know, but . . ."

My gaze bounced back and forth, watching one and then the other.

"Trust—" Auntie broke off as headlights drew up to the house and car doors slammed.

Tens walked to the window and stared out. "It's the sheriff." He went to open the door.

Auntie wobbled as she got to her feet. "Oh my."

"Are you okay?" I asked, reaching for her elbow to steady her.

"Let's see what Sheriff Michaels has to say."

Tens opened the door and the sheriff nodded at each of us. "Evening, Mrs. Fulbright. Tens. Miss." He didn't bother to come into the house. "Have you seen Celia Smithson wandering through your property tonight?"

"No. What's going on?"

"Seems the girl is missing. She was snowmobiling with her older brother and wandered off. He thought she'd gotten a ride home, so we don't know how long she's been missing. They were around the outskirts of where their property meets yours. Thought maybe you'd know something. Girl won't live the night if we don't find her soon."

"Tens, get a chair." I clasped Auntie to me, supporting her weight as she seemed to collapse with this news.

The sheriff helped me hold her in the foyer while Tens brought over a chair.

"I'm fine. Stop fussing." Auntie batted us away.

"You almost fell over!" I shushed her.

"I'm fine. You have to go scout for Celia. She's a precious girl. Lovely. So full of life." Auntie pushed away our hands. "I'm fine. Tired, maybe."

"Will you stay here and rest?" Tens knelt in front of her. His eyes shone with concern.

She patted his hair. "Promise. Take Meridian and go check the property."

"You be careful out there. I don't need my team

searching for you, too. Take a rest, Mrs. Fulbright." Sheriff Michaels tipped his hat and shut the front door as he left.

"I'm fine. Go," Auntie told Tens.

"Okay. You ready for this?" Tens asked me, already pulling on his thick-soled boots and snowpants.

I nodded, trying to at least project confidence, even if I didn't feel any.

"Your mother shipped ski gear in the fall. It should all fit." Auntie pointed to a hall closet.

I rummaged through an assortment of outfits I had shopped for online before school started—Mom had told me she wanted to plan a family ski vacation for winter break. That trip never materialized. How long had Mom been planning this?

Tens hesitated and shared a glance with Auntie. "What if we find Celia and she's dy—"

"She won't be," I interjected. I wasn't willing to go out there already believing it was too late for the little girl.

"It would be very dangerous if that's the case." Auntie struggled to stand. "You're right, I should go instead."

"No!" I shouted. "I'll be fine. And so will she. You'll see. We will *all* be okay."

Auntie nodded. Though she still seemed concerned, she didn't argue. I shot Tens a black stare. Regardless of the danger, a tiny, frail old lady wasn't stronger going out into the snowy wilderness than me.

"If you're ready?" Tens opened the back door.

"Ready." I donned the last of the black and emerald gear. "How do you walk in this stuff?"

"You get used to it." Tens smiled at my stiff-legged waddle. "Let's go."

* * *

We plunged into the snowdrifts at the back of the property, stumbling. The air squeezed my lungs with its crispness. We called "Celia!" every ten feet or so as we walked parallel to the stone bridge, listening to the creek bubble and ice crack in the distance. The world was so beautiful, bright snow covering it all. There were birds everywhere in the late afternoon, chirping and flying, an angel choir with wings. I wanted to pretend we were strolling for the beauty instead of seeking a lost and probably terrified little girl. I hoped she was alive.

I sucked in the fresh air, enduring the unfamiliar snap in my lungs. A light sweat broke out along my brow. I followed Tens along deer tracks and deeper into the forest.

"Celia!" Tens yelled.

"Celia?" I called.

I stopped to listen. I heard something. A whimper. "Did you hear that, Tens?"

"No. Hey, I'm going to head over to the left here. There are Anasazi caves she might have crawled into. Keep me in sight at all times, okay?" He loped off, easily cutting through the snow when he didn't have to worry about me keeping up.

I pushed through the muscle burn and aches. My body wasn't used to exercise. Concentrating on listening and watching, in addition to wading through the snow, was almost more than I could handle. A sound made me freeze in place. I was sure I'd heard something. I wasn't moving until I was positive it wasn't Celia. "Hello?" I whistled, too. "Is someone out there? I'm a friend."

Tens turned in the distance. "You hear her?" he yelled, but I was barely able to make out his words. His outline stood stark against the snow and darkening forest around us.

The birds disappeared with the falling night. I switched on my flashlight, swinging the arc of light over the animal path in front of me. Color at my feet snagged my attention.

I bent down. A pink mitten.

"Celia?" I yelled her name until my voice completely gave out and I couldn't even hear myself. She'd come this way for sure.

Tens shouted, but I couldn't hear the words.

Then, a high keening came. I swung the flashlight. "Hello?" The blood rushed in my ears.

"Mommy?" A little voice sounded tired and far away.

"Celia? Is that you? My name is Meridian. I'm a friend. Where are you?" I frantically shone the flashlight, but the trees all looked the same, snow drifted into piles beneath them. I couldn't find tracks.

"Here . . . I see light. . . . Hurt my leg."

"That's my flashlight. Keep talking to me, Celia. It's so

dark I can't see you. Have you ever played that game called Marco Polo?"

"Yeah." She sounded quieter, as if I were moving away from her, even though I was standing still.

"I'm going to keep calling out 'Marco' and you yell 'Polo' as loud as you can, okay?"

" 'Kay."

"Marco?"

"Polo."

I moved three steps to my left, every cell in my body tuned to listen for, and spot, a little girl. "Marco!" I shouted.

"Po—"

I didn't catch the last syllable. My heart beat itself into a frenzy. There were no other sounds in the forest, no distant lights, no sounds of the snowmobilers the sheriff had said were out searching.

"Marco!" I called again. And waited. And waited. "Marco!" I tried again. *Please, please, please answer me.*

There was rustling behind me. I turned my flashlight to spotlight the movement. "Custos." I'd never been happier to see anyone in my life. I shook the mitten under Custos's nose. "Find Celia, Custos, find the little girl."

I saw a flashlight in the distance coming toward me, but I didn't have time to wait for Tens to reach me. I hoped he'd follow my light.

Custos ran past me about twenty feet, then stopped and waited for me to catch up before running on ahead again. She ran to the edge of my limited vision, then disappeared behind trees.

I heard her whining and moaning and pawing at the snow. I caught up and leaned down under low-hanging branches heavy with snow. A coppery scent I recognized as raw meat hung in the air. "Celia?" I was hoping Custos hadn't led me to the bear's den for dinner. I shoved branches out of my way.

"Mommy?" A tiny, shaking brunette reclined against the trunk of a birch tree. Her face was as pale as the snow around us, her eyes too big for her delicate face. Her ponytail slid to the side under a knit cap; her pink down coat appeared soaked with a dark liquid. She wore only one mitten, and she lifted her hands toward me as her teeth chattered.

"I'm Meridian. Let's get you out of here." I leaned down to haul her upright and then stopped and stilled myself. Followed the deepening dark circle with the light.

"I hurt my foot."

I gagged. Her little foot, in its tiny pink Dora the Explorer boot, was caught in a trap, the kind of jawed trap I'd only ever seen in books about the pioneers of the Wild West. "What the hell?" I gasped. What was a trap like this doing on Auntie's property? There was no way Tens or Auntie would use such a cruel device.

I wanted to run. I'm not brave. I'm not even remotely good in a crisis.

The little girl started crying. "It hurts."

I didn't have the first idea how to get the trap off. "Breathe, Meridian, breathe," I whispered. I lifted my head, hoping that Tens was gaining ground. I had no idea how much time had passed or how long we had before shock and blood loss affected her. I had to act. I had to save her or we were both in trouble.

Custos stood next to me, watching, like she was waiting for me to get on with the part she couldn't do.

"Okay, Celia, do you know how this thing works?"

"You know you're not supposed to leave the trails?" she whimpered.

"Really?" I grappled for a release bar. "Is there a switch?"

"I got lost, so I stopped like I'm s'posed to. Then he said to wait over here for Daddy. That's when it got me, but he didn't come help me."

"It's going to be okay. I'm going to get you back home to your mommy and daddy, okay?"

"You pull it apart. My daddy has some, but he never uses them where people are."

Contemplating her mangled foot, I wanted to ask why anyone would use them at all.

"This is gonna hurt, but I have to get your foot out, okay?"

"I know."

"I want you to yell and scream as loud as you can, okay? I'll yell with you. On the count of three, start screaming, okay?"

" 'Kay."

"One." I braced myself and swallowed.

CHAPTER II

"'Two." I gritted my teeth.

"Three."

She opened her mouth and got the first scream out before the pain hit her brain and she passed out.

"Let me help." Tens appeared at my elbow and steadied my hands.

"Where were you?" I wanted to screech.

"I found her footprints; they circled back here. I lost you in the dark. I'm sorry." Tens finished opening the trap, inching Celia's leg out of it.

I held the jaws of the trap, praying the damn thing wouldn't spring shut and make Celia's wound even worse. We moved her before she regained consciousness. I hoped she'd revive. Blood oozed around the bone, the flesh torn and shredded. Could she survive the injury? She had to. I refused to contemplate the alternative. It was selfish, but if she died there was good chance I might too.

"Dammit, I dropped my scarf." Tens glanced at me. "Give me yours. We have to stop the bleeding." I gave him my scarf to tie around Celia's leg.

"Okay, Custos, you better find people to help us. Find help," Tens commanded. Even bundled in layers, Celia couldn't have weighed forty pounds. "Their ranch is over that next ridge. It's faster to go ahead and meet up with the search party rather than go back to Auntie's. I hope they have an ambulance there."

"But isn't Auntie's just back there?" I pointed behind us, seeing nothing but rolling white and pockets of forest.

"Meridian, we've been out here for four hours. We're nowhere near Auntie's." Tens lifted Celia, tenderly cradling her inert form.

I held the flashlights so he could see in front of him, and followed blindly in his tracks. It made wading through the snow arduous.

Custos bounded ahead, waiting for us, then going on. I hoped she had the sense not to walk into another of the traps, and I prayed my foot wouldn't find one either. Celia's breathing grew shallow and irregular.

"Hurry," I snapped, feeling the urgency, sure that we weren't moving fast enough. Weren't pushing hard enough.

"I can't go any faster." Tens sped up just the same.

"Oh, I know. Sorry." Of course he was doing his best. He knew what was at stake too.

"I'm dizzy." A little voice interrupted us.

Tens paused for a second, "Hi, Celia. We're taking you home, okay?"

I saw lights in the distance headed diagonally across the field. If they stayed that way, they'd miss us. "Tens? Look."

He handed Celia to me. "Hold her. Keep her as warm as you can. I have to get their attention." He grabbed a light and plunged ahead, shouting and waving his arms.

"Custos, bark, help us!" I pleaded.

I unzipped my coat and wrapped it around Celia. The wet cold seeped into my skin and made me grit my teeth. "It's going to be okay, I promise."

Celia was staring up at me in the beam of the flashlight. "You're pretty."

"Thanks."

"It'll be okay, you know," she said.

"I should be reassuring you, not the other way around." I knelt in the snow, worried I'd drop her.

"No, you don't really know, but you will."

"Okay." I hugged her tighter against me.

Her breathing slowed, but she opened her eyes and peered up at me. "Why did the man tell me to go under the tree?" Celia said. "That was mean."

"What man, Celia? Who?" My left leg began throbbing and I felt pressure building inside of me. I looked around us, wondering if she knew what she was saying. I hadn't seen evidence of anyone else. Then I heard the dogs barking in the distance and the soft whir of snowmobiles.

"Over here!" Tens boomed. A flurry of activity headed in our direction.

Celia couldn't die. Not now. Not ever. But definitely not while I was holding her.

"Hang on, Celia, they're almost here." I shook her as gently as I could, trying to keep her awake. A new, unfamiliar pain radiated up my leg. Fear sped up my breathing and my heartbeat.

Tens ran toward us, plowing up powder. I cradled Celia's small form against me.

"It's beautiful here," she said, snuggling into me with a sigh. "Thanks for finding me and fixing my leg. It doesn't hurt anymore."

"Oh, I didn't . . ." I had to get away from her. I had to get her help. There were so many reasons this precious girl couldn't die.

Custos howled. The lights rapidly came closer and Tens was silhouetted against the snowmobile headlights.

I must have looked as terrible as I felt, because when Tens reached us he grabbed Celia from my arms and turned toward the snowmobiles. "Get away—go! Open the window!" he shouted, breaking the painful stupor I was sliding toward.

The hair on the back of my neck stood up. My ears

felt like they needed to pop, and pressure built in my chest as if the air was being sucked out of me. The pain in the pit of my stomach intensified. "No, Celia, no!" I stumbled away, trying to visualize the window, but an irrational part of me wanted to resist—as if I could force her to stay alive by making it harder. Waves of excruciating, piercing pain crashed over me, forcing the breath from my lungs. I couldn't move fast enough. Or get far enough away.

She was dying. I knew this feeling.

My left leg gave out completely. Pain radiated through me as I fell into a snowbank. "No, no, no." Tears poured down my cheeks. I could feel her leaving her body.

I tried to stand, but I couldn't put any weight on my leg. It felt as if the bones poked through the skin. Custos tugged at my jacket and I dragged my leg behind me until I'd hobbled and crawled as far as I could. It didn't matter anymore; in that moment there was nothing left in me to fight. I leaned against a tree and focused on breathing through the scorching pain. My ankle throbbed and I struggled for each breath as I watched the scene unfold around me.

"Celia? Celia? Where's my baby?" An older woman frantically stumbled through the snow toward Tens, falling to the ground with grief. As she ripped the child from his arms, I turned to the side and vomited blood. I heaved until nothing came up. The pressure eased fractionally, and the pain loosened its grip enough that I could lift my head.

From a distance, I surveyed the vaguely familiar

group before me as a tall, blond man said a prayer and made the sign of the cross over Celia and her mother. He seemed to be some sort of preacher, but his vibe was intimidating and oily. Where his features should have been illuminated by the headlights, there was only the black and empty blankness of a human form. I squinted but couldn't quite catch a glimpse of his face.

Like someone had flipped a switch, the feeling of Celia's soul pressing into me, through me, disappeared. The pain began to dissipate like fog in the sun. I forced breath back into my lungs. I felt as if I'd been freed from my own inhumane trap.

My teeth chattered and shivers racked my body. Celia liked Oreos, My Little Ponies, and helping her mom make chocolate chip cookies. I didn't know how I knew this.

Tens came to check on me as the conversation escalated around us. "Are you okay?"

I shook my head. "I don't know. My leg is messed up." The pain was slowly rolling off like a storm passing, but the effort had left me weak and ill.

I heard Celia's mother wail as her father said, "She's gone. Honey, she's gone." He drew his wife up and picked up Celia.

Tens gently brushed the hair from my face. "I'm going to borrow a snowmobile to get us home. Wait here for a minute, okay?"

I nodded without opening my eyes.

" 'What thing is this that thou hast done?' "[1] asked the rich voice of a stranger.

I opened my eyes to blink up at the most handsome

older man I'd ever seen up close. The blond man. A movie star. A Wall Street tycoon. Surely *People* magazine's Sexiest Man Alive. He oozed confidence, class, and charisma. He had such perfectly symmetrical features that I was spellbound until he continued speaking. " 'Cursed be he that taketh reward to slay an innocent person. And all the people shall say, Amen.' "[2] He didn't take his mercurial eyes off me. Eyes that appeared as black holes. No white shone, just swirling, oily voids. I tried unsuccessfully to make my eyes focus in the odd light.

" 'And God saw that the wickedness of man was great in the earth, and that every imagination of the thoughts of his heart was only evil continually.'[3] We're watching, you know. Waiting."

Tens drove back into earshot before I had time to piece together this bizarre monologue.

"Tens, son, I was just introducing myself to Miss Sozu. I'm Reverend Perimo. It's so good to meet you, young lady. Your aunt has told me so much about you." It was as if a full transformation had occurred. "I offered her a ride back to her aunt's, but I think she's delirious from the cold."

"We're fine, thanks. I borrowed transpo." Tens's voice was smooth and modulated, but tension radiated from every sinew in his body.

"You sure? She looks like she's got a bum leg there." The reverend's tone never slipped from friendly and concerned. I almost believed I'd hallucinated his odd language.

"We're good, thanks." Tens helped me stand. I could

almost put weight on my leg. I straddled the seat and kept my mouth shut. Wrapping my arms around Tens's waist, I laid my cheek against his back. Custos ran alongside us. I must have dozed, because I don't remember the ride home.

Auntie met us at the front door, worry etching lines in her face.

Tens lifted me from the back of the snowmobile. When I registered that he intended to carry me, I cried, "Stop! I can walk." I was a complete sissy around him—that had to change.

"Sure. Tomorrow." He didn't stop. "You're a weakling, it's not a hardship." I swore he was teasing me, but he didn't crack a smile, so I didn't laugh.

"Thanks." I wrapped an arm around his neck, trying not to notice how silky straight his hair fell against his neck. Or how nice he smelled. Or how safe I felt with him holding me.

"My goodness, what happened?" Auntie asked, hovering. "Put her down, Tens, she's not a damsel in distress."

"She's hurt." He didn't set me down until he reached the couch. "Okay, Meridian—what happened?"

CHAPTER 12

"It felt like my leg was broken. It felt shredded." I fell back against the pillows and blankets. "I thought I broke it, but now it's getting better."

"Right." Tens exchanged glances with Auntie. He shoved the couch closer to the fire and wrapped a quilt around me like he was rolling a cigar. I noticed his hands shaking.

"You're growling like a damn grizzly with a bellyache. Move back." Auntie shooed him away and perched on the edge of the sofa to feel my forehead.

"I'm feeling better. Really. Must have only been a sprain." I was trying to reassure both of them, but it was also true. Breathing seemed preposterously easy around Auntie. I felt more awake, less fragile, less sick.

Tens loaded logs on the fire until it blazed and crackled. He paced, putting his hands in his pockets and then pulling them out.

"Easy, we're trying to warm her up, not roast her for dinner." Auntie pushed him away. "Go get her clean clothes. Now, let's see about that leg." As Tens ran upstairs, she carefully drew my sock off and rolled up my wet pant leg. She glanced up at my face.

The fire felt so good I could barely force my eyes to stay open. All that fresh air, exertion, and adrenaline about did me in. "Did I sprain it?"

Auntie gently patted my leg, rubbing the skin with soft, whispered strokes. "Little one, what happened out there? Did you see Celia?"

My eyes flew open. For a moment I'd been so happy to be back in this house, I'd forgotten what happened out there. "Celia, she . . ." My voice broke and a tear spilled down my cheek.

Auntie nodded. "She died, yes?"

I confirmed this with a slight nod.

"Did she have an injury of any kind?" Auntie rubbed my other foot and the tingles of warmth became pinpricks as the blood flowed back.

I swallowed the bile rising in my throat and nodded. Tens hurried back into the room with my pajamas. My face flamed at the thought of him pawing through my stuff.

"What's wrong with her ankle?" Tens set my pj's on the coffee table and crossed his arms, keeping a distance.

Auntie sat back and peered at my eyes. "Nothing."

I sat up and stared at my ankle, pale and unswollen. Not an hour ago, it felt as if it were the size of a watermelon. "But—"

"What happened to Celia's leg?" Auntie asked, her expression knowing yet gentle.

I closed my eyes. "A trap. One of those clawed ones."

"And you were with her when she died?"

"Yes." I glanced at Tens.

He shrugged.

"Did you picture the window?" Auntie asked.

"No!" I shouted, pushing Auntie's tender hands away. "She shouldn't have died. She was a baby. I could have done something. I should have done more. If I'd known first aid or if we'd gotten there faster."

"Meridian, all your illnesses, your physical maladies, those are the souls tangling in your energy. If you didn't let Celia go—I mean actively picture your window so she could break through easily and painlessly—then her pain must have transferred. If you felt that much of her pain, you should have died. I don't understand how you're still alive." Auntie was puzzled and thinking hard. "I wasn't there—"

"Do you feel their pain?"

"Not anymore. But it requires practice. Once you're in

control of the window, it never hurts. You feel it, see them pass."

"So my ankle is fine?" I rotated my foot and it didn't hurt at all. Very strange. Then it occurred to me that I always seemed to feel better when Auntie was in the room, "It's you, isn't it?"

"Me what?"

"I feel better around you. Or am I imagining that, too?"

"Don't kid yourself. The pain is real. But yes, you probably do feel better around me. I've never really thought about it, but souls would pick me. I'm easier to pass through, so you're not getting bombarded. As soon as you become confident in your ability, your body will get stronger—you might even grow a few feet. I used to be almost five ten, would you believe that? Age shrinks the spine."

"So there have always been small souls passing through me?"

"All your symptoms are departing energy punching holes in you, trying to get through. When I'm around, they pick the easiest route: me."

Talk about a headache. "But—"

"Once you learn to stay on this side you can have your window open all the time, like me. You'll get to a point where it's painless, easy, second nature. You'll know when a soul is passing on because you'll see their heaven and know a bit of their life, but it'll be like watching a movie preview—simply a moment of their life shared with you."

"Oh." I was too tired to process all this. The fire danced while Tens hovered.

Auntie abruptly got to her feet and said, "Want some brownies? I have a hankering." She was already moving out of the room, muttering to herself.

"Thanks. Chocolate sounds really good."

I closed my eyes, leaning back into the embrace of the pillows. This was so confusing.

Tens stood there, still and silent.

"What?" I asked, keeping my eyes closed.

"Nothing." He moved closer. Cleared his throat. "Do you want, um, need . . . help with your clothes? Or I can ask Auntie to help you instead?" He sounded vulnerable and unsure.

A blush stole over my face. But exhaustion sapped my limbs, making it nearly impossibly to move. "Please."

He tenderly peeled back the blanket and gripped the bottom of my shirt and sweater.

I must have blanched at the intimacy because he said, "I've seen it all before, but I'll close my eyes if you'd rather. Of course, I'm more likely to put my hands in the wrong places with my eyes closed."

I cracked an eyelid to see him smiling shyly. I raised my arms so he could tug the clothes over my head.

He handed me the unbuttoned pajama top and for the first time in my life I wished it was satin or lace— anything more sophisticated and worldly than Sponge-Bob. Sammy had given these pj's to me last Christmas as his idea of a joke, but they were the softest flannel I owned. I unsnapped my snowpants and lowered the zipper. Tens moved to my feet. "Lift your hips."

I did and pushed the nylon down my legs. He carefully and slowly drew the pants off my legs, replacing them with SpongeBob and letting me finish hauling them all the way up. It registered in the girlie part of my heart that he was the first boy to ever see this much of my skin.

Tens stayed at the end of the couch, his fingers idly running over my ankles as if he needed to reassure himself that I was okay.

Auntie came hurrying back in, carrying a tray of milk and brownies, and Tens rose from the couch.

I ate a brownie; it tasted delicious. Auntie settled into a chair by the fire and Tens finished three large brownies before digging around in a basket filled with tools and chunks of wood.

Maybe I'd watched too much television, but I couldn't help wondering. "Auntie?" I didn't know how to ask this question and wasn't sure I really wanted the answer.

She sat in her rocker and pulled out her lap-sized quilting frame. "What is it?"

"Are Fenestras . . . Are we witches?"

"Goodness Gabriel, no!"

"Are the Aterthingies?"

"Aternocti? Not in the traditional sense, no." Auntie held a couple of scraps of cotton together, discarded one and considered another. "They are the DarkNights. Rather than letting souls transition back to the Creator, they ferry the soul to the Destroyer."

"Hell?" Visions of fire and brimstone flashed through my mind.

She nodded. "It has many names."

"Do the Aternocti want to hurt Fenestras?"

"Kill us, you mean? Very much so." Auntie's pronouncement was so matter-of-fact, she could have been giving me a cookie recipe. But she squinted into the fire, frowning.

A horrifying thought rushed into my head. "Do we want to kill *them*?"

"No, that's not our job. There are warrior Sangre angels who do that, but if you're lucky you will never meet a Nocti, nor will you meet a Sangre." She shuddered and stared into the fire, forgetting her sewing.

Even Tens paused and waited.

"Oh." Visions of Buffy danced in my head. I couldn't imagine myself in cute outfits battling demons. That wasn't on my list of things to do before graduating high school. High school—*do I get to go back?* "What about ghosts?"

Auntie started stitching again as if a trance had been broken. "They do exist. Usually, their energy is trapped on this plane. They held on to this world rather than moving on."

"Why?"

"It depends, but it could be to see their children grow up or to protect loved ones. Sometimes they stay to watch over a place or a house. Maybe they're afraid to go on, which is silly since it's simply a change, not an end."

"Are they, uh, mean?" As in, were they trying to kill us too? Because I could swear I was being watched.

Auntie shook her head and shrugged. "The energy has the persona of that which it lived—remember, energy can change form, but doesn't appear or disappear. So if they were evil in one life, that doesn't change simply because their bodies have gone back to the earth. The longer they're here, the harder it is to get them to move on."

"Can they use us?"

"They can be very dangerous, Meridian. Don't start hunting lost souls."

"Why are they dangerous?"

"Their energy is no longer tightly packaged. It's much easier to get tangled in them, especially if they have any reason to want you with them. It can be completely accidental, not malicious in the least. Just be careful."

Lovely, another wrinkle to worry about. "Can anyone see us? I mean, as the light thing rather than just human?" My mind flipped to Señora Portalso calling me *luz*. Should I mention it? I kept my mouth shut. I didn't know yet whether or not it was okay.

"There are a few humans who have evolved over time to be able to see us."

"How?" Maybe Señora Portalso had seen me. I liked the idea of having someone else, an outsider actually know the truth.

"Not every family of Fenestras gives birth to them. But Fenestra progeny without the power itself still have the ability to sense it and notice it. Think of healers and psychics, people who can see auras or move chi around the body with their hands."

And here I'd always thought they faked it. My memory flashed back to the state fair last summer and the fortune-teller's booth I'd visited on a lark with Sam. She'd said I'd be going on a long journey and would be introduced to a future of light and dark, life and death. I'd told Sammy she was full of crap. If I ever saw her again I owed her an enormous apology.

Auntie chuckled to herself. "Enough for tonight. But I have something for you."

I braced myself. So far her gifts hadn't been terribly fun. My expression must have shown my reluctance.

"My journal. Actually it's *our* journal. Over the centuries, Fenestras from our family have added to, rewritten, and guarded the wisdom we've gained. It won't bite, I promise. I've kept notes over the years, hoping you would come. There isn't enough time to tell you all of it, so you'll need this." She handed me a leather-bound tome with gold edging and a ribbon tie. It was worn and mangled, the oil from many fingers leaving streaks on the pages, marks where the ink had run, and smudges on the cover.

"Thanks." The darn thing was so heavy I had to use both hands to hold it.

"It's been many years since my eyes were good enough to read it cover to cover. Perhaps there's a way to fight the Nocti that I don't remember. I will think on it— we should be prepared. Get some sleep." Auntie kissed me on the forehead and then went back to her seat by the fire.

I stood up and put weight on my foot. It was completely normal, as if I'd never felt pain.

"I'll walk you up." Tens shadowed me.

Custos was already snoring on my bed. I laughed.

Tens peeked over my shoulder and chuckled. "Bed warmer?"

"Yeah, I guess."

Custos blinked one eye at us and went back to sleep.

Tens moved around me and turned the space heater up to high.

I crawled onto the bed and picked up a framed photograph of my parents and Sam from the nightstand. How my life had changed since I'd snapped that shot with Sam's camera. Not for the first time I wished I'd been in a family photograph. Now at least I knew why I was always the one behind the camera.

Tens stuffed his hands in his pockets and paused at the doorway, observing me with a brooding expression that made me shiver. He made me feel itchy and hot and unused to my own skin.

"What?" I broke the silence with a bark.

"Night." He turned and walked out the door.

"Wait!" I called.

He poked his head around the corner. "What?"

"What did Auntie mean, there isn't enough time?"

He wouldn't meet my gaze. "You have to learn to let souls pass before . . ."

I thought I saw fear and hurt pass across his face. I prodded, unsure I still wanted the answer. "Before what?"

He swallowed. "Auntie's dying. She has to pass through you or the world loses another Fenestra. If you can't do it . . . well then, you'll go too." His eyes locked with mine.

"What? No!" I crumpled into myself.

"I wasn't supposed to tell you yet, but I—"

"I asked. It's okay. I wanted to know. Needed to know." Didn't I? No wonder. I closed my eyes and tried to inhale immense breaths.

Tens stepped forward and then stopped, rubbing his hands over his face "I— Sorry—" He backed out of the room and shut the door.

I gave up on sleep. Auntie was dying. I turned the lamp back up to high and tugged the enormous volume onto my lap, flipping through the pages.

March 23, 1921

I do not always get to see the souls that pass through me. I only feel the warmth of the light and see a glimpse of their afterlife from my vantage point on this side. But I know the feeling. I know when it is coming and I know when a soul makes use of me. I am only beginning to get accustomed to it, but I wonder if it will ever feel natural?

January 2, 1972

Favorite foods, a song, their first love. I know these things the moment the soul passes through me, but I am unable to share my knowledge with their families. I hate not being able to bring comfort to the living, only the dying. Other people can bridge and pass messages and such. I am not skeptical of their ability to do so, but I cannot. I can never get the words out of my throat, no matter how hard I try. I have come to think it is not my place. I am not a medium. I am a window.

October 18, 1931

There is one who is chasing me. I must remember Atlantis, Aztecs, druids, Gede, Easter Island—they all were swallowed by the Aternoctis. Their energy and their people gone because there were too few Sangre and too few Fenestras to cover the world. It is a battle between good and evil that plays out in those brief moments of transition. If they can scoop up the energy, the darkness grows and the world turns with less good. I have heard rumors the Aternocti have gained terrible power in Europe. I must be everywhere I am needed. Perhaps I will travel to Europe on my own. I must save the souls I can. I wish I had a sister Fenestra to share my burdens.

If Auntie felt this way, how was there any hope for me? "I must save the souls I can." How was I supposed to do this? Before she died? I'd never felt so alone.

The best way to know if she is a Fenestra is to know the date of her birth. She is always first to cry at the stroke of midnight on December the 21st. Our relatives are birthed on the 20th or 22nd, but a Fenestra will always & forever see her first light as a human soul on the day of winter solstice. The darkest morn of the year births the brightest lights.
——Cassie Ailey, 8th of January 1876

CHAPTER 13

I woke to a complete face wash, one long tongue stroke after another. "Custos." I opened my eyes, sticky wolf drool lathered like a wet clay mask on my face. I giggled, letting her nudge and push me toward the edge of the bed.

The chill slapped my bare feet. The space heater's plug had fallen out of the socket. I rubbed my arms, shivering, and tugged a sweater on over my pajamas.

The house was silent. I didn't hear Auntie or Tens anywhere below. My breath caught and sadness washed over me as I remembered Tens's confession the night before. Auntie was dying, and I had to help her pass through. Pass on. Die. Would I be able to do it?

I padded along with Custos by my side, down to the kitchen for a glass of juice. Tens's kitchen skills were spoiling me. Sure enough, there was a pitcher of fresh-squeezed OJ waiting by a glass. He'd given up trying to force me to eat, but this morning I actually felt hungry.

I grabbed a blueberry muffin and decided to explore the house a little more while it was still quiet. I didn't know what time it was, though it was early enough that the light was still soft.

A shadow passed across my peripheral vision, but when I turned toward it there was nothing there. I opened the first downstairs door that creaked under my fingertips, its old-fashioned key not engaged in the lock.

At the far end of the room, a picture window looked out over the snowy field. The room was decorated in grand mahogany tones, with shelves along one wall full of books and shelves along the other crowded with paintings and photographs. I picked up a velvet blocked quilt and wrapped it around my shoulders. Cold air seeped past the rippled glass panes and chilled me.

Huge gilded frames and simple wood ones embraced crowds of people. Shocked, I saw my mother as a little girl with Auntie. A photo of my parents' wedding hung next to one in sepia tones. I flipped on a light to see better.

"That was my wedding day." I jumped as Auntie entered the room.

"Seriously? You look so happy." I motioned toward the rest of the photos. "Who are all these people?"

"Family, some friends." She walked over and stood at my shoulder.

"My wedding-day portrait is the first photograph that developed right." Auntie touched a fingertip to the glass.

"What's the deal? Is it a Fenestra thing too?"

She shot me an amused glance. "Why yes, it is. There's something about the film—or digital processing now—that captures the light in us."

"But it's possible?"

"Have you heard people say that ghosts or spirits in photographs leave a white blur or flashbulb reflection?"

"I guess." I was learning how little I knew about the world. In photographs, my face was always in shadow, like a lunar eclipse. It always seemed like the sun was right behind me, throwing my face into darkness. It was as if I didn't have any identity on film.

"We do that. Until you learn how to close and open your gateway to spirits, then all that people can capture is the light from beyond you."

I'm eclipsed by my role in the world. "But you *can* control it?"

"Yes, you can learn to. Like you learn to control tangling yourself up in other energy. Wasn't my husband handsome?" Her smile bloomed even as her eyes teared up.

"Yes, very. What was his name?"

"He was my Charles. My daredevil pilot. He was one of the first people to fly experimental aircraft."

"Wasn't that dangerous?"

"Of course, but he didn't fear death. He told me that every time he went up as long as he could see my face when he died he'd never fear death."

"He knew?"

"Oh yes. We met at a field hospital in France during the war. I was already well past the age of marriage in those days, but I was a nurse. I went where I was needed, and the boys fighting for us needed a peaceful end if they weren't coming home."

"So you nursed them?"

Sadness filled her eyes. "Some. Mostly I went out with patrols and with the Resistance to the front. Made myself available to any who needed me. My skills as a nurse were not in as high demand as my skills as a Fenestra. The Aternocti built an empire in Europe with Hitler's help. Or vice versa.

"The boys started calling me Angel because the screaming stopped when I was around. Charles paid attention. He'd heard stories from his grandmother about the light people who are angels on earth. He volunteered to escort me.

"Near the war's end we found a camp in Germany. A place of hell on earth."

"The Nazis?"

"Hmmm. I went with the troops that first day. Not afraid, but not prepared. No one could ever be prepared. There were so many. So close. My eyes hurt from the light; I almost couldn't see myself, my skin glowed. I focused on breathing and letting them through, one after another."

"What happened?"

"Most of the soldiers knew I wasn't quite like everyone else. But in wartime, it's easier to believe in things that don't make sense, miracles, the supernatural. They alternated helping me get around the camp, to be with the people who needed me, the ones who couldn't recover. But Charles never left my side. After hours of this, I was so exhausted I could barely stand. I fainted and Charles caught me. Carried me back to the base camp and poured whiskey into me until I cried the pain all out. I told him things I'd never told another human being, but he listened quietly and kept pouring."

"He wasn't scared?"

"Oh, child, you see enough and live enough, death isn't the scary part anymore. War puts our puny human fears in perspective. Plus, he saw what it cost me. I couldn't get out of bed for a week. The doctors diagnosed me with some nonsense like female hysteria or vapors."

I laughed at how insulted she still sounded.

"Charles kept bringing me fresh bread and cheese from local farms. He learned I had a sweet tooth, so he'd barter for sweets, which were terribly difficult to find in those days. He brought me roses and bouquets of wildflowers. Life. He nursed me until I could get back on my feet. He was ten years younger than me. That was quite the scandal in those days, but war is war and, well, you form a bond after living through it that belies propriety. He told me he loved me and asked me to spend the rest of my life with him, to bear him over when his time came, to let him protect me and help me in whatever ways he could."

I wondered if I'd ever know that kind of love and devotion. Or if I could walk through the present-day equivalent of a Nazi death camp because it was the right thing to do for the souls trapped there.

"Have you ever studied a dead human body?" Auntie asked.

"A person? No." Celia was my closest.

"Hmm." She moved down the line of frames to a portrait of a little girl, a wonderful oil painting.

"I was five when that was painted. Had the worst time sitting still." The painting captured a young girl with the world's most earnest expression. So serious and focused. Her eyes were like drill bits; I almost felt the heat of her gaze on my face. It was strange the way the painting seemed alive, glowing with purpose. Dark, glossy curls framed an ivory face with eyes the unfathomable blue of twilight in summer.

Auntie brushed her fingertips across a miniature painting. "Your great-grandmother was seven years older than me. That's her there." She had the faintest glow around her.

I wished my mother had thought to have my portrait painted. "You're actually my great-great-aunt?"

"Yes."

"How old are you, then?"

"One hundred and six. All Fenestras live that long if we make it past the transition. My dad painted this one, too."

"Did he know?"

"He knew there was something different about me, of course. He knew when my mother called me to her side in the middle of birthing my youngest sister. She knew what I was. Her mother had been a Fenestra. But she had kept it from my father, thinking she could shield me from the whispers and the witchcraft fears."

"What happened?"

"Children weren't allowed in the birthing rooms back then. But my father never could refuse her anything."

I felt like I already knew the conclusion of this story. "She died?"

"Hmm, yes, she was the first person I know of who tried to go through me. I was six, but if the soul knows a window, it's easier for them. She couldn't make it without killing me, though; she sensed it was too much and retreated. I can't imagine how hard that was for her. For me, well, it was difficult to recover from. I had the worst stomach pains for weeks afterward. The doctor was called from three towns away and wanted to operate, but my daddy wouldn't let him touch me."

"Did your sister die too?"

"No, Mama pushed her out clear and fast. But something tore inside my mother, and the blood wouldn't stop. She held my hand and wouldn't let go. She asked me to sing the lullaby that she always sang to me. I forgot the second verse. By then it didn't matter. I sang as if my life depended on it. Over and over again, I sang that lullaby. The midwife cleaned up my sister and went into town to find a nursemaid for her. My father broke that night. Something never healed in him."

"I'm sorry."

She continued like she hadn't heard me. "I heard my mother's voice in my head, telling me she loved me and to trust myself no matter what. Then her hand relaxed. Her eyes turned toward me, but I knew she was gone. The way the bedclothes are still warm after you get out of bed in the morning—you're there, but no longer. Mama gave my eldest sister the journal, but I was the only Fenestra in the family, so it came to me."

"I'm sorry." I didn't know what to say. At least my parents were alive in another city or state, as far as I knew.

"Don't be. Death is what makes life possible. It's the balance, Meridian. There always has to be balance. You'll learn. You can sense the souls that need you, before *they* know it, so you can be prepared for their passage rather than taken unawares."

"It becomes second nature?"

"Like breathing or swallowing. You'll have an awareness and you can be deliberate about it, but you can also rest and simply be."

"Why do I need to close the window, then?"

"It's part of learning how it feels, how it works. There will be times when you'll want to shut the window. You'll need to shield when you're ill or vulnerable."

If I shield, can I be completely human? Go back to my family? "Is there any way to shield completely so I'm normal?"

"It's possible to have the appearance of a normal life, yes, but you'll always be a Fenestra. It's who you are." She ran her hand over my hair. "Is your hair naturally this red?"

"What? No, it's brown." A completely nondescript dirty brown.

"So you dye it? Give the appearance of being a red-head or a blonde, right?"

"Yeah."

"That's what shielding does for us—it's temporary camouflage."

"Will I ever see my family again?"

"I hope so, little one, but I can't make any promises. I know what it's like to miss the people you love. I still do. I wish I could spare you that." Her expression filled with longing and loss. She brushed a finger against the photograph of Charles.

"What happened to him?"

Her face clouded and her chin trembled. "He died."

There was more, but I hesitated to push. "Were you—"

"I wasn't there. I'd gone to the restroom. I left his side for a moment. Just a moment." She gripped my hand.

"I'm sure—" I broke off, knowing there was nothing I could say. "Is there a chance?"

I barely heard her whisper, "I don't know."

Did Charles get to heaven or was he recycling into a new life? Or worse still, was he in hell?

"Get your coat," she said.

"Why?"

"Can you drive?"

"I'm still learning."

"Good, you can practice that, too."

"Where are we going?"

"To visit my friend Winnie."

"I thought she died."

"She did."

CHAPTER 14

I was certain a snail could have beaten us to Winnie's doorstep, but at least we arrived in one piece.

"What exactly are we doing here?" My heart thudded while Auntie knocked on the door.

"It's Winnie's wake."

"Why isn't she in a funeral home?"

The door swung open and a heavy, middle-aged woman welcomed us. Her teased hair was as big and round as the rest of her. "Come in, come in. This must be Meridian. I'm Sheila, one of Winnie's daughters. I expect you're here to pay your respects?" She helped remove our coats while she chattered. I had imagined there would be lots of crying and black clothes and organ music. As it turned out, there was lively conversation, the smell of turkey and ham permeating the air. "Mama is right through those doors in the living room, by the Christmas tree, just like she asked to be."

Auntie gripped my elbow and said in a low voice, "Winnie died in her bed, but she didn't want to miss the holiday festivities, so they promised to wash and dress her and have her laying out in there."

If this was my first dead person, it was also my first corpse by a Christmas tree. The tree sparkled with lights, and candy canes hung from every branch. There was a scent in the air I couldn't place, and I wondered if the dead smelled that quickly.

"Mama will be buried tomorrow, back under the oak tree, next to Pop. I'll let you have your time." Sheila closed the doors behind her and it was Auntie and me and Winnie's shell.

"What *exactly* are we doing?" I tried not to stare at Winnie because it didn't feel polite.

"Study her, Meridian. Examine her face."

I uncomfortably trained my gaze upon Winnie's gaunt cheeks. She was yellowing and gray. There was no makeup on her face and she was dressed in what looked like a new, old-fashioned-style flannel nightgown. "Okay?"

"What do you see?"

"Um . . ."

"Have a glance at the photographs on the piano over there." Auntie pointed to the grand piano in the corner. "Bring that one on the end over here."

I picked the photo up and brought it to Auntie. "Is this her?" The woman in the photograph was nothing like the woman lying in front of us.

"Yes. Doesn't look anything like her, does it?"

"Not really."

"Winnie's not there. She's not in the body anymore. The part that made her sparkle and laugh and cry, the animated bits of emotion, her talent on the piano, her sense of humor: those things are all gone. What's left is a shell. When you know the person before they die, rarely do they appear the same afterward."

"Oh. But don't they do makeup and stuff?"

"There's a big business in making corpses look like the people they were no matter how they died. You wouldn't belive the number of funerals I've been to where people murmured about how great the body looked even when it didn't. I always want to shout and shake the living for doing such a thing."

Auntie pressed a palm against Winnie's cheek. "Touch her."

I stepped backward. It felt wrong. "I don't—"

"Many dying people are going to reach out to you. You need to know what death feels like. Touch her." Auntie placed my hand gently on Winnie's hand, watching my face as she did so. "How does she feel?"

"Dead?"

"Exactly. There's nothing left. This is what we do, Meridian. I helped her cross. She was met by her husband and her parents, plus a ton of barnyard animals and pets because she was always taking in strays. There's nothing left of her because she used up her body while she was alive. This is the ending we all hope for and pray for. Most aren't this lucky."

I'd gotten over the willies. Winnie felt like a person, yet also different.

"You'll find yourself holding people while they die. This is a gift to them, but it's also a gift to you. As Fenestras we have daily reminders of what is important in this world."

"I get it."

"Are you sure?"

"I do. I understand better."

"Good. Let's go have a slice of pie before we leave. Sheila does amazing things with homemade crust and frozen fruit." Auntie hugged me and chuckled. "I'm partial to her rhubarb custard."

"I've never had rhubarb."

"Then you'll have to taste hers. You're doing well, little one. I know this can be tough."

* * *

The next morning, I put together a light breakfast for us, thinking Tens would appear at any moment. When he didn't, I began to get worried. Auntie alternately sewed and dozed, her eyelids slipping shut between stitches. Her chin would hit her chest and she'd rally awake.

"Where's Tens?" I asked.

"He had a few things to take care of. He'll be back soon."

I put down the journal and watched her stitch. Her fingers flew through thread and fabric. "Teach me to quilt?" I asked.

She smiled joyfully. "I'd love to." She patted the sofa and hoisted a basket of scraps into my lap. "Pick two pieces." She dug around in another basket for a needle and thread. "I quilt so I can clear out the memories. Every Fenestra has to find her way of coping—some cook, some paint. I quilt."

"Memories?"

"Each soul leaves odd bits of information with us. Things that are important to them."

"That's why!" I exclaimed, dropping the fabric.

"Why what, dear?"

"Celia loved Oreos and Cheerleader Barbie, and her guinea pig was named Shrek. I thought I was making all that up!"

"No, dear. I bet if you thought about it, you'd notice things from animals, too. The sound of mosquitoes is so electric. The smell of spring. The taste of clean water."

I nodded. I had memories and experiences that didn't seem to make any sense. I tried to thread the needle, but on the fifth miss, Auntie took it from me.

"It gets overwhelming. Too much. I make fabric stories from each life that moves through me."

I glanced around at the stacks of quilts that were everywhere. "All of these?" There had to be hundreds—thousands—of stories represented.

"They do add up, don't they?"

I attempted to tie a knot at the bottom of the thread as instructed, but it was hopeless. Auntie patted my leg. "You'll get it eventually. It entails practice."

"Like everything else?"

"Yes." Her face suddenly paled to the color of chalk and her head snapped toward the door.

Custos growled deep in her throat.

I froze. "What?"

Auntie shook her head infinitesimally.

I waited, my heart pounding. I felt the fear in the air. And something else.

Custos skulked over to the front door and waited, her head and tail lowered.

We sat there, frozen like trapped prey, maybe seconds, maybe hours, until Auntie stood. "It's okay."

"What? What is going on?" I asked, licking my dry lips.

Auntie set her quilting aside and removed a shotgun from hooks on the wall.

"What the hell?" I cried, aghast. A tiny old lady holding a shotgun is incongruous at best.

"Stay here," she commanded.

I followed. "No."

She peered out the window by the front door.

"Where is everybody?" Tens suddenly shouted,

banging the back door closed and stomping through the kitchen.

We both skittered and turned around as he came down the hallway.

"What happened?" He rushed to Auntie and tugged the gun from her shaking hands.

"I don't know," I said.

"Did you see anything?" Auntie asked him.

"No. I came through the back woods. What's going on?"

"Someone was here," Auntie answered him.

"Who?"

"It felt like a Fenestra, but maleficent."

"The Nocti?"

"What?" I gasped. I hadn't heard anything.

"I don't know. I've never been in the same room with one. I don't know how their energy feels."

"When?" Tens moved us away from the door. He opened it a crack and told Custos to stay. His shoulders blocked my view, but his reaction had me forcing him away so I could see.

An arrow, its end on fire, was lodged in the front door. A decapitated and disemboweled tabby cat lay on the doorstep. Blood congealed and darkened around her corpse. Her stomach produced the remains of what I knew instinctively were kittens.

I gagged as I scanned the carnage. I moved outside and stumbled down the steps. My breakfast lurched as I knelt in the snow by the side of the house.

"Shit." Tens walked down the steps and surveyed the mess. "Shit." He kicked at the steps and the Land Rover's tires.

Auntie leaned against him. "Oh dear. Not again."

I moved toward clean snow and wiped handfuls of it across my face, reveling in the cool and clean feel.

Auntie came over to me and handed me a handkerchief. "Let's go back inside. We'll make tea."

"But—"

"I'll clean it up. Go on." Tens didn't glance at me as he all but shoved us back into the house.

"Why?" I asked Auntie as I helped her in the kitchen. There was no reason in the world that would suffice. All her strength seemed to have flowed out of her.

"A warning. A promise." She seemed haunted.

"From?"

"Did you feel anything? When we were sewing?" Auntie measured out loose tea leaves into a pot, but her movements were jerky and slow.

I slid out a chair for her and took over brewing the tea. "Fear? My heart sped up. My mouth went dry."

"Good. Good."

"Why?"

"You felt them too. The Nocti were here, little one. You must always remember that feeling, because it's the only warning you'll get. I'd heard they leave behind arrows and desecrated corpses. But I'd never experienced it."

"Has anything happened before?"

"Silly things—toilet paper, eggs, paint—but nothing I couldn't attribute to bored children."

"From the church?"

"Maybe."

"Are the Nocti churchy?"

"To blend in, maybe, but with so many people moving here and those I know leaving? How do we know *who* it could be?"

The teakettle whistled. I poured the boiling water into the teapot and watched the steam rise from its spout as the brew steeped.

"You must trust yourself. Be alert at all times, or they'll capture you. They aren't above murder, but they'd rather make you one of them than lose your energy to the other side. If they can, they will turn you."

"How?"

Auntie wrung her hands. "I don't really know. I've never faced a Nocti. I've heard a Fenestra must kill herself in the presence of one and then, rather than send her soul on, somehow put it back into the body."

"Well, I'm not killing myself, so we're okay."

Auntie's expression was stormy. "I'm sorry, Meridian. I should have prepared better for the Nocti. I should have done more to—"

"Stop." Tens interrupted her as he strode into the kitchen. "You've never done this before either, right?"

"No."

"So you have nothing to apologize for. We can handle it. Right, Meridian?"

I wasn't sure I agreed, but Auntie was beyond troubled by what she seemed to believe were her inadequacies. At the moment, she appeared as if a strong wind could blow right through her. "Right. Tens and I can fig-ure it out."

Thank you, he mouthed.

Auntie pursed her lips, then sighed. "I have to go lie down. I can't seem to stay awake these days. Will you be okay?" She was already shuffling out of the kitchen be-fore she finished speaking.

"Are you sure? Do you need help?" I followed, but she climbed the stairs, not answering me.

"I'm sorry," Tens said, standing in the doorway.

"For what?" I glanced at him, momentarily stunned by the intensity of his expression.

"I should have been here. I should have—"

"What? Used the shotgun?" I tried to make light, but my joke fell flat.

Tens slapped the doorframe, agitated. Clearly, he felt responsible for us. "It's important. I'm supposed to—"

"Tens, you didn't do anything wrong. Why are you apologizing?"

He shrugged out of his coat and folded his long limbs into a chair.

I poured him a cup of tea, unsure of what else to do.

"I should have been here. That's all." He swallowed great gulps of tea, almost as if scalding his throat were an earned punishment.

"We're fine. Forget it."

"How's she doing?"

"Until that, okay, I guess." I chewed on my bottom lip, not sure I wanted to ask my next question but needing to know the answer. "How long? You know, for Auntie? *Do* you know? Before she . . ." I couldn't make myself finish.

"Not long."

"Years? Months?"

Tens frowned and finished his tea without answering.

"Come on." I reached out and gripped his forearm. "Seriously, how long?"

"Days. A week or so if we're lucky."

"What about medical care? Shouldn't she be in a hospital or something?" I hated feeling powerless.

"She made me promise she wouldn't die in a hospital. Meridian, she's one hundred and six. How much longer do you think they could keep her going anyway?"

"That's harsh."

"Am I wrong?"

I swallowed. Tears pooled in my eyes and one slid down my cheek. "You're asking me to—"

"No, I'm not." Tens knelt in front of me and wiped the droplet from my face. "If you can get her to go be checked out by a doctor, maybe they could make her more comfortable. But Fenestras don't live longer than one hundred and six. They just don't. And she wants to die here, in this house. She's not insane, Meridian. She knows exactly what she wants. We can give that to her. This last thing, we can do. Even though it means it's harder in some ways on you, I get that." Tens stopped, seemingly shocked by his long speech. "Can we not do this right now?"

I nodded, not wanting to add to his pain.

"Should I make you a sandwich?" I asked, my appetite completely gone.

"No, thanks. Maybe later."

I picked at my sweater and realized I was still wearing my pajamas. "I, um, I'll go get dressed."

He grunted. His focus lay on the journal I'd forgotten about.

"I was looking up the Aternocti, hoping—"

"If Auntie doesn't know it, it probably doesn't exist."

"Oh."

"I'll check. You go."

"I can stay—"

"*Go!*" He bit off the word, anger vibrating in that one syllable.

I scurried up the stairs, but I could have sworn I felt eyes watching me.

Smoked sausage and a jolly tupping. Ale and folly. Fickle bosoms and bar fights. That is the sum of experiences my souls gathered from their lives. Why do I attract all the unsophisticated fancy men? For once could one love the opera and his mother?
—Lucinda Myer, b. 1702–d. 1808

CHAPTER 15

A crow sat outside my bedroom window and cawed incessantly. I walked over and stared into the one beady eye it turned my way. I expected it to drop out of the tree dead at any moment, but it only called and hopped around the branches.

Movement in the field below caught my attention and I pressed my face against the glass, trying to get a better view.

It was Tens, on snowshoes and carrying an oversized hiking pack. He was loaded down with bulging pockets, and packages tied onto the pack. It had to weigh at least seventy-five or a hundred pounds. He trekked out of sight. Something must have been terribly important, for him to leave us alone again so quickly, especially given his earlier feelings of guilt.

Custos trotted at his side to the edge of the trees, her tail wagging. Then she turned and raced back toward the house. *Where is he going? What is all that stuff on his back?*

I picked out clean clothes, grabbed the stack of fashion magazines Mom had packed for me, and padded down the hall. I hoped to soak away this oppressive reality in a claw-foot tub, the likes of which I'd only ever seen in movies. My chest felt so tight it was difficult to get a full breath. Phone calls were scary, but eviscerating a helpless animal crossed the line of crazy.

I sighed, opening drawers in the ancient vanity, hoping to spot bath salts or bubble bath. No luck.

A brisk knock at the door startled me. "Meridian? It's Auntie."

I opened the door. "Is it okay for me to bathe in here?"

"Of course. I used to spend hours soaking in the tub too. It was like a minivacation, almost as good as the hot springs up the road." She smiled and held out a basket full of bottles. "Bath salts and bubbles and I don't know what else. Use whatever you like."

Guilt flooded me. "Do you need me for anything?"

She smiled. "No, you enjoy."

"Okay."

She closed the door.

I yanked it back open. "Auntie, where did Tens go?"

She paused, but didn't turn around. "He's running an errand for me." She disappeared around a corner.

"On foot?" I asked the empty hallway. I shrugged. Clearly, I wasn't to know. That bothered me. *I'm supposed to be learning and trusting and doing what I'm told, and yet I'm not trusted with the whole truth. I'm either part of this or I'm not.*

Soon the bathroom filled with scents. I stripped my pj's off and dipped a toe in, then a foot and a leg, until I was all but submerged up to my chin. Bubbles tickled my nose like butterflies.

I ran my hands over my body, trying to imagine what it would be like to be the recipient of quick, careless caresses. Sam was the only person in my family who ever touched me without hesitation. Tears leaked from beneath my lids. *What does Sammy think? What has he been told? That his sister just disappeared? Does he think I don't love him anymore? Where are they?*

I grabbed the top magazine from the pile. I'd lugged twenty pounds of magazines across the country, but I knew Mom thought she packed what I wanted most in the world. She always thought I wanted to be a magazine writer or editor. She never understood that in those glossy pages I saw the material world of normalcy. It didn't matter how many issues I read, but that elusive world of everyone else's never looked like mine. There were no happy Christmas scenes photographed with dead reindeer under the tree or the family dog being buried in the backyard beneath fairy lights and falling snow.

I'd never had a friend. Not since I'd made the mistake of telling Jillian the truth after her hamster died in my hands during a playdate. I told her everything died around me. She must have relayed this to her mother, because pretty soon Jillian was always busy. Finally, she told me she didn't want me to kill her, too.

I tossed magazine after magazine toward the wall. None of them brought the distraction they used to. I closed my eyes and a montage of Tens flashed across my eyelids. I remembered the feeling of him carrying me. He was safe and dangerous all at the same time. He made me want to trust him with every dark secret, but also to run away as fast as I could. My lips tingled as I imagined what kissing him might feel like. What I'd give for him to regard me with the warmth and love he showed Custos.

Did he wonder what kissing me might be like? Did he even know me as anything other than Auntie's pesky, sickly niece? Auntie's imminent death loomed above me.

Frustrated, I dunked my head underwater and held my breath.

And held it.

And kept holding it until I was past the point of bursting. Then I pushed to the surface, gasping great gulps of air into my burning lungs.

The tub suddenly felt like a coffin. I grabbed a bar of soap and a razor and shaved my legs for the first time in weeks. I scrubbed my skin with a washcloth until it was red and sensitive. I used a handful of shampoo on my hair. My long gorgeous hair that my mother refused to let me cut, that took forever to wash and even longer to dry. The red color was fading back to its normal dark brown. I lifted the plug in the tub so I could rinse off in clean water.

It took nearly a year to get all the soap out of my hair. Suddenly my eyes snapped open. I had an idea. I needed scissors. Sharp scissors.

There was no one to tell me no. No worlds to collapse if I did this. No one was going to care. I rubbed the towel on the huge antique mirror so I could see myself. My hair hit the curve of my back, right above my tailbone. I dressed in an old turtleneck and jeans.

I dumped my pajamas on my bed and rummaged around in the bureau drawers. I found a set of skeleton keys. Most of the doors in the long hallways of the house were locked. The temptation was irresistible. My mission for scissors shifted as curiosity got the better of me. I felt a bit like a pirate searching for treasure. Behind one of these doors was the tool I needed. I wandered down the hall, trying keys in the locks until one worked.

The door creaked open. A musty cloud of cold air hit my face and shivers broke down my body. Spiderwebs hung like tinsel from the ceiling, and a thick coat of dust made my nose twitch. I tried the light switch. A lamp emitted a soft glow, one made even dimmer by the dense layer of dust on the shade.

I caught a whiff of pipe tobacco. Heavy masculine chairs flanked a fireplace, and easels of stretched canvas with half-finished landscapes on them faced the windows. But the crown jewel of the room was an enormous, intricate desk. The top was bare, but when I opened drawers I found bits and pieces of treasures.

Old photographs of a young man in uniform. A postcard with a hospital on the front and a note in spidery script on the back: *Will be here at least six more months—terrible and exhausting. Much love, M.*

A dried rose crumbled when I picked it up. Pens and pots of ink hid behind carved doors with knobs made of onyx and ivory.

Bundles of letters flanked the desk. Most were yellowed and fragile with age, tied together with grosgrain ribbons, but others were clearly more recent.

I picked up the top batch; the envelopes were still white and smooth. All were addressed to Nurse M. Laine Fulbright.

I glanced at the door and sat down in a chair, ignoring the plume of dust that enveloped me. I untied the ribbon and opened the first letter.

Dear friend,

Our little prophet grows stronger each day. But these weary bones are fading and will be called home soon. I have given him lessons in hunting and scavenging. He does well for a young man of eleven. Gods willing, I will put him on a plane when I know I'm close and let you know when to pick him up. I'd trust

him to no one but you. He will be quite a man, one
we will be very proud of. His mother would have
adored him. He has her eyes and her loyalty. He has
memorized your address so he can find you on his
own if he must. The future is not clear and it frus-
trates me. I can't see the visions as I used to, but I
know he needs you and you him. This I trust.

> *Your friend,*
> *Tyee*

I picked up the next letter. They were spaced about
three months apart. I riffled through the other piles. None
were more recent than this batch, from seven years ago. I
scanned them all—the prophet Tyee wrote about had to
be Tens.

Friend,

I have seen beings—not in a vision, but trailing
steps behind me for the past week. I fear they've
come for Tens—his destiny is tangled in that of your
great-niece, this I feel. I have asked a policeman
friend to watch him this weekend. I must try to lead
them away from him. I pray he'll find you—the fab-
ric of my life is unraveling. Tyee

It was as if Tyee had stopped midstride before finish-
ing the story. His penmanship was sloppy and hurried, as
if he had been writing under great duress. *What does*
Tens know? How are we tied together?

I found letters from my mother chronicling events in

my life and asking Auntie questions about what to tell me. I questioned whether she'd followed any of Auntie's advice, since I'd known nothing of Fenestras before coming here. There were postcards from all over the world, signed by people I'd never heard of.

I opened the bottom drawer and found shears that were perfect for cutting cardboard. They'd do for hair. I grabbed the pile of letters from Tyee and my mom, and the scissors. I didn't lock the door behind me, certain no one would notice.

Back in my room, I spread old newspapers on the floor and positioned the mirrors so I could see the back of my head. I inhaled an ample breath and began hacking.

CHAPTER 16

My head felt lighter instantly. With each chunk of hair that fell to the floor, I stood straighter and felt older. My new haircut curled and cupped my chin and made my eyes look bigger. I evened it up as best I could and decided that while I certainly didn't have any talent for haircutting, it worked.

I smiled at myself.

"I'm pretty." The realization made my eyes light up. I'd never stopped carrying death around long enough to consider my own attractiveness. But the circles under my eyes were now mauve rather than their usual dark plum, and a light pink tinged my cheeks where before there had only been gray or green. Even to my most critical self, I didn't appear as haunted.

I wanted to show Tens. I wanted to show Auntie. I raced out of my room and down the stairs, speeding along until I stopped, worried they wouldn't appreciate the change. I decided to play it cool and wait for one of them to mention it.

I pursued the scent of garlic and onions into the kitchen. Glenn Miller played on an old tape deck, and Tens, his back to me, tapped his foot as he stirred.

I stopped, hesitating, feeling like I was intruding. All my newfound confidence and joy dispersed like smoke. This was the real world. I was an outsider.

"Can I help?" I asked Tens's back.

He didn't glance up. "We're having lazy lasagna. You like Italian food?"

I nodded. "I like trying new things."

"Why don't you butter the bread?" Without looking up, Tens pushed a thick round loaf across the counter to me.

" 'Kay." I gave up and slumped into a chair. He wasn't going to notice anytime soon.

Silence fell like a foot of fresh snow. I watched the muscles play under Tens's thin wool sweater. His shoulders were broad, and straight as a razorblade. I liked the way he flipped his hair out of his eyes with a shrug and a tilt. He needed a haircut, because it kept getting in his way. I remembered tangling my fingers in his hair when he carried me upstairs. It felt as shiny and silky as it looked.

I struggled with the quiet, words clawing at the back of my throat.

"So?" I finished buttering the loaf and wrapped it in foil. I stood and walked over to Tens, who had finished filling a bowl with ricotta, basil, and mozzarella. "What now?" I sidled closer to him. He smelled of woodsmoke and pine sap and soap.

He stepped away, but I couldn't tell if the rejection was intentional. "Layer the sauce, noodles, and cheese. Ladle sauce into the pan to start." All said without a glance at me. Nothing.

I picked up the ladle and dipped it into the pot as I was instructed. "Where are you from?"

"Around." Tens spread the sauce with the end of a noodle, then layered more noodles on top. He'd yet to look at me.

I decided to shock him into at least acknowledging my presence. "Are you Auntie's love child?"

If he'd been drinking, liquid would have come out his nose. As it was, he blinked and shot me a hard glance. "You're kidding, right?"

"I don't know. You're here. She's here. It's like you've been here forever and you belong." I didn't say that he seemed to fit much better than me. "Are you sure you aren't a Fenestra too?"

"What the hell did you do to your hair?" he blurted.

Hurt slapped me, but I lifted my chin. "I like it." I slopped the cheese mixture in globs on top of the noodles and sauce.

Tens all but shoved me out of the way. "Uh-uh. So why?"

"What?"

"Why did you cut your hair?"

"I wanted to. Are you a Fenestra?"

"I don't like it." He turned away.

"I didn't do it for you." But God, I had wished him to like it. I growled, wanting to bare my teeth and bite. "So who are you?"

"No one."

"Yeah, and I'm Oprah."

"Who?" Tens put the lasagna in the oven and turned on the timer.

"Are you going to answer my question?"

"No." He began to walk away.

"That's it? 'Around' and 'no'?" I wanted to stamp my feet like a toddler. He made me regress. And feel like a full-grown woman, both at the same time. How was that possible?

"That's it."

"You have to tell. You have to give me more than that."

"No, I don't."

"You're in a crappy mood."

He shrugged, not disagreeing but not apologizing, either.

"Who wants pizza for dinner?" Auntie glided into the

kitchen as if completely unaware of the tension. She looked at the two of us and stopped. "Oh dear me. What's going on?"

I didn't know what to say.

Tens sighed and wiped his hands on a dish towel, but didn't speak.

Auntie crossed her arms and held her ground. She tried to stare both of us down. "What is it? Tens, I can see the stick up your arse from here. I'm dying, remember? Dying people don't have time for silly moods."

I blanched. *How can she be so nonchalant about it?*

"Little one, what happened to your hair?" She fluffed it with her hands. "I like it."

Tens snorted.

I raised my eyebrows at him.

"Oh, I see. That's it." Her eyes crinkled at the corners. "Tens, cough it up—what's going on? Sit, sit." She shooed us to the table.

"I didn't mean it like that." Tens reached out as if to touch my hand but caught himself. "Sorry."

I wasn't sure if he was apologizing for his comments or for almost touching me. "Thanks."

"And?" Auntie prompted.

"How am I supposed to do this? By myself?" Tens asked her.

"Be a Protector, you mean?" She seemed to know exactly what he was talking about. She turned to me. "Has he told you that part yet?"

Tens shook his head.

"I guess not." I watched him rub the tabletop.

"Shall I?" Auntie asked him.

He nodded.

"The Creators watch over Fenestras with angels—warriors—the Sangre, whom we've already talked about a little. The Creators have humans who are urged to help by their faith or an inner moral compass. Sometimes people don't even know they're acting on behalf of the Creators. And the Creators give most Fenestras a Protector. Sometimes these are angels, but mostly they're human, granted extra gifts of bravery, intelligence, courage, compassion. They can sense the presence of their Fenestra, can empathically know their emotions."

"Okay?" I asked, wanting her to continue. I noticed a red flush creep up Tens's neck.

"In terms of the window metaphor we've been using, they are the walls that hold the window, the structure that helps the window do her job."

"Oh my God, you're Auntie's Protector, aren't you?" I gasped. Jealousy, irrational though it was, sang in my blood.

"Hers?" Tens's gaze snapped to mine.

"No, child, he's yours." Auntie patted my hand.

"Mine?" I swallowed, dumbfounded.

Tens nodded.

"You *can* read my mind, can't you?"

Auntie chuckled. "No, he can't. He can sense your mood, your feelings, but he doesn't always understand what he's sensing. That entails practice. And time."

"Who is yours, then?" I couldn't wrap my mind around this.

Her face changed. "Charles was as close to a Protector as I got. I never had one destined for me. They are even rarer than Fenestras these days. Rarer still are those with the power to fight darkness by themselves."

"Oh."

"I'm hungry for pepperoni. Tens, child, can the lasagna be frozen?"

"Sure," he muttered.

"I'm going to get my coat. Give me a minute." Auntie whisked her fingers through my hair again. "So pretty." She smiled and left the room.

"You probably wanted someone better, right? Someone more worthy?" I asked Tens. I was sure he was upset because he'd expected a real superhero to show up instead of me.

"No. No!" He grabbed my hand. "You were so sad. And lonely. And scared. And I couldn't do anything. I couldn't help. I thought when you got here, it would be better. And now you're here and you're still—"

"Sad and lonely and scared?" I asked with a frown.

"I don't really know how to do this—you're changing and I can't keep up."

"I can't either. I guess we figure it out together."

"I'm ready!" Auntie called from the front door.

He smiled. "I'm sorry—for everything. Your hair is nice."

"Don't apologize. We're fine." I squeezed his fingers,

then dropped them. "Let's start over." I held out my hand. "It's very nice to meet you Tenskatawa Valdes. I'm Meridian Sozu."

"How did you know that?"

"Know what?"

"My full name."

I tilted my chin up and tried to act like I had every right to snoop. "I found a bunch of old letters."

"Letters?"

"From your grandfather to Auntie."

"Where? Were you snooping?"

"In a room upstairs. I was looking for scissors. I'll give the letters to you when we get home, okay?"

But it was too late. The clouds were back in his eyes, and this time I'd put them there.

It is what we are taught. It is what we know. It is our deepest secret, for to know the truth quite literally requires a death. The seeker's death, not ours. Never ours, until the end. So we never tell. When our loved ones begin to fade out of their bodies, & they are able to see us for the first time, well, by then it is too late to explain. So we burn brightly & become the doorway, the path between this life & the beyond.

—Jocelyn Wynn, b. 1770–d. 1876

CHAPTER 17

I hadn't paid any attention to the town when I'd arrived. But now, as ranch lands and wilderness gave way to shuttered factories and abandoned fringes, I saw the skeletons of a once-vibrant place.

"What happened around here?" I asked.

Auntie sighed. "It pains me to see it. It's awful. Simply awful."

Tens spoke up. "Jobs moved, factories shut down, the mine closed. Industry declined for a few years and people left."

Old-style clapboard architecture of the Wild West rubbed shoulders with the brick favored by the early boomers. The newest building looked like its ribbon cutting had happened in the seventies. Paint peeled in strips and signs hung at drunken angles. Potholes spotted the road with a frequency that made them the norm.

As we got closer to town, billboards with Reverend Perimo's smiling face popped up on both sides of the small highway. After the sixth appearance of his Hollywood A-list face inviting us to meet the Almighty on Sunday, I wondered out loud, "Is he for real?"

"There's something about him," Auntie answered me.

"He creeped me out."

"How?" Auntie turned in her seat and gazed at me.

"He recited Bible verses at me when we found Celia. Then he got all friendly when Tens walked up."

"I don't like him," Tens growled.

"He knew my name before I'd even told him."

"That could be small-town America at work." Auntie didn't sound convinced even as she said it.

"But who knew I was here?"

"I don't know."

"He is doing good things for this town, though." Auntie added this as if admitting it pained her.

Gradually, freshly painted houses lit up with Christmas lights started to outnumber the empty shells. Every lawn had a nativity scene or a lit cross. I didn't see any symbols of Hanukkah or Kwanzaa. There weren't any Santa Claus decorations either. "Where's Santa?"

"The town council voted to put Christ back in Christmas."

"No Santa?"

"Nope. Reverend Perimo dabbles in politics, too." Tens spit the words out like they were sour.

All around us new construction and remodeling were evident. Paint so fresh it appeared wet. A general store, a Christian bookstore, a salon. All sparkled. Fake poinsettias and garlands decorated the storefronts along with the three wise men and the Eastern star.

A mammoth cathedral complex shone under huge spotlights like a professional sports stadium. A cross reflected the light as if it had millions of diamonds embedded in it.

"Wow." I wasn't sure if it was a church or a Vegas casino.

"Not much else to say, huh?" Tens smiled over his shoulder at me.

"At least he employed townspeople to rebuild it." Auntie said this as if she was trying to find something positive to say.

Tens parked in front of a small ma-and-pa pizza place.

"This is cute," I said.

"Best pizza in town."

Tens eyed me and mouthed, *Only*. The smells of garlic and yeast bread were comforting. At home, we had pizza once a week.

As we entered the parlor, tinkling bells announced us. A compact man with a full beard walked toward us with an enormous smile. "Ah, Mrs. Fulbright, so good to see you. Perfect timing." He set a menu down and moved away to the counter.

"Why?" I asked as we were seated near the back of the empty restaurant. Tens grabbed the chair next to me.

"There's a big rush when Bible study lets out in about an hour," Tens replied.

"Oh."

"Every night."

"There's Bible study every night?"

"Different groups, different activities, but the church has become the town center."

"The usual?" the man asked, returning with three glasses of water.

"You know me so well, Mr. Lombardo," Auntie said laughing. "Let me introduce you to my niece, Meridian. She's visiting from Portland."

"For the holidays? Such a lovely girl. We will miss seeing you, Mrs. Fulbright."

"Why?" I asked, wondering if he, too, knew she was dying.

Mr. Lombardo dropped his eyes, as if ashamed. "We are moving. At the first of the year."

"Don't say that. Please." Auntie gripped his hands.

He dipped his head. "It's past uncomfortable. We're too old to fight this. Best to leave."

"Like the Mitchells, the Vanderbilts, the Johnsons, and the Smiths?" Auntie asked sadly.

"We've been bought out, so there will still be pizza."

Mr. Lombardo tried to smile, but it looked more like a grimace.

"It won't be the same. Not at all." Auntie wiped away a tear.

As Mr. Lombardo walked off, I dug through Auntie's purse and handed her a Kleenex.

After a minute or two, Tens leaned into me. "They've all been bought out, or they've left."

"Who?"

"Anyone who doesn't agree with Perimo and his believers. No one is exempt. They've even elected the town council and the sheriff, all of whom swore to uphold God's love above man's. Men can 'discipline' their wives and children; the local schools all teach creationism and prayer; taxes go to the church rather than to the government."

"That's not legal. Is it?" I couldn't imagine.

"Legal or not, they've done it. People are moving here because of the church, and Perimo is so charismatic he can make persecution sound logical and rational. The old-timers are dying or leaving."

"But why don't they fight?"

"Little one, human beings always take the path of least resistance. It's the few, the very few, who are willing to stand up to anything," Auntie said grimly.

Mr. Lombardo set down our pizza, but I found that my appetite had deserted me. "Mrs. Fulbright, before they come in here, I have to warn you that there are many rumors, many whispers. About you."

"Tell me."

"The deaths, Mrs. Fulbright, the babies. They say it's because of you. They're angry. The Reverend says Epiphany is the time of new beginnings and that drastic changes have to be made in order to welcome God into the New Year. Sacrifices."

"I'll be okay, Mr. Lombardo."

"These are very serious threats. Very scary. I fear for you. I do not hear everything, but enough. Enough to worry."

"Thank you, but I'll be all right."

He turned to me. "You watch out for her, yes?"

The bells above the door tinkled and a group of families poured in, rosy-cheeked and bright with laughter and merriment. Mr. Lombardo moved quickly away from our table.

I didn't know what to say. Tension radiated from Tens. He was wired to spring, and that made me nervous.

"Shall we get this to go?" I finally asked when none of us move to touch our slices.

"Yes, that's a good idea," Auntie answered.

I walked over to the counter to get a box and pay, while Tens stayed with Auntie at our table. I listened to whispers that followed me as I walked the length of the restaurant.

"She's the witch's—"

"Witch too?"

"Killed those babies—"

"Let the moms die—"

"Wouldn't let them be purified—"

"Burn—"

I turned to meet the stares head-on. The whisperers turned away, averting their eyes as if they hadn't been watching me.

I stood there for a moment, and their conversations resumed as they ignored me completely.

Auntie held her head high as we left. "Rebecca, nice to see you. Evan, Emily, your daughter Eva is getting so big. She's a beautiful baby."

As a group they fidgeted and mumbled without meeting our eyes or returning Auntie's greetings.

"Andrew, you've grown into such a handsome man. Ranching suits you." She kept trying. Some people ignored us, as if we were invisible.

"I helped birth half of them. The other half moved here for the church," she said as we walked out to the Land Rover.

Two of our four tires were slashed. Tens spun around, scrutinizing the shadows.

Auntie sank into the passenger seat. She appeared weary and shrunken, as if walking past all those people had somehow aged her. "They're gone, dear. Did you think to—"

"I bought four spares when I was out. Odds were good we'd need them." Tens shrugged out of his coat and gloves.

"I'll help," I offered, unsure that he'd welcome me.

"Thanks." He handed me a flashlight.

I shut Auntie in the car as Tens hauled out the jack. "What was that all about?"

"Auntie's been a midwife for the town for decades. Before this place had a doctor in residence, before the big hospital two hours away was built. She handled everything. And everyone wanted her help.

"About six months ago, the church elders got together and decided that all pregnant women should be confined for the last three months of their pregnancy. They couched it in terms of extended maternity leave to allow families proper preparation for the arrival of the infant. And they banned midwifery not associated with the church."

"Freaky." I held the flashlight as Tens expertly twisted the wrench and heaved off a flat tire.

"Then they decided that the women needed to be purified for the birthing. There were a bunch of rules that started creeping in. Only bread and juice—Communion foods—for the last two weeks; no air-conditioning—the room should be at body temperature; no medication for pain because women were created to bear the pain of childbirth—"

"These are men making up this list?" I snorted.

"Yep. Anyway, soon Auntie was all but shoved out of the process."

"But this is America—it's the twenty-first century. This doesn't make any sense."

"I know it sounds crazy, but it's like all the people of the church are mesmerized. And Perimo's goons are schooled in how to make his wishes sound plausible. One little tiny thing becomes many big things. He can make individuals feel special—important, even—in a way I've never seen before. He has amazing power over people."

"Why do they think Auntie killed the babies?"

"There were seven women who were all pregnant within weeks of one another, and they were the first group the new rules applied to. Rose Cannady was the first to go into labor. She was weak from only eating bread, and the labor was long. She started passing out and finally her husband called Auntie in a panic. By the time Auntie and I got there, both Rose and the baby were dead. I tell you, their bedroom seemed like something out of a history book. Perimo arrived on our heels and blamed the deaths on Rose's lack of faith. He hinted that Auntie wasn't a believer and perhaps she was even working against the faith."

"Oh my God."

"The same thing played out in different ways over the course of October: a preemie only lived a few hours, one child was born severely disabled, another mother's placenta tore. Each time the family waited until the very end to seek help. Soon they began blaming Auntie and calling her a witch. They're all coincidences. I don't know, terrible luck, bad timing? But when people are scared, it's enough to fan the fires of doubt and blame." Tens shoved the last nut into place. "We're good."

I shivered. "Let's get out of here."

He put a hand on my arm. "Be careful. There's something off about that church. Perimo's never been anything but nice to my face, but there's nothing behind his eyes. This is a very conservative small town that leans toward Bible-thumping anyway, but he's started something. It's like a train with no brakes. I Googled him early on, and I can't find a past. I found church names where he's served, but they're all PO boxes or disconnected phone numbers or voice mail. It's like he appeared out of nothing."

CHAPTER 18

Shouts and the clang of pots and pans woke me with a jerk. I lay in bed, trying to place the voices in the house. Auntie yelled and Tens replied in a low rumble. I slipped out of bed, realizing I felt stronger than I had in years. Maybe ever. I had no pain, no stiffness.

I heard glass breaking as I hurried down the stairs and into the kitchen. "What's going on?"

Auntie's cheeks were flushed. "This, this filthy, disgusting lie." She threw the town newspaper on the table and started pacing. "I knew he wouldn't let well enough alone, but this is too much." A substantial cough wracked her tiny frame. I poured a glass of water for her while Tens rubbed her back. She sat and caught her breath.

"Who lied?" I said, reaching for the paper.

"Mr. Google Reverend."

"I think you mean Internet," Tens inserted, sipping coffee from a mug that held a gallon if not more.

"Whatever. He sure as bat crap didn't study theology to get his credentials." She pointed at Tens as if she didn't like his correction. He didn't seem shaken to see her so worked up.

"What did he say?" I asked. Custos padded over and put her head in my lap with a whine. I stroked her ears, enjoying the texture, so soft. She made me think of Sammy, who demanded attention and touch at every opportunity.

"He instructed his twelve lackeys to write and publish garbage. Read it! Read that filth! Read it out loud, even. Go on." She shooed me until I picked up the newspaper.

OUTSIDERS BEAR GIFTS OF SIN,
GREED, AND SLOTH.
WRITTEN BY THE BOARD OF DIRECTORS,
CHURCH OF FORGING PURITY

We all know the Christmas story. The three wise men who bring gifts to the Christ child. We know Mary and Joseph sought refuge in a town not unlike ours, and that the miracle of Christ's birth was witnessed by simple folks like us.

But the world is changing, and no longer is our town the pure American classic that it was for so many years.

We have been invaded by the lax work ethic of the consumer. We don't have to tell you, our neighbors, how badly the closing of our town's largest employer, Furnace Steel Manufacturing, and the closing of the Cristos coal fields have affected our town. You have felt that pain personally. Hardworking, God-fearing members of this congregation have been shamed into standing in line at the food bank. But have you stopped to think why they were closed? Because of profit margins and numbers. Human beings are not numbers and God does not condone His children suffering in vain. And this is vanity.

This week we lost a precious soul to an outsider's illegal animal trap. An outsider found our darling, but we can't help but wonder—if she'd been rescued by a member of this congregation, would she still be with us today? What took so long to rescue the child? Who coerced her to wander so far afield?

The wolves have begun attacking our cattle at God's insistence. A pestilence plagues other herds so that we will bow down before Him. To those who are righteous, they are wealthy. God despises the sinner. He degrades the greedy, lashes at the luxury peddled by the Devil around us. Band together, brothers and sisters. Bow down before the Lord, that He might smite the sinner and save the pure. Drive out the enemy of God, purify yourselves and your children.

Our children will be born healthy instead of dying before leaving their mother's womb. There is evil at work in this town, and it is our duty as Christian soldiers to fight. Fight with our faith, our words, and our fists if it comes to that. The Devil fights dirty. We must reevaluate those we associate with. We must quarantine the evil and safeguard the pure.

But if we do nothing, if we ignore the commandments, if we forsake the covenant that we made with the rebirth of our spirits, then we deserve what the good Lord metes out upon us. We must compel evil to leave us, we must drive the enemy of the Lord away from our boundaries, for only then will we find everlasting life with the Almighty in Heaven.

We are instituting a prayer list that we will publish weekly to help believers save these desperate souls among us. Outsiders, those who do not follow the faith, need strong encouragement to search their hearts for the Almighty's truth. Let these neighbors know you pray for them, for their eternal happiness, and let those who turn you away shudder with the wrath only He can bestow upon the wicked. We live in Revelation for a reason—the time has come when the earth shall see the glory of God and know His judgment.

Dumbfounded, I asked, "This is today's paper? The front page?"

"Yes." Auntie bit off the word.

I raised my eyebrows and gave her a small smile, trying to lighten the tension in the room. "It sounds like something from a history book. Is 'smite' even a word anymore?"

She gave me an expression that burned with 106 years of experience. "Look closer, Meridian. Read the other one now."

YOUR SPIRIT REVEALED

SCRIPTURE LESSON

WRITTEN BY THE LORD OUR GOD,

REMINDED TO YOU BY REVEREND PERIMO

"... keep all my statutes, and all my judgments, and do them: that the land, whither I bring you to dwell therein, spue you not out.⁴" The Lord is clear. Those who are impure will be cast out. Those who do not follow His judgments and statutes will be destroyed. The Devil does everything to entice you, your spouse, and your children. You must be ever vigilant. Ever on guard against his evil works. "A man also or woman that hath a familiar spirit, or that is a wizard, shall surely be put to death . . ."⁵

Brothers and Sisters, I have received word that the Epiphany is coming, and with it will come the Almighty's judgment on our hearts. A great evil will befall innocents soon, and you will know that I speak the truth as the Almighty commands it. The Devil got Celia Smithson; will he lure your children from their families too?

We must band together. None will be saved from judgment, we will all stand before the Almighty and He will chronicle our sins. Will He note that we purified this place in His name, or will He repeat that we disobeyed His commandments and His laws? He says, "Thou shalt not suffer a witch to live.[6] . . . As the Lord liveth, the man that hath done this thing shall surely die . . ."[7] Will you be surprised when you are received in Hell or will you stand before the Almighty in paradise? We must act *now*. We must work together to prepare for the way of the pure. January sixth is coming. Will you be ready? I will be. Join me. Amen.

I stopped smiling. Clearly, I was missing the bigger picture. It was an editorial with Bible quotes in a small-town newspaper, and the guy was clearly whacked. No one was going to pay attention to his fanatical blathering. Right? "What's the problem?"

Auntie sat down across from me and gripped my wrist. "They all but said you killed Celia."

"What?" I checked again, but the words blurred on the page. "She wouldn't have made it," I whispered, barely able to get the words out. "You said she wouldn't have made it."

Auntie nodded. "I'm no longer welcome in the birthing room. Carson asked me to get my groceries in the next town. Billie hasn't had an appointment free to do my hair in months."

"Perimo's targeting you." Tens pushed away from the counter to pace the length of the kitchen.

I was working frantically to process what I was hearing, but I couldn't quite get up to speed.

"I'm working with the devil, according to this prophet." Auntie snatched the paper and threw it across the room. I'd never seen her so upset.

I felt like I needed to reassure her. "That's ridiculous. No one believes that stuff anymore."

Tens guffawed. "Then what's with all the slashed tires, phone calls, blood-draped carcasses, and arrows lodged in the front door?" He raised his eyebrows, daring me to connect the dots.

I shrank further into myself, as if to protect me, us, the way I thought the world worked. "Do you mean— if the Aternocti are here and the church is doing bad stuff—then maybe they're working together?"

Auntie considered this for a moment. "The Nocti are supposed to be like us—they don't cause death, they merely move souls to the Destroyers, given the chance. But I don't know. I've never met a Fenestra who'd survived contact."

"So what do we do?"

Custos pawed at the back door and pranced away smiling when Tens let her out.

Auntie stood and stared out the window. The silence stretched. "We go to church. Let's have him say this to my face."

I shook my head. "I don't think that's a good idea."

That felt like taunting the cobra; wasn't it better to walk away before being bitten?

Tens joined me. "Neither do I."

Auntie waved her hands like our opinions weren't part of the discussion. "You get to be one hundred six and you don't need permission from youngsters. Go get ready, and for God's sake look proper and God-fearing." She stomped out.

"What's God-fearing look like?" I asked Tens.

"Probably not SpongeBob," he answered with a smile and a nod at my pj's before grabbing an apple and leaving the kitchen.

I sound insane, I know that. But I am not crazy. I cannot prove it, of course. The only way to know for sure I am telling the truth is for a soul to transition through me, and by that time, they are not going to wire their friends and family to tell them I'm not a loon. They have other things to think about when they see the light instead of me.

—Meridian Laine, April 13, 1946

CHAPTER 19

I picked at the skirt of my school uniform, mortified to know that Tens had washed it and pressed each pleat. I thought of the other clothes he'd delivered to me last night. He hadn't glanced at me, hadn't even grunted when I'd stammered a thank-you after seeing my pink undies with embroidered silver stars at the top of the pile.

Clearly, Mom hadn't gotten the memo that I was going to have to seem God-fearing for a radical congregation that thought I was a devil-worshipping witch. My school skirt and an ancient ecru lace blouse I scrounged from a closet were the closest I could get to what I thought might appear acceptable. I rolled on a pair of dark green leggings. My tights were ruined seven ways, but "God-fearing" didn't include bare knees.

I ambled down the stairs with fifteen minutes to go. It was a good thing my hand was tight on the railing because I hardly recognized the suited man with his back to me. *Oh gracious, Tens cleans up well.* Charcoal gray pinstripes ran the length of material with a lustrous black sheen. Maybe the pants were a little short and the sleeves a little long. He fussed with a tie in the hall mirror. I must have been reflected in it, because he froze like a rabbit sensing danger. Poised to flee.

He'd cut his hair too. Now it tucked right behind his ears. He was watching me in the mirror. I couldn't read his expression; it was closed, guarded, maybe a little afraid.

"Nice." I swallowed the other ooey gooey words that wanted to tumble out of my mouth.

He grunted and went back to mangling the tie.

"Here, I can do it." I held out my hand. "I have to tie it on me, but you can tighten it on you."

He stopped and considered my offer.

"Really. Hand it over. My dad taught me." It was one of the few father-daughter moments I remembered.

Tens reluctantly handed me the gray silk tie, which smelled of cedar. I wrapped it around my neck, trying to ignore the heat clinging to it. I closed my eyes and visualized the steps, hoping I wasn't about to make an ass of myself.

With a final tug, I tied the straightest knot of my life. I lifted the tie over my head and passed it to Tens. He grunted again and tucked it around his neck, tightening the knot, straightening the lay. He smoothed down his starched white shirt collar, but missed a bit in the back that edged into his hair. I reached up and turned it down, noticing the quick glide of his hair over my fingers and the stillness of his body at my touch.

"Let's get this show on the road." Auntie's voice marched ahead of her down the stairs.

I jumped back from Tens, as though I'd been caught doing something terribly naughty.

"Thanks," he mumbled, and moved away from me. I think he blushed.

I turned to Auntie, expecting an outfit that was maybe a step up from her usual impeccable classic. My jaw dropped.

Auntie was resplendent in a purple velvet skirt suit. She carried herself like the Queen of England, and the ensemble was one that would have made Victorian Elizabeth proud. Layers of petticoats peeked out from beneath a full skirt. A jacket corseted her tiny torso and accentuated the bust I hadn't been aware she had. Even Custos seemed caught off guard.

Auntie smoothed on a pair of white gloves and handed a set to me. She placed a navy blue pillbox hat, complete with navy blue half-veil, on my head and patted it down for effect. "You'll wear this as well."

"Do I—"

"Yes, you have to. I will not have those Believers saying we didn't follow their customs."

"They wear gloves and hats?"

She gave me a hard look and wrapped a thick scarf around her neck. "Have you ever heard of a religion that preached getting naked? Don't answer that. They require covering up. So we cover up."

I had the feeling that I would be the only person under the age of eighty wearing a hat, veil, and gloves, but this was Auntie's show.

"Whatever," I said, adamantly ignoring the mirror as I walked past it.

Tens drew on a black trench coat of the softest leather, broken in and worn for years.

"You're almost as handsome as my Charles in that." Auntie opened the coat closet and pointed to a stack of hatboxes on the top shelf. She was way too short to reach them. "The second to the top will make your outfit."

Tens reached up and lifted a hatbox down. Auntie removed the lid and peeled back the yellowed tissue paper. She drew out a charcoal fedora with a blue satin band and said to Tens, "Lean down."

He bent, scrunching his knees until Auntie could reach his head easily. She perched the hat at an angle.

My heart stuttered and I reminded myself to breathe. Tens towered like one of those black-and-white movie stars—a gangster, dangerous, possessive.

"You like?" He turned to me.

I couldn't get words out; I just nodded.

"Dashing," Auntie proclaimed with a clap of her

hands. She marched out ahead of us to the Land Rover. "We're going to be late if we don't hurry."

I tried to glide past Tens rather than trip over my feet. I didn't quite accomplish a glide, but I didn't make an ass of myself.

"Wanna trade?" he whispered to me.

I choked back a laugh. The vision of him wearing Auntie's ancient tulle on his head sent giggles fizzing in my stomach. "Absolutely," I said over my shoulder as he locked the dead bolt on the front door.

* * *

Tens turned another corner. Packed parking lots spread out in front of us. In the distance, set against the backdrop of the Sangre de Cristos Mountains, was the enormous structure of cement and chrome we'd driven past the night before. It was a building better suited to a population of ten times what Revelation boasted. "Is that a church or an airport?"

"Yeah, I always think it looks like it's missing the planes," Tens muttered.

"Wait till you see inside this monstrosity. I snuck in once to see what the fuss was about," Auntie said, patting my shoulder.

We turned right and it seemed like the world got brighter, as if the sun came out and this street was happier.

"I'll drop you off and go park," Tens said, addressing Auntie.

"You don't have to—"

"Yes, I do." He weaved his way between pedestrians smiling and laughing like they were heading to a party and not to church. The women's hats, veils, and heels complemented the men's three-piece suits and shined shoes.

Tens braked in the drop zone and I unbuckled my seat belt. "Brace yourself," he said to me, then glanced away as if he wanted to say more but didn't know how.

"Come on, child. Let's face this head-on."

I opened the door and held on to Auntie's arm as she avoided snowdrifts and ice piles along the curb. The hair on the back of my neck bristled.

Tens met my eyes, but I couldn't read his expression. "I'll be right back."

I nodded and put my gloved hand over Auntie's.

"We'll wait here for Tens," she said, patting me.

Cheerful conversation seemed to cease around us. A man I didn't recognize, in resplendent robes of pure white, stood in the doorway and greeted each person. He leaned toward another man, who whispered and pointed at us.

"Are they talking about us?" I asked, embarrassment flushing my cheeks.

"Let's go say hello." Auntie pretended not to notice and marched over.

"Do we have to?" I muttered.

"Jack, how nice to see you today. May I introduce you to my niece, Meridian?" Turning to me she said, "Jack and his wife, Nicole, have six beautiful children I helped deliver. The eldest is heading to college next year. How are the kids, Jack?"

"Fine. I'm glad you came, Merry. We pray for your soul at dinner every night."

"Isn't that nice." Auntie touched his arm and ignored his wince. "Have you found a job yet?"

"The Reverend helped me get a position at the high school."

I pretended not to notice the whispers and stares as people moved around us, giving us a wide berth.

"If you'll excuse me, I need to welcome the people behind you." Jack turned away before he'd even finished the sentence.

"Don't you know all of these people?" I asked Auntie.

She nodded, not once looking at me. "I used to. They decided knowing me wasn't worth the risk. Or they moved here to rid the town of people like me," she said, answering my unspoken question. "Oh, here comes your young man." She smiled at Tens's approach.

"Oh, he's not—"

"Of course he is." She chuckled.

Tens strode up to us in the long trench and debonair hat. I could almost see a smile in his eyes. He presented Auntie with his arm. "Shall we?"

"Yes, thank you." She took his arm and I could see a flash of the young woman she'd once been with her Charles.

I started to follow them and realized my hands shook.

Tens reached over and linked his fingers through mine. "I'm here," he said.

I nodded, unsure why fear clamped my gut. I had to close my mouth several times while we walked through the spacious hallways. They were lined with stained-glass windows depicting scenes from the Bible, and music from a huge organ filled the space with hymns. This building, and these people, made me feel very small.

CHAPTER 20

The greeter passing out programs ignored us even though Auntie addressed him directly. "Nice to see you, Devlin. I trust your children are healthy?" We didn't pause, but walked right by him.

I kept my eyes straight ahead as Auntie led us down the center of the sanctuary. It was huge, with gleaming organ pipes and a clear Lucite pulpit that floated above the congregation. I knew my neck would hurt by the end of the service.

A fly buzzed near my ear for just a minute and then

fell silent as it hit the floor behind me. I prayed there were no dying people in the church with us.

The low hum of whispers and the creaking of people shifting in their pews trailed behind us. It felt as though the entire town was present.

"I think they're expecting me to go up in flames." Auntie shook her head in admonishment. "Almost everyone I know is here, save a few."

She stopped at a half-filled pew and gestured for me to enter. I didn't want to let go of Tens's hand, so I didn't. I clung to it as a mother with three small children scooted down to the far end of the pew, then moved several rows back.

The familiar strains of a Sunday-school song swelled through the amplifiers and camouflaged speakers around us. With every song change, the energy and fervor rose. The congregation sang, clapped, and danced as one. Sweat glazed the faces around us, but the singing continued.

A roar from the crowd made me turn. Forming an inverted V, Perimo and a gang of robed men with the walk and carriage of bodyguards came down the center aisle.

Auntie leaned over Tens to say to me, "His twelve quasi disciples."

The last three, including Perimo, were inhuman in their beauty. They were the After photographs of the best plastic surgeons.

Reverend Perimo was the point of the V, clearly absorbing the energy around him. He paused to greet people and touch the hands of a lucky few on his march down the aisle. His step didn't falter when he reached our pew; instead he dipped his head to Auntie and gave me a smile that was both sinister and secretive. I didn't know if that was a good thing or a challenge accepted, but I had a feeling I'd find out.

He spoke into a tiny flesh-colored head mike when the music paused. " 'I will sing praise to the Lord God of Israel.' "[8]

He raised his hands like he was blessing the choir and used a conductor's move to shut down the sound. Everyone fell silent. I hung on to Tens's hand and he squeezed back.

Reverend Perimo then faced the congregation. "First off, I see new faces in the seats today. We have prayed you'd hear the Almighty's word in your life and join us in this holy place. Can I get an Amen?"

The people replied as one. "Amen."

Reverend Perimo continued. " 'When I blow with a trumpet, I and all that are with me, then blow ye the trumpets also on every side . . .' "[9] He raised his hands, and trumpets sounded as if from everywhere at once.

"Amen. Amen." Reverend Perimo stepped up to the pulpit. His posse settled in huge, ornate velvet-covered chairs behind him.

"I am not eloquent . . . 'And the Lord said unto him . . . I will be with thy mouth, and teach thee what thou shall say.'[10] I have been asked why I use the Bible as the foundation of my ministry. I am but a man, like you, human and fallible. But the Lord's word was given to us at creation. It's a great gift. The answer to every question is in here." He lifted an enormous Bible off the podium in front of him. "Your souls know the truth. You know that like Moses I only speak as the Almighty commands. I have proven this to you time and again. Who told you to watch your cattle?"

"You did!" a woman shouted.

"Who warned you that wandering children are the devil's playthings?"

"You did!" A man raised his fist.

His voice was mesmerizing. This was the Bible as if delivered from heaven above. The acoustics of the church gave a rich timbre to his voice and absoluteness to the words as he continued quoting the Old Testament.

Tens nudged me and I surveyed the other impeccably groomed men flanking Perimo. "Those tallest ones came to town right after he got here."

One of his twelve stood, his gaze gathering in everyone seated below. " 'Beware of him, and obey his voice, provoke him not; for he will not pardon your transgressions: for my name is in him.' "[11]

The nodding and quiet "Amen's" in the audience unnerved me.

Reverend Perimo stomped his feet. " 'And he that blasphemeth the name of the Lord, he shall surely be put to death. . . .'[12] These are strong words, brother and sisters, but the Almighty does not mince his meaning. There is a tug-of-war going on for your soul. You must make sure your family, your friends, and your neighbors are all helping to tug our way. Better one perish to hell than all of us. Amen?"

"Amen!" the congregation shouted. A few people stood and clapped. Auntie shifted her position and muttered to herself.

" 'If ye walk in my statutes, and keep my commandments, and do them; then I will give you rain in due season, and the land shall yield her increase. . . .'[13] Where is Branson McAfee?"

A man stood. "Here."

"Branson, how were your corn yields this season?"

"Up two hundred percent from last year."

"What was different?"

"I was saved last Christmastime."

"And the Almighty provided for you in abundance."

"Yes, sir, He did. And my back doesn't hurt none either."

"And a healing! Praises, Amen!"

"Amen!"

" 'And if you walk contrary unto me, and will not hearken unto me; I will bring seven times more plagues upon you according to your sins. I will also send wild beasts among you, which shall rob you of your children, and destroy your cattle. . . .'[14] The Lord knows." Perimo motioned to another man in his posse.

The man stood. "This week little Celia was ripped from us and there were two miscarriages. Before we were saved, who saw the town dying each day? The highway was empty, no one stopped, no one moved here. But now, four families moved in last week—will the Stones, Rogers, Greggs, and Pattersons please stand?"

Four young families stood and were applauded.

Reverend Perimo then said, " 'And when the people complained, it displeased the Lord: and the Lord heard it; and His anger was kindled; and the fire of the Lord burnt among them, and consumed them. . . .'[15] I don't know if you've heard or not, but the Lombardos' house caught on fire last night. They escaped, but we must pray, for their souls, that they hear this warning from the Lord."

Auntie gasped.

"There are people who will tell you God doesn't start fires. That He doesn't increase the crops of believers. That He doesn't care who our friends are or how we treat non-believers." Perimo shook his head. "The Bible tells us differently: 'And thou shalt stone him with stones, that he die; because he hath sought to thrust thee away from the Lord thy God. . . .' "[16] He never took his eyes off us. Not once. I wasn't sure he even blinked.

A woman in the audience stood and yelled, "I repent, I repent. Save me, O Lord, save me."

Tens muttered, "Mrs. Devlin. Wonder how often she had to rehearse that line."

Reverend Perimo held up a hand for silence and the people quieted. " 'But ye that did cleave unto the Lord your God are alive every one of you this day.'[17]

"Now, those who would like a special blessing may stand before me. Who needs the touch of the Lord? Who else repents? Who believes in the Lord our Almighty?" The band started playing a contemporary Christian hymn and Perimo said, " 'Who is on the Lord's side? Let him come unto me.' "[18] Rows of people stood and were ushered single file past the front of the church. Perimo made the sign of the cross and nodded. The organ belched and the choir sang down the rafters.

"Stand up," Auntie instructed Tens, but when the ushers came to our row, they skipped us. The crowd didn't pause to allow us to join the procession.

Auntie waved to Perimo. "Excuse me, but we were accidentally skipped."

I had no idea her voice could carry so clearly or loudly. I prayed I wouldn't faint from embarrassment.

The ushers glanced toward the pulpit for instruction. Reverend Perimo walked toward us through the parting stragglers.

"We want a blessing," Auntie said as Perimo approached, towering over us.

"Blessings are for believers. Do you believe in the Almighty? In His purpose for your life? In His judgments and commandments?" He leaned down until he was eye to eye with Auntie, not blinking once.

Her chin tipped up, and if her spine could have straightened completely she'd have stood to his full height and then some. "I believe in the Creator," she said in a rich, confident voice that brooked no argument.

He gave her a half-smile, half-smirk and cocked his head to the side as if pondering a bratty rebuttal from a child. "Do you repent of your evil ways and exorcise the devil that has inhabited your soul?" He leaned into her, his tone lulling and kind.

"I am a child of the Creator. I am not evil. I have never been evil. I am a child of the light."

His voice softened even further, as if he were talking to a young and stupid child. "The devil has a strong grip on your heart, doesn't he?"

"The devil isn't in my heart, Mr. Perimo. I have lived here most of my life and know most of these people. They will tell you I have done nothing evil."

I knew even as Auntie said it that we wouldn't find anyone here to stand beside us.

"Unless you repent, the Almighty cannot work on you. I can do nothing for you. You can have the sign of the cross made over you, but it will not be of the Almighty until you push the devil from your soul." He spoke clearly into the mike again. " 'For on that day shall the priest make an atonement for you, to cleanse you, that ye may be clean from all your sins before the Lord.' "[19]

"I am clean. And you are the devil himself, aren't you?" Auntie whispered to him, but the mike caught it.

The congregation gasped in unison, and Tens moved as if to protect Auntie.

"I'll escort them out?" Jack appeared at Perimo's elbow.

"No, they stay. Perhaps we can work on their souls and save them yet. Before they leave us for good." Perimo walked back to the pulpit and continued the service as if nothing had happened. " 'And ye said, behold, the Lord our God hath shewed us His glory and His greatness, and we have heard His voice out of the midst of the fire. . . . Go thou near, and hear all that the Lord our God shall say . . . and do it.' "[20]

His twelve henchmen rose as one and said, "Amen unto the Lord." The congregation repeated the words while trumpets blared in the background.

Leers were aimed at us from every direction.

"Let's get the hell out of here." Tens gripped my hand and all but carried Auntie and me up the aisle. I don't think we stopped to breathe until we were in the Land Rover and the church was nowhere in sight.

* * *

By the time we got home, Auntie had dozed off. She was pale and her skin looked paper-thin, as if she'd sunken into herself.

The phone was ringing when we walked in the door. I wasn't sure we should answer it. Before I could voice my concern, though, Auntie picked up the phone. She grew more and more agitated, until finally she replaced the receiver.

"What's wrong?" I asked, not sure I could handle one more thing.

"How are you feeling?" She cupped my face in her hands and peered into my eyes.

"Okay?"

"I think it's time you went with me."

"Who was that?"

"An old friend. There's no time to change. He hasn't got long."

"Where are we going?" I shrugged my coat back on.

"To get you your next lesson."

"What's that?"

"How to let a willing but strong soul through your window."

"Who?"

"My Charlie's best friend, Jasper Lodge. His granddaughter's asking for me. He won't mind if you're there too."

"For what?"

"For his death, little one. For his death."

December 21, 1974

There is no gender. No male or female. There is no singular. No plural. The few humans who use more than three percent of their brain know this. Think of Einstein. He knew things few people can comprehend even with visual aids. So while most people can't wrap their heads around the idea of no gender and no quantity when it comes to Creators, as Fenestras we have to try. So I try. I don't always succeed, but that's my path.

—Linea M. Wynn, b. 1900–d. 1975 (Killed by Aternocti, never proven, death declared accidental drowning)—her cousin Meridian Fulbright, March 3, 1975

CHAPTER 21

We braked in front of an ancient clapboard rambler. A couple of cats slinked over to us and a dog barked in the distance. Hay was scattered over the thick mud and slush, but I still picked my way carefully up the walkway to the expansive porch. The cats meowed and escorted us inside when Auntie entered.

She headed straight for the bedroom, making introductions on the move. She'd been in this house many times. "Hello! Jasper, this is my niece, Meridian. She's one of us."

I hesitated in the bedroom doorway, letting my heart adjust to the fear. Why did an old man frighten me?

I jumped as a voice spoke from behind me. "My granddaddy Jasper is one of the last living World War Two veterans. A B-17 gunner, there on D-Day storming the beaches with his friends. Couldn't get through introductions without mentioning that." A woman with long braids and a peasant skirt moved into the room and took a place opposite Auntie. "Hello, Auntie, it's nice to see you again." She smiled. The scent of patchouli and pine floated like a cloud behind her.

"Sarah, it's been too long." Auntie touched her arm across the quilt-draped form. The idea of an Army man reduced to this small frame was incongruent.

"He's barely hanging on, Auntie. There's not much left of him here. It said in his papers to call you when it was time."

"Your granddaddy and I go way back. He was always so proud of you moving to New York and making something of yourself."

Sarah laughed and then sipped from her mug. "He did love to brag, now, didn't he?"

Auntie motioned to me. I slowly stepped to the side of the bed. "This is my niece, Meridian. I made this quilt when your grandmother died, Sarah."

Jasper's eyelids didn't flutter, and his breathing had a rhythmic, automated cadence, though he wasn't hooked up to anything.

Auntie grasped my hand. Hers felt as if I were clutching the full blazing sun in my palm. So hot, and mine so cold. "You have anything else to say, Sarah?"

Sarah stood and put her mug down. "He knows. It's been said."

"Well then, Meridian, I want you to close your eyes and picture that window. You're going to do this by yourself." Auntie gripped my hand. "I'm losing my strength to shield you."

I shot a glance at Sarah, not sure how she'd react. "I'm a clairvoyant," she said with a shrug. "You're not going to shock me."

I nodded, not trusting my voice, and closed my eyes. I squeezed them too tight and got those rainbow-colored blobs and sparks behind my eyelids.

"Relax," Auntie cautioned me. "Breathe."

I tried to relax my shoulders and force oxygen into my uncooperative lungs.

"Now, picture that window. You got it?" she asked.

I nodded. I visualized a big window, white lace curtains framing the glass like snow.

"Now open it. Let the wind roar through. What's outside that window?"

I kept my eyes closed and leaned toward it.

"Not too far. You stay on this side of it, you hear me?" Auntie's voice brought me back from the urge to step through, the compulsion to keep going. "Tell me what you see, Meridian."

"R-r-r—" I cleared my throat and tried again. "Red, lots of red flowers."

"Are they poppies?" Sarah asked.

In that moment I knew they were the red poppies of Flanders Fields, though how I knew that, I couldn't say. "Yes." I felt someone standing at my back.

"That's good. Now you have to step aside," Auntie said. "Move out of Jasper's way—stand clear of the window and of him."

I turned around, trying to move out of the way. I felt tangled up, like I was playing Twister with a bunch of invisible beings. "I can't." I started to move toward the window again. My arms started to ache and a headache lanced my temples. In the background, I heard Auntie's voice. I was back in the bathtub, holding my breath and then gasping for air.

"Yes, you can. Step aside like you're in line for a movie and you haven't bought your ticket yet. There are people going around you, but you're still in line. Right? Can you see that? You hold your ground. You are strong."

"Yes. Yes." I felt myself move to the side. I could see the poppies, but now I saw the room, my yellow room with the daisy throw rug and white four-poster bed. Jasper turned from the window to face me.

"Thank you. Tell your Auntie I owe her one." Jasper touched my cheek the littlest bit and stepped over the sill into the poppies. There was movement in the meadow and I could see people coming toward him.

I felt like I was swimming against an undertow. Part of me wanted to go with him.

Keep going.

It was so beautiful and so peaceful. *So bright.*

I didn't know the people, didn't need to—I felt the immense joy. A blinding, overwhelming need wracked my body with spasms.

CHAPTER 22

There was a loud crack and I jumped, my eyes open wide, back into Jasper's bedroom. I gripped Auntie's hand.

"I closed the window for you. You almost made it on your own." Auntie patted my cheek. "How do you feel?"

I gaped, surprised to be back in my body. It was odd to feel the heavy sensation of arms and legs again. My headache faded, but didn't disappear. My stomach flipped, but I didn't think I'd vomit. My bones hurt considerably, but that, too, was a passing feeling.

"Are you okay?" Sarah moved around the bed to stand by me.

"I think . . . I'll be fine." I couldn't keep the surprise out of my voice. "He said he owed you one, Auntie."

Sarah wiped tears away. "I won't ask how you knew that, but I'm sure he'll come through."

I turned to her, feeling a desperate need to share. "There were people. He was happy."

"Thank you." She hugged me. "I'm sure most people are unsure of your gifts, but thank you. You made it easy on him."

I guess that's the gist of it, isn't it? Most people are afraid. But are they freaked out by me or by death itself?

"It's death, not you. They don't even really see you, they're so caught up in the fear of dying." Sarah said.

I looked at her. "Did I say that out loud?"

"No." She smiled. "Do you want tea or hot chocolate before you head back out?"

"No, thank you, Sarah. Meridian needs a nap, I think." Auntie laughed. "Or I do!"

"I'll be here another couple of weeks settling his affairs—you call me if you need anything." Sarah dug around in her purse and handed me a business card. "You call me if you're ever in New York and need a place to crash. It's not much, but it's home and it's yours."

"Thanks." I tucked the card in my back pocket and returned her smile. I could see myself as friends with her, even though she was in her thirties and had the polished veneer of a New Yorker despite her designer hippie accessories.

Auntie handed me the car keys. "Drive it slow and we'll be fine."

I wanted to argue with her. But she had a gray tinge to her cheeks and her lips were stained a severe blue. I closed my mouth and said a prayer that we'd make it home in one piece.

I drove the whole way back at five miles per hour, but I didn't hit anything and we stayed on the road. Auntie's snores were the only sound track for the ride. Once home, I peeled my fingers off the steering wheel and took my first big breath since we'd gotten in the car. "Do we have any licorice?"

"Maybe in the pantry. You got a craving for it?" Auntie paused as she unbuckled her seat belt.

"Yeah, a black licorice and honey sandwich, actually."

"Jasper's favorite?"

I thought about it and nodded. "From his childhood. It sounds disgusting. I totally have to try it."

I held on to Auntie's elbow as we walked up the steps. Custos greeted us with a whine and a quick lick of my hand.

"You should know you'll want to be trying lots of stuff once you get a buildup of memories. I remember a night when I drank whiskey straight from the bottle because one guy said it tasted different in a glass—I don't remember his name but I know that's what he got out of life."

I giggled as we stamped our boots and started peeling off the layers. "Did it taste different?"

"No." Auntie swayed and I caught her.

"What's wrong?"

"Tired, I guess."

"Are you sure? Do you need a doctor?"

"Not right now. I'll swallow a couple of aspirin and see how I feel."

I could tell there was something more she wasn't saying. "But—"

"No."

"I could call—"

"Stop. Don't fuss." She held up a hand, then rubbed her eyes.

I didn't push, but I wasn't happy about it.

Auntie made her way to the parlor and settled down on the sofa.

"I'll make you tea, okay?"

"Two lumps and a bit of milk," she said, her eyes closed.

I poked around the pantry while the water boiled, but couldn't find any black licorice. *What if I called an ambulance? What if I asked Tens to carry her to the car? Could I force her to use medicine? What if I'm not okay just letting her be?*

The outside door slammed and heavy boots stomped to the kitchen door. The old screened-in porch wasn't much more than a mudroom in the wintertime.

I waited in the kitchen doorway and studied Tens as he unlaced his boots and pried his feet out of them. I wondered at the giddy, joyful feeling at the base of my spine. Did I love him? Could I love him? What other name could I give this feeling of fever and itch?

His was the face of a statue, all angles and planes, as if he'd never had enough to eat. His hands—how was it possible to be so captivated by something I saw every day? I'd never paid attention to hands before, but his drew my eyes. I wondered what they'd feel like holding me, if he'd be as gentle with me as he was with Custos.

"You done yet or do you need a few more minutes?" Tens asked, not glancing up.

I cleared my throat and moved toward the teakettle. "Oh, there you are." Brilliant.

"Here I am." Tens smiled at me and pulled out a chair at the kitchen table. I could feel the weight of his scrutiny on my back.

"Where were you?" I asked.

"Out and about. You do okay?"

"Yeah, actually. I couldn't do it by myself, but I'm getting better." The kettle whistled and I sprang into action like this was more important than just making tea.

"Any pain?"

"Nothing that hung around long." I made him hot chocolate and placed it in front of him.

"Thanks." He brushed my arm and sent zings up it.

I nodded, moving away and dunking the tea bags absently.

"I think that tea is done."

I blinked down at tea that could very well have held up its own bag. "I like it like that." I dug out two sugar cubes and splashed in milk for Auntie. "Where did you say you were?"

"Around."

I glanced at his shuttered expression and dropped it. Maybe he was dating someone. That would top it off, falling in love with a guy who loved someone else. "I should take the tea to Auntie." I picked up the cup and saucer.

"Let her sleep." Tens reached out and stopped me. I slopped tea onto the floor.

"Crap." I set the cup down and grabbed a towel. Always graceful, that's me.

"Don't worry about it. Auntie's been having a hard time sleeping; she's walking around at night. She's very worried about leaving us to face the Nocti alone. I don't think we should wake her. That's all." Clearly, Tens thought I was upset by his suggestion, not about making a mess in front of him.

"Once I can do it, won't they leave us alone?" I tossed the towel into the laundry room and sat down.

"I don't know. You're really going to drink that?" Tens nodded to my tea.

It was such a dark brown it seemed black. "Of course." I sipped and tried to keep my expression bland.

He chuckled but didn't say anything. He had this way of answering questions without actually saying anything. I always ended up confused about what I had asked in the first place. Was it his presence that messed me up or something else?

I needed to change the conversation. "By the way, how did you get here?"

"I walked. You guys had the car."

I had a feeling he was deliberately interpreting my question literally. "Not today. I meant, in the beginning, how did you find Auntie?"

Tens set down his mug and spun it on the tabletop. I had just decided he wasn't going to answer me when he said, "My grandfather." He drew in a pained breath and continued. "I was twelve when he died. They put me in foster care. I ran away a couple of times before I didn't get caught and sent back. I wasn't real bright about hiding."

"You were a kid."

"Maybe. Maybe not. At fourteen, with a broken lip and a couple of busted ribs, I finally got smart about what to fear."

"You were beaten on the streets?"

"No, the monster was in the nice, safe house, not out on the streets. Nobody cared. Nobody asked me why I was always covered in bruises. They just saw this nice middle-class white family who accepted foster kids no one else wanted."

I swallowed. "You left, right?"

He nodded. "Stole some cash. Started walking."

"Where were you?"

"Seattle."

My jaw dropped. "That's a long walk. Why come here?"

"Tyee had told me to. He told me if I was ever in trouble to come here and ask for Auntie or Charles. He said my destiny was tied up in a war of people and light. To protect them. There was more, but we ran out of time."

"So you walked here?"

"I hitched rides, stole wallets, worked odd jobs where I could. I got here about two years later. I lived off the land mostly. Tyee had taught me well. Made me memorize which plants could be eaten, and learn how to make a fire with nothing but wet wood. How to keep warm. He talked to me in my dreams. Told me what I needed to know to stay hidden."

"You still see him?"

His voice turned sad. "No, he stopped coming to me the day I set foot on this front porch. Then I started dreaming of . . ." He trailed off.

I didn't want the conversation to end. "You miss him? Never mind, stupid question. I miss my family and they're not dead."

For a few seconds, we listened to the creaks of the old house and the wind in the trees.

"You're not afraid of being around me?" I asked Tens.

"Why would I be?"

"People die around me." *Okay, stating the obvious here.*

"I'm not scared. Although you did just massacre a perfectly good cup of tea."

I crossed my arms over my chest. "You're not afraid of Auntie, either."

"She's pretty feisty. Maybe she was a serial criminal in her youth." Tens stood and walked over to me. He peered down at me.

"I'm serious." I rolled my eyes, hoping just once he'd take me seriously and not make me feel stupid.

"So am I." He shrugged, prying profoundly into me

with his eyes, as if measuring my ability to handle a truth. "I saw you when I was little, before my grandfather died. And after. You're who replaced him. In my dreams."

"Huh?" This was not what I expected to hear.

"He'd told me to think about what my life as a man would be. He always tried to get me to grow up faster than I wanted. Preparing me, testing me. Making sure I was ready for you."

I got stuck on the dreaming-of-me part. "You saw me in your dreams?"

"Mmm-hmm. You were playing in a fort in your backyard. You'd poked dandelions in your hair and were making up stories."

I'd always liked my make-believe world more than the real one because there was no death.

"There was a terrible commotion, a howling."

I knew what was coming next. "The mama cat, right?"

He nodded. "She crawled into your fort, birthed two kittens at your feet, and died."

Tears flooded my eyes. "The kittens were dead too. She'd been an alley cat. She didn't belong to anyone. After Dad buried her, I never went back to the fort. I thought it was haunted."

"I didn't understand it at the time, but when I woke I asked my grandfather about it."

"And he said?"

"Nothing. Not a thing. I couldn't get him to explain the dream at all. He just shook his head and smiled at me."

"Oh." Disappointed, I bit my lip and blinked at the cracked tiles on the kitchen floor.

"Where's that tea, my girl?" Auntie shuffled into the kitchen seeming even more fragile.

Tens tugged a chair out for Auntie. "You seem ready to fall over."

"Your grandfather ever tell you about his time in the army?" she asked wistfully before a cough wracked her.

"We need to get you into bed." Tens and I exchanged a glance.

"Hmm, the army, that's how we met—" A loud thump on the porch startled all of us, but it was the animal whimpering that followed that had Tens grabbing the shotgun and wrenching open the front door.

Beware of the Aternocti—they changed my sisters forever. I do not know how, but two Fenestra I used to know as well as myself are now walking with the Destroyer as Nocti.

—Luca Lenci, b. 1750–d. 1858

CHAPTER 23

"No, no, no, no, no!" I slipped on the ice and snow Custos had dragged onto the porch with her.

"Careful, Meridian. We don't know if she trusts us right now."

I leaned over the injured wolf. "You trust me, don't you, girl?"

A low rumble in her belly was her only response.

"Careful." Tens kept his voice even and made slow, careful progress over to us. "Easy."

Custos whimpered and lay down on her good side,

giving us a clear view of her injury. An arrow, the same kind that had accompanied the dead cat, was lodged in the meaty part of her left shoulder. She panted up at me expectantly.

I swallowed a gag. I'm not good with blood. Funny, you'd think being okay with gore would be part of the Fenestra job description.

"That's good." Tens walked wide around us to make sure no one waited nearby.

I reached out and laid the tips of my fingers against Custos's toenails. Just enough to touch, but not more than she could handle. "Why? Why would they do this?" She lifted her head and licked my hand, trying to nudge me closer.

Tens inspected her side, soothing her with his fingertips. "I don't think it's that bad a wound. The arrow's stuck in her skin and fur, but it's running the length of her body, not puncturing any organs. Let's see if she'll go inside and then we'll clean her up. She should be okay."

"I'm not a vet—are you a vet?"

"The only vet in Revelation left when the believers gained a majority; we're the best she's got."

Why didn't that surprise me?

Custos lifted herself to her feet, keeping her weight off the left front leg as best she could. She panted hard, her tongue lolling out of her mouth, in between boundless sighs. The crude oil of clotting blood matted her coat and dripped as she hopped toward the door.

"Help her!" Tears streamed down my face.

"We can't until she's inside and we get what we need to clean her up." Tens held the door open and motioned to me. "Go with her. Get the fire roaring, offer her fresh water. I'll bring Auntie in and then we'll get that arrow out."

I nodded.

I worked in a fury, placing a pillow under Custos's limp head, then blowing on the fire's last few red embers, begging them to catch. When wood crackled in the fireplace, I raced into the kitchen and grabbed a bowl of water.

Tens was settling Auntie on the sofa when I came back in.

"You should be in bed," I told her, unable to make my voice gentle.

"I'm fine, child. Feeling better already. Besides, my room is lonely and you need a guiding mind to fix up this girl. Years as a nurse have qualified me to teach you." Auntie's color was back and her eyes sparkled in the lamp light. "Tens, close that door and let's get lots of light in here." Tens left the room, silent.

"Meridian, see if Custos wants to drink. She's lost quite a bit of blood."

I knelt and held the trusting gaze of my newest friend. She lifted her head and tried to drink, but I could tell she only wanted to appease me.

"We'll try chicken broth later," Auntie said, breaking into another hacking cough.

Tens returned with the first-aid kit.

"You find the razor where I told you to check?" she asked.

"Yep." Tens lifted a straight razor from the kit.

"Good. Now, Meridian, find a large sewing needle and thick thread in my basket."

My stomach fell. Dying was almost easier to handle than the blood. "You're not—"

"No, child, you are," she said with confidence. "Sterilize the needle in the fire or the firewater—doesn't matter which."

I dug through the basket and found a needle, then held it to a match to clean it. I handed Tens the thread to dip in the alcohol.

Auntie struggled to sit up and catch her breath. "We need to get the arrow out without doing more damage. The best way to do that is to cut the skin around it just enough to remove it. We're lucky it's right under her skin; whoever shot her had lousy aim."

I swallowed back bile, but Tens didn't seem fazed.

Auntie stopped him from shrugging out of his overcoat. "Don't remove your leather coat—it'll give you a bit of protection if she doesn't understand we're trying to help. You hold Custos's head. You're going to have to grip her so she doesn't bite Meridian."

That left me to do the cutting and stitching. "I can't even quilt. You said yourself I'm a terrible sewer; I have no talent for it."

She shushed me. "This can be ugly and crooked and ain't nobody going to care. You have to. Now get to it."

My hands quaked as I leaned over Custos. The only sounds in the room were the fire and her heavy, panting breaths. I closed my eyes and said a quick prayer to whatever god might be listening. I didn't want to cause Custos any pain.

"Steady yourself, Meridian. Work fast, it'll hurt less. You'll need to clean the wound with the alcohol, then sew her up."

Tens sat down and put Custos's head in his lap. He didn't take his eyes off me. "You can do this. You owe her."

I remembered falling asleep on the hike up the hill, the pleasant feelings of warmth, Custos's growls to get me moving to the safety of the house. He was right. I owed Custos my life. Even if I sewed like shit and was just as likely to cut myself with the razor as her. I swallowed, trying to channel every medical television program I'd ever seen to my fingers.

Custos didn't move, other than to hold her breath through the hard parts. The cuts were easier to make than I expected because the arrow lay shallowly under her skin. I dabbed alcohol on the wound and she whined, but didn't make any moves away from me or Tens.

"Almost there." Tens nodded at me. "You're doing great."

I readied the needle and held the jagged edges of her flesh together. I sewed seven stitches, smeared antibiotic cream on top of them, and placed a handful of gauze over it all.

"Here, I'll lift her and you can wrap the bandage all the way around so it's secured." Tens leaned over Custos and lifted. My hair brushed his face and his fell in mine. He smelled of pine and fir and wet dog. It made me smile.

"Done." I sat back, collapsing against the chair legs.

"Good, good." Auntie smiled. "Your grandfather would be proud, Tens. You're a good medic."

"You knew him well?" Tens seemed shocked.

Auntie chortled. "Of course I knew your grandfather. Did you think he told you to come to this place on a lark?"

"I always thought it was profound. That he wanted me in a place, not with a particular person."

"It was about the place. It was where you were meant to come next on your journey. You're from a long line of Protectors, on your mother's side. But if I correctly re-member Ty's soft heart for the ladies, then I daresay he might have known about the person, too." *Does she mean me? Are we destined to be together?* However much I felt for Tens, the idea of predestined relationships both-ered me.

Tens's face flushed a breathtaking crimson and he stared down at the carpet. "Do you know anything about my parents? My father? Mother?"

"No, not much, I'm sorry. Your grandfather didn't like to talk about it. Your father was an illegal immigrant from Cuba. Your mother was too young and she didn't survive childbirth."

Auntie turned to Custos. "She'll sleep here tonight.

Let's give her broth in a little while and see if we can't get her to drink it. I'm thirsty for real hot chocolate. Anyone else? Have I told you about the marshmallows my grandmother made during the winters?" Auntie's face melted into an expression of childhood bliss.

Tens jumped up, clearly ready for a change of topic. "I'll get it."

"Do you love him?" Auntie asked after he left the room, shoving her hair from her face and wiping her cheeks with the edge of a quilt.

"How do I know?" I chewed on my lip, scared to admit to feelings I wasn't completely sure of.

"It's different for everyone. For me, with Charles, it was the littlest things. I was able to live to my full potential and not ever apologize for being a Fenestra. He took my destiny in stride. Even when I wasn't able to keep my promise to him."

"What promise?" That familiar shadow in my peripheral vision hovered.

"I promised him that I'd be there when he died. That he would see heaven through me."

"You couldn't have known."

"I should have. There was a doctor with him. He said it was peaceful. But he won't be waiting for me, not after this life. I know that."

The pipe-smoke scent got stronger. "Do you smell that?"

"What, child?"

I shook my head. "Nothing, I guess."

"If you love him, if you think you love him, hang on

to him. Your destinies are intertwined. Your choices and his choices are tangled. This I do know."

"What makes you so sure?"

"Faith."

"In God?"

"The Creators have many names: singular, plural. Names are more about the humans and the time than the Creators themselves."

I wondered if she was going to dredge out the crystals and start chanting.

She laughed at me. "You think I'm an old crazy lady."

"No." But my denial was halfhearted at best.

"You do. I know because I thought my grandmother was nuts too."

"You did?"

"Of course. But then I started listening and looking, really observing the world around me. After my mother died, my grandmother lived with us. She was a Fenestra. She taught us the history to pass on. Gods are male and female because that's the human limitation. But there's no gender to energy. Do you call your batteries he or she? Do you name the lightbulb Fred or Ginger? No, it's energy. It's timeless, it's faceless, it's sexless."

I nodded.

"Meridian, you're special. You've been given the greatest gift of the Creator: the ability to help souls find their nirvana, their enlightenment, their heaven. Humans have many names for it, but it has a sameness to it. I wish we had more time, but we're running out."

"Why?" I croaked the word. I'd miss Auntie, more

than I'd ever thought possible. I wanted to slow down time.

"Hot chocolate." Tens carried in a tray and set it in front of Auntie.

We sipped in silence and I kept an eye on Custos.

"Tens, you need to hear this too. Have you heard of Atlantis? The Aztecs? Easter Island? Gede in Kenya?" Auntie's voice sounded stronger.

Some of the names rang bells from her journal, so I'd hazard a guess. "Gone?" I asked.

"All work of the Aternocti. All because there were too few of us to reclaim energy for good."

"What am I going to do about it?"

"We." Tens tugged on my hair, making me smile.

Without warning, Auntie seemed to doze, her chin hitting her chest. The mug slipped from her hands and the noise of it falling on the floor startled her awake. "Oh dear me."

"Don't worry about it."

"Let's finish this tomorrow, okay?" Auntie stood. "Tens, hand me the cane by the door, please. I think I need it tonight."

"Let me carry you." Tens scooped her up and I followed, up the stairs and to her bedroom.

"She's got a fever," I whispered to Tens as a chill shook Auntie and the bed. "I don't think aspirin's going to cut it. I think we should call a doctor." I didn't try to conceal my concern.

"Let's talk in the hallway, Meridian." Tens motioned me toward the door and Auntie blinked her eyes open.

"You don't have to talk about me like I've lost my mind. I know I'm dying, remember? No doctors—sleep. I've got more days in me yet." A cough wracked her body.

I glanced at Tens, who bent to check one of the space heaters. He shrugged. "Are you sure? Maybe they can help."

Auntie patted my hand. "Don't worry, you're not light yet. It's not time." Then she gripped me with surprising strength. "Promise me that I won't die in a hospital. Promise me." Her skin was dry and flaky, superhot.

"I don't think—"

"Promise me!" Her eyes grew wide and panicked.

I licked my lips. "I promise," I whispered, wondering if there could possibly be anything more difficult to face.

I started to paw through piles of quilts, looking for the warmest and coziest. Each was precisely sewn with diamond shapes, trees, circles, or stripes. Some of them were intricate as tapestries, depicting scenes like the ancient story tableaus hanging in museums. Tiny faces made of bitty scraps of tans and taupes, browns and creams. Animals and landscapes. Stitches so fine I couldn't see them. Velvets and brocades, linens and polished cottons. Sari-like patterns and batiks, Japanese silks and dark-washed denims. Snowflakes and sunshine, rainbows and rivers.

"Shoo. I need sleep." Auntie's snores accompanied us as we finished tucking her in and making sure she had water within reach.

"I'll stay with her tonight."

I glanced at Tens. "You don't look good either. Are you feeling okay?"

"I'm fine. Why don't you check on Custos and then hit the sack?"

I nodded, watching him settle down on the floor next to Auntie's bed.

"Are you—" *Sure?*

"Go." Tens jerked off his boots and closed his eyes.

CHAPTER 24

I lay down on the sofa next to Custos; I'd grown accustomed to her night noises. Sleep eluded me. When I finally fell asleep, though, I dreamed.

I dreamed of the only family vacation we ever went on—to Australia, of all places. I think my parents hoped we could outrun the death that followed me like a conjoined twin.

On our first full day in Australia, we rode in a cab to the Australia Zoo. Dad wanted to see the oldest living giant sea turtle. There'd been lots of controversy over whether or not Darwin really brought her back to England from the Galapagos Islands. I was nine. I didn't much care, but my dad thought we should see the turtle that might have been in the presence of the great Charles Darwin.

The zoo was crowded with school groups and other tourists. We waited in line for what seemed like hours. My father kept talking to everyone around us, "gathering intel" as he liked to say. The turtle's name was Harriet, "Etta" for short. She'd been sick with a respiratory bug a couple of weeks earlier, but on this day she'd recovered enough to go out into her habitat. People lined up to gawk at her, and I wondered if she minded the same way I did when people stared at me.

I pressed up to the glass, jostled by a bunch of people. I watched the turtle drag herself closer to the glass and to me. Everyone thought it was so cool that she was coming over to say hello to us. But I remember the terror I felt. I wanted her to go the other way because she was huge and beautiful. Her shell reminded me of giant sand dunes. And her eyes were fathomless.

I knew what was coming, and there was nothing I could do about it.

I tried closing my eyes, but she kept moving toward me. The day had been overcast, but the clouds suddenly parted. There was a sunbeam and the turtle paused in it. She turned her head, so I could see one eye. One perfect, cavernous, clear eye. I saw to the beginning of time in that eye. I locked gazes with her.

She put her head down in the sand and sun and heaved a sigh. Everyone thought she'd gone to sleep. But I stood there for a good fifteen minutes, frozen, my parents trying to get me to snap out of it. I remember Etta said she'd been waiting for me. She had something to tell me.

On the couch, I woke enough to flip over restlessly. Then Etta's eyes sucked me back into dreamland.

The eyes morphed into ones I recognized as Reverend Perimo's. The irises fell away, swirling like sunspots, until the only thing that remained was a blackness so dark, so molten I was afraid I'd fall in. He spoke to me: "Don't believe them, Meridian. You can have it all. You can have him back. You can live forever. 'Is the child dead? And they said, He is dead.' "21 Celia's hands reached for me and I sprang away. I ran.

I ran alongside an old train. A smiling young man in a soldier's uniform reached for me and called out, but I was caught from behind.

I wrenched myself from the iron grip and found myself on the floor beside the couch, tangled in my blankets. Custos lifted her head and whined.

"I'm okay. Go back to sleep." I stood and wrapped a quilt around myself, then padded to the kitchen. I dug a spoon into a carton of mocha fudge chunk ice cream.

When Tens walked into the room, he said, "Her fever broke."

I jumped. "Crap, you scared me."

"Sorry." Tens got another spoon out of the drawer and sat across from me.

"I'm missing something. I can feel it," I said, frustrated with myself.

Tens just waited and ate the ice cream.

I could barely taste my favorite flavor. "It's right there. I know it is."

"Maybe you're trying too hard." He kept eating, watching me.

I gazed out the window at the night. "I had this crazy dream. God, it was so real."

"You'll figure it out. Stop thinking about it and it'll come to you. I'll sit with you if you want," Tens offered.

"No, I'm okay."

"Then go up to bed. I'll check on Custos. No one could sleep well on that spiny sofa."

I smiled. "Sure. Thanks."

* * *

The next morning, I put water on to boil for tea and mixed up pancake batter. I found an unopened package of bacon in the fridge and set it on to cook.

I jumped when Auntie suddenly greeted me from behind. "Good morning, little one."

"You guys have got to stop doing that!" I placed tea in front of her. "How are you?"

"Much better. Right as spring rain on the wheat fields."

I didn't believe her, but her expression didn't leave me

room to question her further. I nodded, deciding to go along with her until I had an opportunity to suggest a hospital again. "Hungry?" I asked.

"Famished."

"Me too." I grinned as Tens wandered in barefoot and wearing a threadbare T-shirt and jeans with holes at the knees.

"Smells good." He perched on the counter, grabbed an apple, and bit into it.

"Always hungry." Auntie chuckled. "I have an idea. We should go to the hot springs up the road and soak."

"Hot springs?" I asked.

"They're beautiful. Just the right temperature. They're also healing for the body and soul. I haven't been in years. I don't know why; they're one of my favorite places on earth." Auntie's expression grew wistful.

"Then we should go," Tens said.

"Sure." I flipped a couple of pancakes off the griddle and added bacon to the plate, then set it down in front of Auntie. "Dig in."

"I couldn't possibly eat all of this."

"Try. I'm sure the human vacuum can help if there are leftovers." I giggled at Tens's fake offended expression.

I served Tens and then myself. We munched in companionable silence. There was peace in the kitchen, a calm I hadn't felt since my birthday. I realized with a shock that this was what happy felt like.

We piled into the Rover after breakfast and Auntie directed us to the hot springs. I'd borrowed one of her ancient bathing suits with shorts and a long-sleeved top. I would have showed more skin in a wet suit, but I didn't care.

She seemed young, free, happy. She reminded me of the grouse that skittered around us, which were ever changing with the seasons, now winter white and in perfect harmony with the world.

We splashed and soaked and tried each pool. We had the place to ourselves.

"I'm so glad we came." Auntie cuddled against me and gazed up into the sky. She peered so intently, I wondered if she could see the rings of Saturn with her naked eye. "Everything changes, Meridian. Everything is temporary, except the sky. When you find yourself caught up in the horrors or the heroes of a lifetime, look up. Don't look down. That which is beneath our feet is liquid, but the sky, the sky is solid, constant, ever ready and ever hopeful that the sun will rise in the morning and the moon will rise at night. They don't really set, you know. They're always rising, just rising for someone else."

"Right." I glanced around for Tens, who'd gone back to the car for towels. Auntie and I were alone with this moment.

"This too shall pass. It's rising for you now. I only have to finish the quilt. Yellow ginghams of first love, steely blues of family branches. I do believe you are an intense red of youth's passion. I forgot. It seems so long ago I turned sixteen."

I swallowed. I couldn't imagine seeing the stories in the scraps of fabric Auntie had found and pieced together with the hands of a surgeon. I decided to ask the question that had been plaguing me. "Auntie, what about souls who don't want to go?"

"They either are borne through by those meeting them on the other side, or they stay here with whomever they're afraid to leave behind."

"And if one of us isn't there—then what?"

"Reincarnation. Another cycle. It's not as simple as all that, but that's the gist of it. Death isn't the end people fear it is. Everything rises, child."

Tens came back, carrying towels. "I think you two are all wrinkly."

"That's age, dear one." Auntie cackled. "Not water."

"Hey!" I cried in protest.

"We should go before the sun sets and the roads freeze up again."

"Rises," I said automatically.

"Exactly." Auntie kissed my cheek and let Tens help her from the pool.

I gazed up into the sky, trying to see what she saw, trying to find the peace she exuded with each breath. I sighed.

"You coming, slowpoke?"

"That's Madame slowpoke to you!" I sloshed from the pool and ran to the car, hoping the heater would drive the chatter from my teeth as the water cooled to the temperature of the air around us.

By the time we made the turn up the hill, the sun was on its downward slope. "What's so bright? Did we leave that many lights on?" I asked.

"Oh no." Auntie's words hung in the air as we got closer.

If you live long enough, you learn time is an illusion created by men who fear death. The clocks and watches worshipped by those who deny the inevitable. There is power in acknowledging we are not the ones in control.

—Melynda Laine

CHAPTER 25

A giant wooden arrow reeking of gasoline burned on the front lawn. Red and black spray paint covered the porch with words and phrases in a language I didn't recognize. The front picture window was smashed.

"Those assholes!" Tens slammed the steering wheel with his fists.

"We're not hurt, we'll be okay," Auntie assured him.

I wasn't sure I believed her. "Where's Custos?"

"I left her inside." Tens and I raced up the steps. As Tens juggled the keys I felt watched. I glanced around and saw black shapes move farther into the cover of the trees.

I grabbed Tens. "Did you see that?"

He followed my finger. "What?"

"I thought I saw something—I guess not." Maybe I'd seen deer.

Custos greeted us from the top of the stairs.

"Good girl. Good girl." I buried my face in her fur.

Auntie followed us in, smiling with relief. "She's okay?"

Tens went out to extinguish the arrow. I began cleaning up the glass and stoking the fire in the hearth.

"Auntie, what's with the gibberish sprayed on the porch? Do you recognize it?"

She nodded. "The Nocti. They speak a language older than Latin, older than Christ's Aramaic, older than that of the druids or Sumerians."

"Oh."

"I know only a little of their language, but the words I recognized translate as 'watching and waiting.' "

I shivered. What would we do if they came? "Do they attack? Do I need a weapon?"

"Love is your greatest weapon. Trust your heart, Meridian. Listen to yourself. They're insidious; they prey on uncertainty and insecurity. There is little we can do to defeat them outright without the help of a Sangre. I wish I knew how to solicit their help."

"Yeah, where do we get one of those?"

Auntie wrung her hands. I'd never seen her so upset

and unsure. "You can't make a phone call for one. I don't know. I don't know." She fought back tears.

I hugged her. "It'll be okay." I wasn't sure how to help her, but she needed to calm down.

Auntie continued. "I've never seen a Nocti. I hope I never will. To need a Sangre's interference means the world is out of balance. They are the beings we whisper about."

"We'll handle it. I promise." I kissed her forehead. "Custos, stay here," I commanded the wolf as she leaned against Auntie's legs and put her head in Auntie's lap.

Tens came back in. "Meridian, I need help holding the plywood over the window. It's the best we can do until after the holiday."

I left Auntie staring into the fire. "Today was too much for her," I whispered to Tens.

"Maybe."

"Are they going to come back?"

"It's escalating."

"What exactly do they want, though? They want Auntie to move out too?"

"It's not just the Brotherhood."

"When did the attacks start?"

"Soon after I got here. The church was up and running, but it was normal. Then there was a shake-up, a scandal, and Perimo seized control. At first it was little things. A new name. A new board. Quiet gossip that no one could ever attribute but that people believed. Then unemployment skyrocketed with the closings. Perimo attracted more people with work and food. I don't know. If I could just put my finger on it."

"When did the dead animals and slashed tires and stuff start?"

"In October, rumors began about Auntie and she started getting fewer invitations to visit people. The phone stopped ringing—with friendly calls, anyway."

"So October?"

"The phone calls. Someone let the air out of the tires when she went to the grocery store. The grocer stopped carrying the brands she bought reguarly. Our power was cut off."

"I could be wrong, but what if the Nocti and the church are working together?"

"But why?" Tens sat down and slapped the table.

"What's changed?" I asked.

"That's it—it's you. Auntie said she could sense Nocti, right?"

"Which means Nocti can sense us." I exhaled. "And she's one hundred six."

"They knew someone from the family would come to help her pass. They knew a young Fenestra would show up. It wouldn't be hard to find out where you were, watch you, wait."

"Try to kill me in Portland before I even got here?"

"Exactly." Tens nodded.

"Why drive Auntie out?"

"When the church couldn't bring her in—"

"They cut her off from support, from friends."

"I bet they don't even know what the bigger plan is."

"Do you think Perimo knows?" I asked.

"He has to. He's not Christian in his teachings—he preaches bloodletting and anger—"

"And the babies? The deaths? The traps—Celia?" I could see the pieces falling together.

"All souls for the Nocti. But in exchange for what?"

I tapped my fingers. "They have to be getting something out of it." My head hurt from thinking so hard. "But I don't know what."

Tens stood. "See what you can find in the journal, okay? I wish she'd let me read it years ago."

"Auntie wouldn't let you read it?"

"Eyes of the Fenestra only." He finished pounding the last nails into the wood. "We'll hang layers of quilts inside to keep out the cold. It'll have to work."

We shut up the front of the house, leaving the graffiti to be dealt with tomorrow. We found Auntie in the kitchen. "It's time. I packed the last of it." She nodded at Tens.

I'd never seen such a bleak expression on his face. "Are you sure?"

She appeared defeated.

His expression turned grave as he pulled on his heaviest hiking boots and coat.

"Where are you going?" I asked.

"Out." The venom in his tone made me blink.

My expression must have shown the hurt I felt because he softened and said, "Sorry. I need to go check on a few things. I'll be back for dinner. You'll be fine. See if

you can't find out anything about what we talked about."
He brushed past me on his way to the porch, pausing long
enough to plant a quick kiss in my hair.

"I'm in the mood for chocolate cake. Let me teach you
the family recipes, okay?" Auntie tugged my hand and I
lagged behind.

Tens swung a huge pack onto his back and opened
the back door. He whistled and Custos appeared, slipping
out the door next to him. "I'll be back." He winked at me,
but I didn't get any comfort from the gesture.

"Why does he have to go?" I asked Auntie.

"Can you reach the top shelf, please, dear? That's
where I keep the special cocoa powder. Doesn't chocolate
cake sound good to you? Let's make macaroni and cheese,
too. From scratch. My grandmother always had the best
recipes for comfort food. Write the steps down, you
should know how to make these dishes."

She turned the radio to a station that played big band
music and old scratchy recordings of singers from the
thirties and forties. "Listen. Ella Fitzgerald. She'll make
you feel better."

I dutifully wrote down the instructions for the mac
and cheese. My stomach rumbled as the aromas of butter
and cheddar filled the kitchen. I was hungry, but terribly
worried at the same time. We pulled the casserole out of
the oven and put the cake in. Darkness fully settled and I
jumped with every noise, moving often to the window to
scan for Tens and Custos.

"Are my parents safe?" I asked.

"Safe enough." Auntie pursed her lips.

"From me?" I couldn't help asking.

She glanced up, shocked. "Heavens no, child. From the Aternocti, from the fearful. Why do you think we send Fenestras away from their immediate family? It's not to be mean."

"Will I ever see them again?"

"In time, you can go to them." Auntie grasped my hand and held it with a strength that surprised me. "We have to protect the ones we love. Anyone who is with us is vulnerable, is in danger. In the olden days we had warrior Protectors. There aren't many anymore. You have Tens. He may turn out to be one of the warriors, but only time will tell. There isn't a quick test to see what his destiny is."

"So, I can't have a family?"

"No, you *must* have a family, but every day of their lives they'll be at risk. It's the way, Meridian."

"Then why can't I have my parents right now?"

"If you don't make your change, make your choice, then you'll snatch anyone around you and force them through too. You know how to open the window, but not how to close it. If you're not careful, you'll get tangled in living energy."

"I'll kill anyone around me?"

"Not directly, dear." Auntie dished up pasta like she'd just told me it would rain tomorrow. "You'll be fine. I know these things. Now, have some of the world's best mac and cheese."

I wasn't sure I believed her, but she wanted so badly for me to not worry, to not pace and panic, that I tried. And when I put the first bite in my mouth I was lost in a world of cream and custard and cheese. "Oh my God, that's good," I hummed.

"I know." Auntie giggled like a child.

We finished eating. The cake cooled, and we iced it. Tens still hadn't returned. Finally, I broke down and had a piece of cake with a tall glass of cold milk.

"Did my mum know how to cook or what? These recipes are from before I was six. Can you imagine? She wrote these down in pencil on the backs of catalog pages. My daddy saved them, made every cook we ever had make them every month or so. Grandmother made sure I memorized them."

"It's all so good," I said. I tried to peek at the window without drawing her notice.

"He'll be back shortly. I promise." Auntie patted my hand. "Come keep me company while I finish this quilt."

"Whose quilt is it?" I asked, sitting down in a chair across from her perch by the fire in the library. We couldn't keep the heat going in the living room because of the broken window. Auntie lovingly unfolded a lap-sized quilt as if unwrapping the richest of presents.

She smiled, a small sad tilt of her lips. "Mine."

My stomach dropped. "But you said . . . These are all . . . You said—"

"I said that I made quilts of each life that passed through me."

"Right?" Tears burned at the back of my throat. I wanted to plug my ears and hum at the top of my lungs.

"This one reflects everything I've learned, ingested. It's an indelible reflection of each face and story that touched my soul."

"I love you. Why do I . . ." I whispered past the waterworks lump in my throat. *Why do I have to be the one?*

"I know, child. Only a Fenestra can transition another. If we die without help, the Fenestra energy changes form. We lose our numbers. It's why we're so few in this millennium. It's why the Aternocti try to murder us or change us into one of them. It's almost time for you to take your place. It's nearly time for me to rise again. I want to see Charles in my next life."

I began pacing the floor. "But I don't know everything yet. I can't possibly—"

"You can and you will." The steel in her voice demanded that I simmer down. "You must go find more of us before they steal the last of us. We're dying out, Meridian, and more souls will be trapped between, more life energy sucked into the dark forever by the Aternocti."

"How am I supposed to . . ." I choked, barely able to catch my breath. Me. Out there. Hunted and hunting.

"If the Aternocti succeed in weeding out Fenestras, then they will have direct access to millions of innocent souls. Think of the energy. The destruction this could wreak. You must find us first. Help us. Teach us. Keep the lore, the history. Use your instincts and the help the Creators will send to guide you."

"But where are they? These other Fenestras? Why don't they come here? To you?"

"Not everyone is as blessed as you are to have a family together, faithful to traditions and the old ways. People in this century prefer things they can see and touch. They don't believe; they lose the stories, the magic. They don't know what they are."

Heavy boots stamped on the porch. Tens shouted, "Just me," before he opened the door and marched in without his pack. "I'm sorry, it took longer than I thought." He didn't bother to remove his boots, tracking bits of snow and mud along the hallway.

Auntie shooed me back to the kitchen. "Go feed him some of that cake. I'll be right here by the fire."

The scent of pipe smoke and roses filled the hallway. "Tens, do you smoke?"

"Never. Why?"

"Does Auntie?"

"Not in front of me."

"Do you smell that?"

"Nope."

"Someone's here. I'd swear someone smokes a pipe here all the time." A clatter above our heads had us glancing up at the ceiling.

"Stay down here," Ten said.

"No. I'm coming with you."

Even his sternest expression wouldn't have allowed

me to let him go up there alone. We got to the top of the stairs and everything seemed normal. The door to the room where I'd found the scissors was wide open.

I pointed, inching toward the doorway. Tens marched into the room. At first we didn't see anything. Then Custos whined and dropped a pipe at my feet.

CHAPTER 26

"That's it." Excitement flooded through me.

"What?"

"Charles. He's here. He stayed. He's waiting for Auntie."

"What are you talking about? He's gone."

"No, I don't think he is. I think he's been trying to tell me he's still here. But why didn't he use Auntie? That doesn't make any sense."

Pounding on the front door had us scrambling out of the room and clambering down the stairs.

Tens swore. "It's Perimo! What's he doing here?"

"You'll protect me?" I asked, and opened the door when he nodded.

"Good evening. I heard there was a bit of trouble up here. I thought I'd offer my services. How is the elder Meridian handling things?"

Tens stood stiffly behind me. My instincts were screaming, but I couldn't tell what they were saying. "She's fine," I answered.

"Are you sure? I heard she was feeling poorly. Perhaps I could pray with her? There's time yet to save her soul." Perimo stepped forward as if to enter the house.

I stood my ground and didn't let him enter. "Time before what?"

"She's not young, Miss Sozu. Time is running out for her."

I heard Auntie call out to us. Tens hesitated until I nudged him to go check on her. "What do you mean, time is running out?"

"It's almost a new year, isn't it? The dawn of a new day. I came to minister to her. As I minister to all my brethren."

I knew when Tens turned the corner behind me because the Reverend's eyes darkened immediately. He drew himself up to tower over me. Fear struck me dumb.

Perimo's voice grew low and scratchy. "The time is coming. The end is near. You don't want to be rude to me."

"I don't?" I asked.

"Little children, it is the last time: 'And as ye have heard that antichrist shall come, even now are there many antichrists; whereby we know that it is the last time.' "22

I slammed the door in his face. "Don't come back!" Once I heard him finally walk down the porch steps, all I could do was rest my forehead against the door and wonder if he had the power to make me regret what I'd just done.

*   *   *

I found Tens in Auntie's bedroom having a murmured conversation with her, the gist of which seemed to be about Auntie leaving us unprepared to defend ourselves. Tens couldn't convince her she wasn't, so I interrupted. "Can I do anything for you?"

Tens wouldn't meet my eyes.

Auntie shook her head slightly and seemed to settle back into a half-sleep.

Ask her. Ask her. Ask her. "Auntie." I dragged a chair close and leaned toward her. "I need to ask you something."

She didn't open her eyes. "What is it?"

"I think Charles is a ghost. I think he's here."

"My Charles is gone, little one." She sighed.

"Let just say I'm right. Why hasn't he gone through you?"

"He couldn't . . . in book . . . energy changes . . . invitation . . ." With each word her voice became quieter, the effort greater.

"Auntie?" I asked.

Tens sidled closer. "She's sleeping, Meridian. I don't think she can answer you."

"What if I'm right?"

"Is there anything in the journal?" Tens asked.

"Let's hope so." I raced out of the room to grab the book. I'd only read about a thumb's width of pages. A lot of the handwriting was microscopic quill-and-ink script. It was like deciphering code.

I lugged the tome into the study and turned on a lamp, flipping through pages until my eyes crossed. Hours passed. Custos wandered in and sat at my feet.

Tens brought in a pot of tea and more chocolate cake. "Can I help?"

"If I could divide the book up, sure." Of course, that wasn't possible. "Just keep me company?"

"Sure." Tens settled next to me and extracted his whittling. Every few minutes he crept out to check on Auntie.

We drank the teapot dry. I tried not to watch the hands on the clock spin.

Finally, I heaved a frustrated sigh, ready to give up for the night.

"For what it's worth, I think you're on to something."

"Really?" I glanced at him.

"You have good instincts when you listen to them." He appeared sheepish. "And I had a dream about this. It's a little déjà vu. I didn't know what we were searching for."

"Why didn't you tell me?"

"I'm still figuring out how to tell dreams from visions. I thought maybe we were just sitting together. You know, cuddling." He blushed.

I giggled at his expression.

Hurt filled his eyes, and he started to draw away.

"Wait, no! I didn't mean to laugh. I wasn't laughing *at* you. I—you looked so cute saying the word 'cuddling.' I just didn't—I didn't expect it."

He nodded, but still stared down at his hands.

I opened to a random page in the journal. He needed to hear how I felt about him. "Tens, I like—" I gasped as the words under my fingers grabbed my attention. "Oh my God, that's it. He needs an invitation."

"Show me." Tens leaned over the book with me.

"The energy of a dead soul weakens," I read aloud. "It needs to be asked to pass through the window. It needs to be coerced over, but it can rip the life energy out of the one transporting it. Fenestras must focus on the soul and—"

"It also says it's dangerous and should only be attempted by Fenestras in their prime—"

Am I risking too much? "But—"

"Just consider it, okay? Stop and think about it. I can't lose—"

"Auntie would do it for me."

"Probably." Tens nodded in agreement. "She's also got a hell of a lot more experience. You're a beginner. What if we wait? What if we get Auntie through and then work on Charles?"

"And if she doesn't go? If I die helping her?"

"You won't."

"I could." I didn't want to contemplate that reality, but I found myself stuck on it.

Tens invaded my space. "You *won't!*"

I nodded, wishing some of his certainty would seep into me. We sat in silence for a moment and I caught another whiff of roses and pipe smoke. I knew I was right. "You said if I trust my instincts I'm usually right. Right?"

Tens's expression darkened. "Throwing my own words back at me?"

I gripped his hand. "I *have* to. Don't you see? Auntie needs him in heaven, waiting. He wants to go. Tens, I'm telling you I can do this. I *have* to do this."

He grasped my chin and gazed into my eyes. His were full of an emotion I couldn't begin to fathom. "I'm right here. Okay?"

I nodded, comforted by his strength.

"What now?"

"Now I call out Charles."

The details were vague. It wasn't like following step-by-step recipe instructions. I gathered their wedding portrait, photographs of Charles through the years, and his pipe. I shut Custos out of the study because I was afraid Charles's energy might accidentally hurt her if she was too close.

"What do you want me to do?" Tens had built a roaring fire that crackled and spit in the hearth.

"Slap me if I faint?" *Or worse.* As always, my joke fell flat.

"How do you call him out?"

"I don't know. What's it suggest in the book?"

Tens smiled. "Come out, come out, wherever you are?"

"Nice."

"It doesn't suggest anything. I think you're on your own." He shrugged.

"Okay, Charles, Auntie needs you. I'm here. Let's get this show on the road." I repeated myself, over and over. My eyes tightly shut, I pictured my window. I tried to imagine what Charles looked like in real life. My breathing leveled and I let myself go deeper.

"Over here, little one." Charles was standing behind me.

"That's what Auntie calls me."

"Whom do you think she picked it up from?" Charles lit his pipe. "Took you long enough. I thought I was going to have to flick the lights or bang the doors."

"I figured it out, didn't I?"

"Just in the nick of time too."

"Are you ready?" I watched a room exactly like this one unfold behind my eyelids.

"Did she tell you her daddy built this house? That she grew up here? I added on over the years, fixed it up."

"No."

He sounded wistful. "She's going to hate what's coming."

"What's coming?" I asked, but he didn't hear me.

"You tell her I'll be waiting. Tell her to come to me and not glance back." Charles stepped through and I realized he was tugging on my arm.

"Let go."

He didn't hear me. Our fingers were entwined. My hand passed the windowsill. My wrist. My elbow. My feet dug in, trying to find purchase while I slid further into the opening.

I felt panic shiver up my spine. My mouth went dry. "Let go. Charles, let go of me! You have to let go."

"Things are not what they appear." Charles spoke to me while he continued to wrestle me through. "It's safe here. Come with me. Wait for Merry with me, here." His face bore an intense expression that scared me, as if he didn't even know what he was saying.

I tried to yell. I braced a foot against the wall and prayed. I twisted and turned, yanking and heaving. "Let go! I can't. She needs me here. Charles, you won't have her with you if you don't let me go."

"You're not safe. They're coming. They'll find you. Come with me." He grimaced, struggling to hang on to me.

Sweat slickened my arms and hands. I inhaled a deep breath and willed our hands apart. In the distance I heard my name. Tens sounded upset. Scared.

Charles seemed to snap back into himself, struggling to untangle from me as well. His expression once again grew calm and caring. "Tell her one-four-three. Tell her I love her, that I'm waiting."

"Meridian!" Tens shouted again. I drew on his strength. I felt him push Charles away and haul me in the opposite direction.

I screamed and snapped the window down with a bang. I opened my eyes, feeling Tens's hands brushing my hair from my face. Sweat drenched my body and I was breathing as if I'd sprinted a hundred yards.

"You're okay. I've got you." Tens cradled me and pressed kisses along my forehead and jaw.

I clung to him. Burrowing closer, letting his heat warm me and chase away my lingering fear.

"I've got you. You're safe. You did it," he murmured into my hair.

I was so spent I couldn't even answer him. Eventually, exhausted, I drifted off to sleep.

Love is the greatest act of Faith.

—Lucinda Myer

CHAPTER 27

I woke in Tens's arms. Dried drool coated the sides of my mouth, and my eyes felt scratchy.

"Hi," he said.

I blinked up at him. "What time is it?"

"Early, very early. Are you okay? You scared me."

I stretched. Aside from the normal stiffness from sleeping on the floor, I felt okay. "Excellent."

Tens grinned. "Excellent?"

I sat up. "Really. Really wonderful." All my former pains and aches that I'd lived with for so long were gone.

The constant nausea and fatigue had vanished. "I feel good."

I loved the way Tens's eyes crinkled when he was truly happy and relaxed. *He's going to kiss me. He's going to kiss me.*

I leaned toward him, closing my eyes, holding my breath. I waited for his lips to brush mine as time slowed; I felt every thud of my heart.

Just as I almost felt his mouth flutter against mine, the ground shook and the doors rattled. Explosions buffeted the house. Metal screamed and glass broke.

The force of the explosions rocked the house. I ran out onto the front porch, Tens right behind me. Custos barked from her place by the fire.

"What's going on?" Auntie called, her voice weak.

"Don't move," Tens shouted to her.

We skidded to a stop, staring down over the valley below us. We could see fireballs billowing up into the sky. Inky black smoke billowed in the wind like the sail of a pirate ship. Hell had come to earth.

"The train," I breathed. From this distance it looked like a child's train set. Ash and debris hung in the air and blew against us. The smell—I can't even begin to describe the smell. Hot metal, gas, fuel, and the sickening stench of human flesh.

"Damn." Tens gripped my shoulders. He checked his watch. "That's the five o'clock."

"Freight? Or people?" I let the question dangle.

"I don't know. You ask Auntie. I'm going to check the

house." He raced through the hallway to the back of the house.

I ran to Auntie's room. "The train—it's all jumbled, it's bad."

Auntie opened her eyes. "Derailed?"

"I don't know," I said.

"It's a freight train that hooks on passenger cars."

"There are people on that?"

"Probably." She struggled to stand. "We have to go." I struggled to convince her to stay.

Tens jogged back in. "You're not going anywhere." Tens gently pushed Auntie back down. "The house looks sound."

"I'm a nurse." She fought him, but it was like a butterfly against a bear.

"You're a patient." Tens's tone brooked no argument.

She glanced past him to lock gazes with me. "There will be dying." The implication hovered between us.

Am I ready? Can I handle multiples? I don't know.

I swallowed. "You'll stay here?"

"She's not ready for so many. You haven't taught her enough." Tens's voice gained octaves and volume. I heard fear in it, so I rushed to reassure him.

"I am. I know how to close the window," I said, trying to sound positive and sure. But my insecurities screamed. *How can I escape tangling in the energy of so many? How can I keep from being pulled through?*

"She's not ready." Tens stepped in front of me and

clasped my hands. "I'll go. I'll see how bad it is and come back. I'll drive you later."

I put my hand on his cheek. I loved that he wanted to protect me, but I knew he couldn't. I wouldn't let him. When it came down to it, I had to do this my way. "We'll be back when we're back. You can drive," I said to Tens, then brushed my lips against Auntie's forehead.

She whispered, "As long as you keep the window wide open and yourself firmly planted in the room, you'll be okay. Don't close the window until it's safe or a soul may break you trying to get through it. Use your instincts."

"But if I keep it open all the time—"

"Open isn't the problem. Stay where you can only barely feel the breeze, as if a fan blows at you but doesn't reach that far across the room. Then you won't tangle. Keep it big. Souls in pain like to get across fast. They'll crowd you. Stand your ground. You will make me proud. You will make your family proud." Auntie patted my shoulder. "I love you. Feel that. Know it. Love will see you through this. You are ready."

I nodded, grabbing the first-aid kit and my coat and gloves. The world felt unseasonably warm. Tens followed me.

* * *

We couldn't get very close to the scene of the crash because of the terrain and the heat, so we parked and started running toward the train. A few volunteer firefighters screeched to a stop behind us, and I could hear sirens in the far distance. But not enough, not nearly enough. This was a big, underpopulated land; it was going to be several minutes, if not hours, before any experts arrived.

All around me, I heard a cacophony of pain. I felt it tug at me. Train cars scattered ahead of me in an almost unending path. They leaned in all directions as if kicked by a petulant child. Rails had been ripped apart, and a crater the size of a luxury car was all that was left of the engine and front of the train. Fires burned, luggage was strewn in the slush. Corn poured out of one car while boxes of mail rolled to a stop down a hill and envelopes fluttered in the wind.

Tens tried to stay right next to me, guarding me. It took me a minute to realize he was trying to shield me as we got closer. What once had been full lives, bodies full of life, were now scattered in pieces. I tried to detach, but I couldn't completely. I choked back the urge to vomit, trying not to get lost mourning the dead. Just then, a man yelled at Tens to help lift a steel door off a woman who'd been pinned. I pushed him into action and kept walking toward the worst-hit passenger cars.

The world seemed to move in slow motion, like the frame-by-frame feature on DVDs. I saw, I stepped, I moved in fragmented moments of time.

I swallowed against fear. This is what war must look like, smell like. Sticky smoke clung to me. Surveying the devastation, I couldn't imagine anyone surviving.

Cries got louder as I drew closer to the passenger cars. I tried to peer through a window.

Coughing, I felt a malevolent presence behind me.

" 'Yet ye have forsaken me, and served other gods: wherefore I will deliver you no more. Go and cry unto the gods which ye have chosen; let them deliver you in the time of your tribulation.'[23] I like that one, I should use it more often."

I knew that voice. I turned to confront Reverend Perimo's chuckling face. He had a hand in this disaster. I don't know how I knew that, but I did. I felt it with every breath. "Did you do this?"

" 'Moreover all these curses shall come upon thee, and shall pursue thee, and overtake thee, till thou be destroyed; because thou hearkenedst not unto the voice of the Lord thy God.'[24] It's catchy, isn't it? The Almighty delivers swift punishment to those who don't do what they're told. More people should keep that in mind."

"You did this, didn't you?" I felt the inexplicable tug of energy. Behind me, somewhere in that train car, was a dying person. More than one. The feeling that someone needed me was becoming more and more recognizable.

Perimo gripped my arm and feverishly whispered, " 'The thoughts of the wicked are an abomination of the Lord: but the words of the pure are pleasant words. . . . The Lord is far from the wicked.'[25] Does the Creator hear you when you cry, Meridian?"

"Let go of me." I shoved him, throwing my full weight

into him, and turned away, not stopping until I reached the entrance to the car.

"I'll have you yet!" he screamed into the night.

Several volunteers were breaking the windows out of train cars. I climbed up the side of one car using debris as stairs to get to an entrance on the top, since the car lay on its side. I saw shapes in the yawning depths below.

Using the handrail like a fireman's pole, I slid down the stairs into darkness and smoke. Burnt rubber and the stench of human waste sucked the breath out of me.

Immediately, wave after wave of longing hit me. More souls than I could count pushed at me. It was like a rock concert and the front row was trying to touch the star. Me.

I closed my eyes and made sure the window I envisioned was wide open. Wind billowed through the curtains with the force of a hurricane. The landscape outside the window spun furiously as each soul tried to make it their own. I opened my eyes quickly before I got too dizzy to move.

The screams and yells were muffled. "Help me, please?" A hand reached up out of the darkness and a lady's fingers wiggled as if waving.

Instinctively, I grasped her hand, unable to see where the rest of her lay beneath the piles of wreckage. The contact sucked at me like an undertow. She was afraid, terrified of dying. She didn't want to go. I didn't know what to do or say. Auntie hadn't told me what to do with uncertain souls. I felt as if the woman wanted to push me through instead. We grappled in my room because she wouldn't let go. I kept fighting her off long enough to catch my breath, until she tugged again and I went under.

CHAPTER 28

I shook her off and caught my breath. I spoke quiet reassurances, struggling to keep myself together. The other volunteers were wrapping survivors in blankets and trying to staunch the bleeding of open wounds. I focused on the dying since that was my supposed specialty. Another mortally wounded person grabbed my leg, my vision blurred, and vertigo hit me at the speed with which the man leapt through the window to his favorite beach in Hawaii.

Viscous liquids dripped on me; the smell of human

urine and sulfur overpowered me. I bent and heaved nothing but air. I felt woozy and disoriented. I visualized the window and tried to feel a fresh breeze on my face.

"Get my baby out. Please." I moved in a careful crawl because I couldn't stand upright in the capsized car. My hands were slimy with what I was sure was a mixture of blood and other fluids I didn't want to think about. I wrenched a suitcase off a woman. She was impaled on a large wedge of metal that might have been a door, but she was conscious and aware. She held an infant who seemed long past dead, limp and lifeless in a T-shirt and diaper. She tried to lift the little body toward me and her breath hitched. "Please . . ."

I was in one of the glass-domed viewing cars—the glass was webbed with cracks, but not smashed completely. I leaned back and kicked against the panes—the shatterproof glass groaned. I kicked again. Fresh air and help was on the other side of that window. I kept my visualization going as another soul passed through me.

Finally, I made a hole. Smoke and heat poured out as clean, cold air roared in. I grabbed a coat and wrapped it around my arm to widen a hole big enough for a person. For me. I grabbed the baby, my hand touching the mother's.

"Thank you," she said, and was gone, leaving me with the fleeting impressions of cinnamon and Bob Marley's music.

The baby's energy was also gone, though I felt peace as the woman was met by a young man in uniform on the other side. I coughed and crawled out, shards of glass poking and cutting. Carefully, I wrapped the baby in another coat and placed it on the ground, away from the car. Shouts and sirens, screams and the roar of fire filled my ears to overflowing.

I tried to catch a glimpse of Tens. I wondered where he was, what he was doing. I gasped the clean air. I wanted to wander until I felt unsoiled and whole again, but I didn't. Firefighters and neighbors were doing the same thing in other cars around me; a few even worked side by side with me. There was so much immediate need and too few to help. There weren't enough of us for me to pause for long. I turned and went back in through the hole I'd made in the window. Of the people in this car, many were dead, others gravely injured.

I don't know how many trips I made. Enough that my pile of coats and blankets covering the dead began to take on a shape and life of its own. A small mountain mimicking the larger Sangre de Cristos Mountains around us. I shoved aside luggage and debris so I could clearly see the passengers who still needed help. The train must have been full to capacity with postholiday travelers.

"My leg is broken. Get me out of here." A man grabbed me, and for the first time since I'd gotten there, I felt only his desperation and fear, not a need to transition. He had to weigh two hundred pounds and he was over six feet tall. He continued, "I'll help you. I can use one leg. I can push off with it. Please, I'm claustrophobic, I don't know how much more I can stomach. It's so dark in here."

I nodded. "I don't know how to make this not hurt."

He tried to smile. "Pain means I'm alive. Just help me get out of here."

I hugged him tight, my chest against his back. "Okay, on three you push and I'll push and we'll get out of here."

He nodded.

"One." I wedged my feet against what solid surface I could find and made sure there wasn't anything in my way to the hole I'd been widening with each trip. "Two."

He braced himself and inhaled a substantial breath. "Three." We said it together and fell out onto the snow and mud, my back and head absorbing the brunt of the landing. Glass shards tangled in my hair like ice crystals and I felt warmth dripping down my back. I wasn't sure if it was sweat or blood. Probably both. The man's moan poured the pain out around us, but he was strong and full of life.

With the help of adrenaline, I hauled him over to a clear spot, grabbing coats that moments ago had been shielding the eyes of the dead from those of the living. I balled one up and put it under his head, then draped another over his torso and around his legs. I wished for medical training. "This is all I can do."

"Find my wife? Please?"

I nodded. My legs felt like waterlogged noodles. I coughed, then turned and dove back into the chaos.

Over the course of the next few hours, I was joined by more helpers. They found the man's wife, three teenagers, and several kids. Paramedics were putting the living on backboards and getting them out of there as fast as we brought them out, but the dead vastly outnumbered the survivors. Reverend Perimo leaned over several of the wounded. He appeared to be praying, but the hair on the back of my neck stood up. I couldn't feel them die, but he closed their eyes and moved on. *To the next victim?*

A single tanker truck battled blazes that crept closer and grew larger each time I lifted my head to check them.

"Are you hurt?" It took me a moment to realize that a face was peering into mine with concern. A fireman whose face was blackened with soot and blood leaned over me.

"No," I croaked out.

"Can you walk? You need to get out of here. See those vehicles? Move toward them." He pointed a football field or farther away.

"There are more people," I said. I felt heat waves, one after another, pulsing like a heartbeat, from the tail of the train.

"I know. We're moving back for now, though; a couple of tanks could blow any minute. You have to get out of here." The fireman's face reflected the pain that I felt. I was sure he wasn't used to walking away from the needy.

In the distance, I watched Reverend Perimo disappear deeper into the smoke. He wasn't stopped by anyone.

"We can't leave them!" I cried, struggling against the fireman's strong grip.

"We have to." He picked me up and threw me over his shoulder, carrying me away from the wreckage.

Upside down, I saw the churned-up earth, red and dark. Then the world went black and I faded with it.

* * *

"Meridian! Meridian!" Etta's voice came to me against the roaring backdrop of Armageddon. We were in hell, and a sea turtle was telling me her secrets. But I kept hearing my name and it confused me.

I opened my eyes to see Tens inches from my face.

He smiled. "You're awake."

I nodded, dragging off the oxygen mask that covered my face.

"You needed oxygen because of all the smoke you inhaled."

"I'm fine. Let's go home." I wanted space to think about what I saw.

"There's glass everywhere. Do you need me to carry you?"

"No." I stood. The adrenaline crash carried me into an abyss and I started shivering. "We should get back in there."

"They're not letting anyone near it. There's a chemical spill. We won't do any good waiting at the periphery." Tens helped me into the Rover. "Stay with me, Meridian. We don't know how that many souls will affect you yet. Just stay awake. Talk to me." I heard Tens slide into the driver's side and start the Rover. "Talk to me!" he commanded.

"Etta. Said to learn the lesson," I mumbled.

"Uh-huh. What else did she say?" He accelerated into a turn so fast that I pressed against the door. I couldn't hold back a groan. "Sorry. What'd she say?"

I struggled to keep my eyes open, but my brain felt drugged and woozy.

"A gift. Take fear away."

"Really? What else?" he shouted. So loud.

"Trapped between without me."

"Uh-huh?"

"Hug." My words didn't keep up with my thoughts.

"Hug?"

"No, 'brace."

"Embrace?" He slapped my cheek, jerking me back.

"Yeah. Perimo is bad. Stole Celia. "

"Hang on, we're almost home." Tens must have been speeding like a race car driver.

He slammed to a stop and apologized when I cried out. "Sorry, sorry." He carried me into the house. "Let's get you cleaned up."

"Fine. I'm fine." The words came in mumbles and sputters.

I felt pain and gentle hands, but the rest of the night slid by in an oblivion of hot water and reassurances.

Memento te mortalem esse sed vim in perpetuum durare.

Remember you are mortal but energy lives forever.

—Luca Lenci

CHAPTER 29

I stretched like a chicken in the sun without opening my eyes. My head was clear and my heart light. I sniffed, smelled the smoke, and grimaced at the stench.

"Sorry, no shower yet." Tens brushed the hair from my face. "You're awake."

I blinked up at him. "I am. Did you stay with me?"

"You slept over a full day."

"How's Auntie? What day is it?"

"She's sleeping. It's New Year's Eve." I sensed there was more behind his words.

"What aren't you telling me? She's alive, isn't she?"

"She's breathing."

"I want to see her, tell her about it."

"Sure, in a minute. Get your bearings."

I rubbed my eyes and wiped goo off my cheek. I sniffed at it. "Is that honey?"

"Yeah. Auntie used to say it works better than antibiotic cream, plus the bears will eat you first." He moved back as I sat up, swimming in a button-down men's pajama top that I didn't recognize. "Those are Charles's old pj's. I didn't think you'd want anything too clingy. Aside from a couple of small cuts on your back, the one on your cheek, and skinned knees, you weren't hurt badly."

" 'Kay." I felt an odd intimacy with him. As if we'd traveled beyond wherever it was we'd started and now were two people united.

"I'll go shower now. I didn't want to leave you alone too long at a time." The circles under his eyes were pronounced enough to worry me.

I nodded. I felt both stronger for having gone in without Auntie and sad for the same reason. "Custos?"

"Much better. She demanded to go out running early this morning."

" 'Kay."

Tens opened the bedroom door and slipped out.

"Tens?"

He poked his head back in.

"Thanks." So inadequate a word for how I felt about him. He was steady and solid and always seemed to be there for me.

He smiled a lopsided naughty grin. "Yeah." He disappeared.

I eased back onto the pillows, sure I should move, and yet I didn't want the warmth in my stomach to dissolve. I wasn't sure why I felt so good, but I didn't want to question it.

Until I remembered Reverend Perimo's comments and pictured him snatching Celia's soul to hell.

CHAPTER 30

Auntie wasn't in her bedroom when I went to check on her. "Tens?" I yelled in the hallway, unsure of where he might be. I raced to the staircase, looking into each room as I went by. "Auntie?" I shouted.

"Meridian!" Tens grabbed me as I stumbled.

One glance at his face and I knew Auntie wasn't drinking tea in the kitchen, feeling right as rain on wheat. "Tell me," I demanded, crumpling onto the stairs.

"When we got home she'd moved."

"Moved where?"

"To the attic tower."

"Why?" A sinking sensation accompanied my question.

"It's time. Soon."

I ran to the tower, out of breath and heaving. I'd clearly not fully recovered from my work at the accident. There she was, tucked under a large pile of quilts, sleeping. Her breathing was even, but she wouldn't wake, no matter how loud I shouted or pleaded. Tears slid down my cheeks unchecked.

"Meridian, here." Tens handed me a card and a package wrapped in rose-printed flannel.

I didn't want to open it. I knew it was her quilt. By opening it and holding the story of her life in my hands, I would accept her death. I opened the card, Auntie's handwriting so like my mother's looping script. In a few short weeks, my life had turned inside out.

"I can't." I handed the card to Tens.

He took it from me and read it out loud.

"Dearest Little One, you have come so far, so fast. It seems like only yesterday I was sixteen myself, the world so big and unknown. I sit here with hands no longer capable of writing legibly, no longer willing to quilt a stitch. My spirit is tired. I have done what I came to this earth to do, and so I leave it, and all its possibilities, to you. You have a strong ally in Tens—trust his soul. Learn from your mistakes and from your accomplishments. I came up here, to the room that Charles crafted for me, to be as close to heaven as possible. I am ready for a party; I only wish Charles could be by my side. I will watch you and love you from wherever I am. This is my final birthday quilt for you. Forever, Auntie."

Tens closed the card and I pushed aside the flannel to unfold the blanket. Gardens of roses filled the front of an almost perfect replica of the house. The borders were filled with airplanes and outlines of countries. Words and recipes were embroidered into the fabric. Portraits of people and stacks of books were interspersed with miniquilts made from tiny pieces of fabric. It was the most beautiful thing I'd ever seen.

"I wish I'd told her about Charles."

"So tell her. She isn't gone yet."

"But can she hear me?"

"Does it matter?"

"Oh, Auntie, Charles didn't leave you. He's waiting for you. He said to tell you one-four-three."

We sat with her in the attic bedroom she'd claimed as her final resting place. She'd waited her whole life for that party in the sky.

So there we sat, in the upper parapet of the great old house. Tens brought up a space heater and we wrapped ourselves in stacks of quilts so old they'd yellowed and frayed. I could hear her voice in my head: "What good is a quilt if it's unused? The same as a life unused. They're meant to be wrung out and frayed around the edges. That's the way of things. Always has been. Always will be."

I held her hand. Her fingers were gnarled and crooked

like the roots of the oldest swamp trees. Not prissy roots of trees that grew in manicured parks and didn't understand the mess of life. These were roots forced to grow around, and down, and through, to survive. Those trees reminded me of Auntie. She got knee-deep in the muck and managed never to lose her hope or her innocence.

Time narrowed to each breath. Her chest rose and fell. Her eyelids fluttered. The sun rose high in the sky and dipped back below the horizon. I waited, ready to visualize my window, to see Charles on the other side, to let her go and make sure I didn't tangle. I tried to keep my insecurities tamped down. *Can I let go? Can I stay on this side?*

I thought back to before my birthday. I didn't know if I was starting with as much hope in humanity as Auntie was dying with. *Have I paid enough attention? Have I learned the stories well enough to recite them in the vivid, vibrant detail she did?* Part of me had always known she was there. Behind me. Steadying me. The windbreak for those terrible storms.

And now?

Now I must find my strength on my own. Was I strong enough for this? Did I want to be?

Tens handed me a plate with a sandwich and a quartered apple. "Meridian, you have to eat. And you haven't showered since the train accident."

I didn't take my eyes from Auntie's mouth. Open. Inhale. Close. Exhale. One breath. One heartbeat. I waited for the next one. "I'm afraid to leave the room. What if I'm not here? I have to be here."

"It will happen as it's supposed to."

I blinked. "That's very Zen."

Tens stomped into my space; he leaned down and got right in my face. "Making yourself sick isn't going to help anyone. You have to be strong so you don't—" He broke off, bracketing my face with his hands so I had to look at him. I had to gaze into those amazing infinite eyes of his and see the reflection of a girl I didn't know anymore. "The world needs you." He rested his forehead against mine as tears dropped from his cheeks onto mine. "I need you, Meridian."

I sighed and leaned into him.

"I love you. Don't you know that?" He'd closed his eyes with his confession.

I let go of Auntie's hand and wrapped my arms around him. I buried my face in the curve of his neck and inhaled the soap and woods and wolf he always smelled of. I pulled back and searched his expression. I closed my eyes and took a breath around my tears.

Charles's secret code for "I love you" flashed through my mind. I smiled when it came to me, "One-four-three, too." As I heard those words come out of my mouth I knew, I knew that I'd listened. That while I might not have gotten every detail, I knew enough of the lore to keep going. I knew enough of Auntie to make her quilt myself.

Tens raised his eyebrows. "Wow, a math equation. That's romantic."

I laughed, stepping back. "I love you, too." It was as if life were held in the balance, stuttered, then moved forward again. Like a grandfather clock slowing for a heartbeat, then ticking like normal. Still, a part of me waited for Auntie to open her eyes and applaud our young love.

"Little one?"

I closed my eyes and opened them. I was in my room, standing next to Auntie. Through the window, I watched a crowd of people in the distance walking, running, skipping toward us, full of joy. The sky was the bright blue of Auntie's eyes and the sun was warm and smooth where its rays fell across us as we stood at the window. Crimson petals rained from the sky like confetti, and Charles led the group with his arms outstretched.

"He waited for you."

"I heard you. Thank you, little one. That's your family in the distance. Generations of us. Except the few Fenestras who have been reborn. One day I hope we'll meet again. It's time."

I nodded, embracing her, unwilling to let go.

"You take care of your young man, okay? It's not over. We'll be right there with you. You have the strength of light on your side, you hear me? I wish I knew how to tell you to fight the Nocti. But trust love, light, life. You've made me proud. Now finish it." She drifted out the window and I reached behind me for something to grab on to as I closed it. I opened my eyes. I was clinging to Tens's hand. My knuckles were white and my nails drew blood along the top of his hand.

"What happened?" Tens asked as my legs collapsed under me. He lowered me gently into a chair.

I turned back to Auntie. Her mouth didn't open,

didn't close, didn't move. "Gone?" The question in my heart mirrored in my voice.

Tens felt for a pulse in her neck. "She's gone."

Part of me hadn't thought I could resist the attraction and stay in this world.

Tens gathered me to him. "You did it. I knew you would."

"I know you did." I watched the light from the bedside lamp leap and dance against the tiny bits of candy-colored fabric. "That's what she was waiting for, wasn't it? There wasn't unfinished business. She was just waiting for me to decide." And I'd picked love. I'd picked life. "Tens—I—"

A howl went up from the yard, startling both of us. And then another, farther afield. Then a pack seemed to take up the chorus.

"That's Custos, isn't it?" The sound of automobiles approached, drowning out the coyotes. "What day is it?"

Tens became a flurry of activity, but didn't answer me. "It's New Year's Eve, right?"

"Meridian, get your bag. We have to go."

"Go? We can't go. Where are we going?"

December 22, 1835
I glimpsed the face of a dear Fenestra friend
yesterday. She now walks as one of them. At
her side was her Protector, her lover, turned
Dark as well. The Nocti grow stronger upon
our weaknesses & I know not how to battle
them. I fear facing one as I fear nothing else.
—Jocelyn Wynn

CHAPTER 31

"You hear it?" Tens shook my shoulders. "Do you?"

"It's people. They're yelling." I glanced at the ceiling. That wasn't the lamplight dancing, those were flames.

"We need to go. Now!" Tens brushed his hand over Auntie's forehead, a final gesture of goodbye.

"We can't leave her here. It's just people from the church. They're not going to do anything. They want to scare us. I won't let them!"

"No, Meridian. Auntie made me promise. She knew she'd never leave this room. Think about it. She never said anything about services or burial, right?"

"But that's because she knew I wasn't ready to hear it."

"No, she knew she'd never leave this room. But we have to."

A roar of wind blasted and rattled the windows. "That's smoke." I sniffed the air. "They're burning another arrow on the lawn?"

Tens grabbed my arm. "Do you trust me?"

"But—"

"Do you trust me?" he asked again.

"Yes." I grabbed my bag and touched Auntie's still-warm hand one last time. "Where are we going?"

"Follow me," Tens instructed.

"Wait, I have to get—"

"We don't have time."

I dragged my feet even as I saw the flames dance along the porch beneath us. A shattering crash and a violent cheer intensified the stench of fire. "I need her basket. I'm a quilter now too. And the journal." It was the most tangible connection I had to Fenestras, to the only Fenestra I truly knew.

"Safe. I have the basket already. The journal's in your pack."

"What?"

"Auntie. She knew, I listened. Let's go." Tens shook me to get my attention.

I slung my arms through the straps of my backpack and hitched it up as Tens ran his hands beneath a stack of quilts that were piled on the shelves of the armoire in the far corner. "What are you doing?"

"There's a latch here somewhere."

I started shoving quilts aside and off the shelves. The roar of the fire was hungry and the people outside sang hymns at the top of their lungs. Someone shouted, "And the witches shall be burned out of the promised land!"

"Here we go." Four empty spools of thread decorated the top of the shelves like gingerbread detailing, evenly spaced. "Shit, what's the code? She told me. Months ago. What the hell was it?"

"There's a code?"

He turned to me. "What did you say earlier? The 'I love you,' what was it?"

"One-four-three."

"That's it." Tens pressed the first spool into the top of the unit until it disappeared completely. Then he pressed the fourth and the third and finally we heard a pop. A musty smell blew into the room.

"Stairs?"

Tens turned on his flashlight and took my hand. "Trust me."

I nodded. Downstairs, another window shattered and footsteps stampeded on the first floor.

Tens closed the unit behind us. When we heard a click, we knew it had locked. Would they think to search for a secret passageway?

We went down the stairs as quickly as we could, descending in a tight spiral of iron and wood. The noises became louder and smoke began seeping through cracks in the chute. It required all my fortitude not to cough, but my eyes watered.

A voice shouted by my shoulder, "Look in the storm cellar! They're here somewhere. Find them."

I turned a panicked face to Tens. He gently placed a finger along my lips. *Trust. Trust. Trust.* With each heartbeat I felt the word.

We slowed down, praying we wouldn't make a noise. We went past the third and second floors, past the first and into the basement. I didn't know where we were or where in the world we would come out. I gripped Tens's hand and he turned to me. "Almost there."

I pressed against Tens's back, mimicking his movements. Down a long tunnel.

"We're here. It's safe to talk now, they can't hear us."

I glanced around. "Where are we?"

"The old icebox. The stream flows past just ahead."

"The stream? That's like a football field away from the house."

"Right."

"How?"

"There's time later to explain, but we have to keep moving. We aren't safe yet."

We heard splashing in the water ahead. Tens turned off his light and handed it to me. He bent down and drew a gun from a holster on his ankle.

The footsteps got closer, as did the panting. And finally, a low growl that was Custos's hello. I flicked on the light and knelt down. She licked my face.

I turned to Tens as he holstered his gun. "Is that a gun?"

"Yep."

"Would you have . . ." I broke off, unable to say it out loud.

"Of course." He regarded me the way every warrior has looked at the smaller and the helpless they've sworn to protect. I didn't appreciate his expression. I wasn't helpless and I wan't in need of rescuing.

I opened my mouth, but he beat me to it. "I know how to shoot. I've hunted for years. A gun is more efficient than a bow and arrow, especially when you're hungry. Would I pull the trigger to protect you? Absolutely. Would I let you pull the trigger to protect me? Hell, yes. But do you know how to shoot? Have you ever held a gun?"

"No."

"So, if this is something I know how to do and you don't, there isn't anything sexist in that—it's smart."

I nodded. He was right, as much as I hated to admit it. "When this is over, you'll teach me, right?"

"Sure. I'll even let you skin and gut dinner." He smiled.

"Thanks." My stomach rolled at the thought.

Custos fell into step with us, occasionally running ahead, then waiting. Her ears never stopped moving and her nose tilted up to catch the scents floating in the wind. We came to the end of the tunnel and Tens pushed against a bundle of branches until it moved far enough for us to squeeze through.

"How did Custos fit through there?" I asked as we pushed the camouflage back into place. We were under the huge curving stone bridge I'd crossed that first day.

"No idea. Come on." Tens grabbed my bag and my hand. "Quiet." He moved out from under the bridge, lit with the frantic flames and echoing with fanatical cries in a language I didn't understand.

People clad in long white robes were running about in the distance. I realized one stood apart and directed the others. Where the light from the fire should have reflected off his robes and face, it disappeared into blackness. The pieces clicked and I knew this wasn't about witches, but about Aternocti versus Fenestra. Perimo had positioned himself in a community that was desperate for answers, and instead of hope he'd fed them a diet of blame.

The bridge afforded us a bit of shelter, but the fire's heat was tangible even from there. We listened to the angry roll of thunder as the fire engulfed the house one board and one stone at a time. Hail and snow battled with warm wind, as if the earth was engaged in a larger conflict.

I let the cold of the rock sink through my coat and into my back, keeping me grounded and in the now. It seemed like months ago I'd crawled and stumbled my way across this structure, unsure of what awaited me at the house. Now, my heart broke and grief swamped me—the house, the love, the stories, Auntie—all reduced to a pile of ash.

Thank God the main structure of the house was stone,

or we might not have made it out. Black smoke billowed, and the people stood so close, the sweat and soot on their faces made them appear like they'd crawled out of a coal mine. As we moved closer, keeping our cover in the tree line, I recognized faces from the church service, but there were also others, ones who, like Perimo, absorbed the light around them. Biblical verses were interspersed with guttural proclamations and what I could only guess were curses.

Freezing rain evaporated before it got within yards of the fire, but it covered other noises as it smacked the trees and cars on the road. The heat from the fire was only deepened by the unseasonably warm weather that melted a lot of the snow and raised the level of the creek, its splashes and trickles covering our footsteps and scent. Custos led the way.

I struggled to keep up with Tens's clearheaded purpose and long strides. The shadows and firelight grew dim behind us; the shouts and high temperature faded away.

And still we plodded on. We headed in the opposite direction of where I'd gotten lost trying to find Celia, but the forest all looked the same. Huge water droplets dripped down on us from the trees above, but the hail had either stopped falling or it wasn't making it through the foliage to hurt us. The cold that had frozen my lungs for days was gone, replaced by a crispness that woke me up and kept me going.

Tens stopped and listened. I ran into his back, my

eyes down, focused on each footstep. "Sor—" I whispered.

He shook his head, cutting off my apology.

I stood stock-still behind him, wondering what he was listening for. The forest wasn't quiet, but neither was it noisy. How did he pick out the sounds to worry about?

"We're okay." He turned to me. "Right?"

"Right."

"We're almost there. Can you keep going?"

"Or you'll carry me?" I asked with a hint of a smile.

Clearly, he didn't know I was teasing, "I pulled something at the train, so my back is really sore. I don't think I can—"

"Then give me my bag." I didn't need to be coddled anymore. Granted I'd been a mess when I first got here, but I was better every day. Stronger. Healthier.

"You sure?" Tens asked, flicking the flashlight to my face. He handed over my bag.

"You really don't look very good," I said, studying him in the little light cast by the flashlight.

"It's nothing." He dismissed me. "I've got hot chocolate and dry clothes when we get there."

"That's motivation. Lead on." I grinned.

We hiked on. Occasionally Tens paused, turned out the light, and listened. He stumbled once or twice, unlike his normal agile self, but we were both exhausted.

Finally, we turned into a steep canyon filled with Douglas fir and ferns. The piles of snow that had slid down the side of the cliffs created a tunnel of ice and snow around us. It was a cool blue in the early-morning light.

Custos whined and waited for us.

"I dug a path. It's melting but still fairly stable. It's not long and there's a cave on the other side."

"When? All those treks and errands?"

Tens squeezed my hand. "Wait till you see it. It's the four-star Hilton resort of your dreams."

"Really?" I laughed. My standards had surely fallen if a cave and a resort could be compared in the same sentence.

"Really." He crouched, following Custos.

Tens lifted a branch at the end of the tunnel, then pushed against a door that appeared to be rock, but was clearly much lighter. He stepped back. "Ladies first." He handed me the flashlight, which I shone into the dark hole, ducking down.

Custos pushed past me and yipped a welcome I'd never heard from her before.

I gasped, shocked by what greeted me.

CHAPTER 32

"Holy crap!" I dropped my bag and shrugged out of my drenched coat. The interior temperature was amazingly cozy.

Tens flicked a switch and several lamps hung from the ceiling illuminated. I pointed at them.

"Battery rigged." He shrugged. "Charles."

The rock walls were decorated with ancient paintings like ones I'd seen only in books. Paintings of huge people with spears, and animals.

An old Oriental rug in noble burgundy and blue tones graced the rock floor. Shelves made of branches held books, knickknacks, and stacks of Auntie's quilts; a rod made from a sapling held a curtain I recognized as identical to the ones in the library. "This is amazing! What is this place?"

I realized I was dripping water all over a discarded piece of linoleum.

"Please remove your boots in the mudroom." Tens cracked a smile, clearly pleased with my delight.

I bent and tugged at my soaked laces until they gave, then I toed out of my boots.

"Your hideout, my lady." Tens also removed his coat and gloves. "Superheated by geothermal energy and the very occasional battery-powered space heater, but it has to be way below zero for that to be necessary. Towels are to your left. Get out of that stuff, Meri. We can't afford to get sick." Tens sounded tired.

I shivered as my cold, wet clothes were replaced by warm cotton bathsheets.

Tens rambled on about the cave. "It's an old Anasazi settlement. About fifty years ago Charles found it while out exploring and began making improvements. He called it their vacation home. Come on, I'll give you a tour."

I nodded, suddenly feeling shy.

"You've just entered the living area. I have a couple of inflatable chairs for warmer weather and I have a bench that's in progress." Pillows were piled haphazardly on the rug, which felt warm against my bare feet.

Tens pushed the curtain to the side. "The kitchen and dining area. We don't have refrigeration for the summer figured out, and we don't really want to attract bears, so the food—mostly camping stuff or canned—is locked in metal boxes. But right now we're okay, and there are a couple of hollows in the rack that make perfect iceboxes. These burners run on gas cartridges or battery power, even solar if we want to use them in the summer."

"How? When? Wha—" I felt like I'd fallen down the rabbit hole. This was a palace. I explored the stocked kitchen, the mismatched dishes, the plastic tub that made a sink of sorts.

"Charles did a lot of it. I cleaned the place up, evicted a few tenants, and restocked. Auntie hadn't been out here in years, but it held up pretty well. And I'm kidding about the bears—no entrance to this place is big enough for one, and I haven't seen evidence of any in the years I've been coming out here."

"This was all your mysterious disappearances, wasn't it?"

He nodded. "Behind that curtain is the toilet. Charles figured out it's deeper than five hundred feet. So it's also a garbage chute."

I peeked behind the curtain. "There's a toilet seat."

"I added that part." Tens sheepishly glanced away.

"Nice." I smiled at him.

"The bedroom." He motioned me ahead. "There are inflatable mattresses, but also thick mats and plenty of—"

"Quilts?" I interrupted.

"Yeah. Plus down sleeping bags and battery-powered warmers, so we'll be toasty even if the temp dips way low again. Want to see the best part?"

"There's more?"

"Of course. It has its own personal hot spring for bathing, a heated vent, courtesy of Mother Earth, for drying wet clothes on, and—"

"I can't believe this place." I turned in a full circle as the high ceiling reached cathedral-like heights. There were murals above us, and the air was warm and thick with humidity.

"Charles did the paintings."

"Wow." I recognized scenes from Auntie's stories, depicting her childhood and marriage. The mural wasn't finished.

"He died before he could complete it." Tens pointed to the old paint cans and brushes in the corner. "I didn't want to clean them up."

I nodded.

"You hungry? I could use food."

"I think I heard the promise of hot chocolate?"

"Want a candy cane with that?" Tens lifted a lantern and we moved back the way we had come. "Oh, and through that passageway is the way out on the other side. Very easy to navigate, and I've got a motorcycle there in case we need to get gone."

"Have you missed anything?" I asked, incredulous.

"Thank Auntie. She's the one who told me we'd need this."

Okay, modesty only took him so far. This wasn't exactly near the house and he'd made lots of trips.

"I've brought lots of clothes—your SpongeBob pj's are hanging in the bedroom. If you want them."

SpongeBob. I hadn't noticed they weren't in my room. I slid behind the dressing screen and shimmied out of my wet bra and panties. Pulling the very dry and almost warm flannel over my thawing skin felt wonderful.

"Wool socks are in the Ritz cracker tin," Tens called.

Sure enough, there was an assortment of bright colors. I grabbed a pair and pulled them on.

"Let me help?" I asked, joining Tens. I pulled a chocolate brown fuzzy sweater over my head and wrapped a quilt around my shoulders. I almost felt human. I reached for the wooden spoon and pushed him toward the clothes. "Your turn."

I stirred the canned soup until it boiled and the scent of chicken broth filled the space. I lit candles, and Custos settled herself snoring in front of a space heater.

We ate in silence, slurping down the heat and noodles. What now?

"We're safe. Not a bad way to start the New Year." Tens seemed to read my mind.

"But what now?"

"Let's take a few days, then I'll go down and scout. We can stay here for a while, but . . ."

"Perimo is a Nocti. I saw him at the fire. I remember he took Celia. How do we fight him?"

"Auntie told you to go find other Fenestras, right? Maybe one of them can help?"

"You mean leave?"

"Why stay? Let them have their church—at least until we know how to take Perimo down for good. If he can kill you, he will."

"I know. I just wish I knew more about the Sangre and how to call for one."

"We can try dreaming and praying for one. We don't have to figure it out tonight. I'm beat. You ready for sleep? We can clean up later." He seemed about ready to fall over, his cheeks flushed and red, his eyes liquid and bright.

Tens and I unrolled the zero-temp sleeping bags and unfolded the heavy mats for padding. I didn't know whether I was sleeping near him or across the cave. I wanted to press against him, to know I wasn't alone even in the deepest of sleep. But I didn't know how to ask him. I blew out the candles and turned all but one of the lanterns off. Tens crawled into his bag and sleep claimed him immediately. His breathing evened and deepened. I glanced at Custos for guidance.

Finally, I tucked myself into my sleeping bag and scooted close to Tens. He woke enough to pull me closer; my head fit perfectly in the crook between his head and shoulder. I turned off the lantern, plunging the cave into the deepest of blacks. Tens shifted closer still and I listened to his breathing and Custos's snores. He was so warm, I fell asleep immediately. But I didn't dream.

*　*　*

When I woke, I blinked in the darkness and reached until I found the lamp switch. I glanced at the watch Tens wore faithfully. It was two o'clock, but whether that was daytime or nighttime I had not a clue. I peeled myself as quietly as I could out of the sleeping bag. Tens didn't move.

I dressed and took our wet clothes to the back room and draped them over the vent on the cast-iron grill. I brushed my teeth and poked around. Knowing I'd gotten more sleep than Tens over the past few days, I wanted him to catch up as much as possible.

I found my backpack and opened it. Inside, a cheap cell phone was actually charged and had minutes on it, but there was no signal. I found Auntie's leather-bound journal, the letter she'd written me, a few stacks of cash, and bank records that were in my name. There were also a couple of the graphic novels I'd carted around since the beginning of this adventure.

I flipped to the back of the journal, hoping Auntie had added a postscript, and I smiled.

Dearest Child,

Let me go. If you're reading this, then you made the right decision. Trust Tens. In turn, keep watch over him. Love is a precious gift—one without strings. Always want what's best for him, even when you disagree. As he'll want what's best for you.

I lived one hundred six packed years. They are frayed at the edges and ready for repair. I am ready for a rest. I do not know how many changes in the seasons you will see, but I hope it's the full one hundred six. Keep your eyes open and rise to your experiences. I am proud of you, my child, and I will be watching.

Auntie

I blew my nose and wiped my eyes. There was no normal now. I broke open a bag of trail mix and popped open a can of juice. I checked on the drying clothes and studied Charles's mural, glad he and Auntie found each other in the beyond.

Tens still slept, but with an increasing restlessness. When he threw his blankets off, I walked over. I brought the lantern closer to him and gasped at the red blotches on his face, arms, and hands.

"Tens! Tens! Wake up." I bent over his face. He was burning up, so hot his skin was both fragile and rough.

"Meri." He tried to move. "Too bright light. Sick."

"What's wrong? Do you know what's wrong?"

"Bad sick. Bad." He lapsed back into feverish shaking. "Barely see you."

Did he mean he saw the light, the window? No! I wouldn't let him die. I couldn't let him die. *Think. Think. Trust my instincts. Trust my instincts?*

Custos padded over and pawed at the front of my backpack. I watched her determined efforts to get into the zippered compartment. *Great, now I'm letting a wolf make decisions.* I leaned down to see what she was after.

"Holy shit," I exclaimed, pulling out the papers with the cabbie's name and phone number on it and Doctor Portalso-Marquez's business card with her home number on it. The señora and her daughter could help. So would Josiah. I knew it.

Think. Think.

"Trust your instincts. Trust your instincts," I said as

Custos's hackles rose and she growled, baring her teeth. She moved around me, backing me toward Tens. As I reached down to comfort her, a shadow fell across the entrance of the cave. The stench of expensive cologne and incense told me Perimo had found us.

"Oh, isn't this cute, the little witch talks to herself." He clapped.

I straightened, ready to protect Tens. "Reverend Perimo? What's your real name?"

"Oh, Klaus Perimo is so catchy. I like being a reverend, too. People trust you. It works for me."

"You're an Aternocti. You took Celia—that's why I felt such relief when you arrived that night, isn't it? You took her? She didn't push against me anymore."

"Congrats. Call off your dog, Meridian. I won't hesitate to use this." He pointed a gun at Custos.

I laid my hand on her head, but she refused to budge. "She doesn't like you."

"Call her off." He waved the gun.

I bent to her ear. "If you can understand me, I need help to save Tens. Run, go. Find help."

She backed away toward the rear of the cave.

"Go," I shouted. Custos raced into the blackness.

"Sending a dog. So very Lassie. I find you amusing. Vexing, but amply entertaining." Perimo shrugged out of his jacket and pocketed the gun again. "It *is* toasty in here."

"Bet you're used to heat, huh?" I asked, taking a washcloth and soaking it in melted snow.

"Is that a hell reference?" He chuckled. "We are so

misunderstood. I brought you a little present. Your first photograph." He unfolded the town newspaper and tossed it on the floor between us.

I didn't move to pick it up. Instead, I placed the rag lovingly on Tens's forehead. My heart broke a little as he tried to move away from my touch.

"Don't be that way. I'll even tell you what the headline says: 'Visiting Teen Anarchist Blows Up Train'—that's you in the photograph holding a dead baby. Not your best hair day. You killed one hundred fifty-seven people all headed home for New Year's."

"I didn't kill anyone."

"Didn't you? Seems there are witnesses who saw you at that junction earlier in the day, and then you happened to be one of the first people on the scene. When your concerned pastor came to offer you spiritual guidance, you confessed and showed him where you'd stashed the last of the explosives used to blow up the tracks and train. Seems you burned your house down and killed your aunt to cover your tracks. You even have a criminal record in Oregon. We are nothing if not thorough."

"No one is going to believe you. You did it. Where would I get explosives? You were there too."

"But I'm a good guy and you're a bad one. Didn't you get that memo? Plus, you can buy anything on the Internet—haven't you heard it's the devil's own tool?" He chuckled.

Tens moaned.

"His fever is getting worse. His organs will start cooking and shutting down within the next few hours. I can feel his heart weakening. Snakebite?"

Snake? Were there poisonous snakes here? "You're wrong."

"I'm rarely wrong about death, little girl, or hadn't you noticed?"

"What do you want?"

"Oh, finally. Aren't you going to offer me a beverage?"

"No."

"Manners get you everywhere."

"You are a lunatic," I muttered. I opened tins and cupboards searching for a first-aid kit, anything with aspirin or Tylenol. Something to bring down Tens's fever.

"Au contraire. I am one of the sanest men I know."

"What do you want?"

"A trade."

"You have nothing I want."

"Are you sure?" He tossed a photograph to me of my parents and Sammy. There were palm trees in the background and they lounged by a pool. I'd never seen this photograph.

Lux tenebras semper vincit.

Light always conquers the darkness.

—Luca Lenci

CHAPTER 33

"My family is fine." My pulse fluttered in my throat. I hoped he couldn't see it.

Tens thrashed around and threw off the washcloth. I gave up on finding medicine and poured cool water over his head and torso. I didn't know what else to do. When I tried to get him to swallow some water, he choked on it.

Perimo sat and tsked at me. "Tick tock. Tick tock."

"Oh, shut up."

"You should be nicer to me."

"Or what? You'll kill me?" At this point I was tired of playing games.

"I don't have to do that. Why don't we play twenty questions, Bible version? I spout off a verse and you tell me what book of the Bible it's in."

"No." What did he mean, he didn't have to kill me?

"I'm just trying to keep you company in the final hours. I can just sit here." He pouted, leaning against the wall.

I started to pack snow around Tens's head and arms, but by the time I worked my way around him, it had melted.

"If there's anything you want to tell him before you two go to my side of the stadium for eternity, I would get cracking. Confess those enormous teenage emotions. Man, I'm glad I'm not a teen anymore. Shakespeare made it all romantic, but the stench. You don't know how nice you've had it. I promise your bodies will be found and the note you wrote confessing to all the terrible things that have been happening around here will get to the authorities. Your parents will never have to know what a hellion they raised. Cross my heart."

Don't do it. Don't do it. "What are you talking about?"

"Didn't Granny tell you? Shame on her. He dies, you do. And he's dying. Right soon, as they say in these parts." He cackled.

"That's not true."

"It's not? Really? Because last time I checked, I'd been at this a lot longer than you. He's dying."

"You're lying."

"Okay, okay, you caught me. It's not a snakebite,

nope—it's poison. Got him at the train accident. Slow acting, but kills one hundred percent within ninety-six hours. Tick tock."

"You're lying."

"And you're getting on my nerves. What part of this don't you understand?"

My mind spun, trying to figure out if there was any truth in what he said or if it was all a lie. But why?

"He's had muscle aches, right? A headache? Dark circles under his eyes."

"I was with him at the train."

"Not the whole time."

"So what do you want?"

"Now you ask? First you refuse me hospitality? Call me names? Accuse me of lying? And just *now* get to the good part? I have so much to teach you."

"What do you want?"

"Who."

My heart sped up again. "Who?"

"You."

"See, you *are* lying." I leapt to my feet. "I knew it." I wouldn't die just because Tens did.

"How many times do we have to go over this? I am not lying. I am offering you a trade. You, alive, become my apprentice, and I'll let you take your boy toy to your side and let your parents live. I'm not sure I'm ready to give up Sammy, though, he's so cute. Loves his fudge ripple, doesn't he?"

"Or?"

"You die, Tens dies, and your whole family dies."

That didn't sound like much of a trade.

"If Tens here dies, you're going too. The fam is bonus for having to put up with your granny for the last few years. Bitch refused to see the light."

When Charles died, Auntie didn't die. Maybe Perimo was lying. Of *course* he was lying.

"You become a Nocti and learn from the best. My team is the best there is. We are everywhere and anyone."

"How?" I wasn't seriously contemplating the offer, but I needed time.

"You have to kill yourself—sort of. You pull the trigger, I blow you back into your body, and then you get to spend forever with Tens. I'll save him, too."

"And my parents?" If he handed me the gun, then I would have control.

"If you insist. Have I told you that Celia was accommodating? She was really quite easy to convince to step in the trap. Then to suck her away from the tea party she was having in your head. Delightful."

My stomach churned. "How do I know you have my parents?"

He pulled out a phone.

"No reception in here," I told him.

"Satellite. We have the good toys on our side. Money. Power. Beauty. Eternal life." He dialed a number and held the phone out to me.

I took it and listened to it ring. My breath hitched when I heard, "Mer-D?"

"Sammy?"

Then Mom's voice came on the line. "Meridian? Our caller ID says this is Meridian. Who is this?"

"Mom, it's me," I cried as Perimo yanked the phone out of my hands.

"See? Not lying."

I sank down next to Tens. His pulse was rapid and erratic. The hair on the back of my neck rose and I felt a soul push against me.

"Oh, he's dying. Look at that." Perimo tapped his fingers on the cave wall.

This wasn't a feeling that could be faked. I knew this was real. Tears blurred my vision as I waited for Tens to open his eyes and reassure me. If he was going to die, I'd just have to live enough for both of us.

"Okay, I'll do it. Give me the gun."

CHAPTER 34

"I'm impressed. I thought it was going to take you actually feeling the pull of death to see my point."

"I'll do it." I watched Tens's breathing slow and grow more shallow. "You win."

Perimo handed over the gun. "Put it in your mouth. That temple position doesn't work so well."

"Let me say goodbye first." I leaned down and kissed Tens's lips. "I love you. So much."

I took a steadying breath, raised the gun, and pulled the trigger. Red bloomed from Perimo's stomach and he crumpled, then slowly stood back up, glaring.

"Oh, that was sneaky. Didn't see that coming. Were you listening to nothing I said? I am *done* being nice to you. Your brother dies now, no matter what!" Rage pulsed from his words.

My eyes widened as I watched him shake the blood off his shirt.

"Did you not hear the eternal life part? You think you're the first Fenestra to try to kill me?"

"But—"

"But?" he mimicked.

I'd let down my family, Tens, everyone. So much for my big plan. "Then I'll die with him."

"He doesn't have to die, you moron. Do you need me to speak more slowly?"

"I don't want to be a—"

"Why not? We're fun. You think Destroyers are less than Creators? Without us there would be nothing to create from, or on, or with. We are an integral part of making this world work. You should be grateful to get the invitation."

"You tried to kill Auntie. You terrorized a whole town. Where's the justice?"

"Justice? You *are* young, aren't you? The world is full of assholes, Meridian. It's a choice between being vanilla or chocolate, you can't be both."

Tens jerked me into my head. Suddenly, we stood together at the window. "What's going on?" he asked.

"You're dying."

"No, I'm not."

"I think you are."

"I'm not leaving you, Supergirl. I won't go. I'll wait like Charles." Tens crossed his arms and planted his feet.

I panicked. "Don't! You have to go. You have to. I need to know you're safe. No matter what. Please."

I blinked and scrutinized Perimo. "You let me take Tens across. Then I'll do as you say, for my family's safety."

"That's fair. You're a top negotiator." He shrugged like we were trading baseball cards.

I closed my eyes and visualized my bedroom at home. Tens leaned against the window frame and faced me. "I don't like this."

"We don't have a choice. I tried to kill him. I can't."

"I'm not leaving you to him."

"You have to. It's either hell or both of us working for him, and one is more than enough. Tens, I'll figure it out, but if you're dying, you need to go to Auntie. Your family will be waiting."

"I love you. I'm supposed to protect you."

"You have. I can do this because of you. I have to save my parents and Sammy."

Tens nodded sadly, moving to kiss me.

I didn't feel his lips against mine, because blinding light filled the cave.

"You can't behave, can you, old man?" A rich voice echoed off the walls, its accent one I found familiar.

I leaned over Tens and peered up at a huge man dressed in combat boots, old army surplus fatigues, and a long black leather trench. Aviators covered his eyes.

"Hell's bells." Perimo paled and eyed the gun just out

of his reach. His eyes darkened to black pits, and the light in the room spilled toward the pitch-black of his outline.

The warrior laughed. "You no think a gun touch me, do you?"

I blinked. "Josiah?"

" 'Ello, missy. Sorry I be late." He peeled off his sunglasses and the light that streamed from his eyes almost blinded me. "Put these on. Cover the Proc's eyes too. Your family be fine. I'll see them next, 'kay?"

I slid the mirrored glasses onto my face, nodded, and laid my arm across Tens's eyes.

"Ha-ha, just seeing if you're paying attention. Guess you are." Perimo tried to scurry away.

"You be goin' nowhere."

Perimo turned to face Josiah, drawing up to his full height. "I'll extinguish your light, Sangre. There are more of us. An army trained in the modern world. I'm only following orders. You don't know whom you're messing with."

"No, *you* don'. You been messing wit souls for too long. Free will is sacred, Nocti, and you break that rule too many times."

"My friends will carry on with or without me. I've started a revolution. You don't know whom I work for—"

"Enough. What chase darkness, Meridian?"

"Uh, light?" I answered.

"That be right. Light it up!" Josiah raised his arms and I lowered my head as rays of pure white light poured out of him.

I heard Perimo scream and I lifted my head to catch a glimpse.

He sucked up light, agonizing as if it burned. But slowly the blackness lightened, degree by degree, until his outline began changing. Inch by inch, he was erased.

I stayed crouched over Tens long after the screaming ended and the light flickered back down to normal.

I raised my head at the gentle touch on my head and dog kisses on my face.

"*Luz, luz.* Okay?" Señora Portalso held my face and peered into it.

"Josiah?" I glanced around, but the only thing he'd left were his sunglasses.

"No Josiah," the señora answered quizzically.

"Hi, Meridian, let me have a look here." I recognized the señora's daughter. "I'm a doctor. Remember?"

I gave her space to examine Tens. "I think he was poisoned. I think he's dead—"

"Has he been in the woods a lot? Making trips up here?"

"I guess, yes." I watched the señora empty one of the bags she carried, while her daughter took Tens's temperature.

"Any muscle pain or aches? Headache? Has he had this rash long?"

"He mentioned his back hurt, and he definitely has a rash. He rubbed his temples a lot and light hurt his eyes."

"Do you know if he's been bitten by a tick?"

"A tick?"

"That's a no."

"Would I know that?" What the hell did a tick look like?

"Not necessarily, but it's highly likely we're dealing with Rocky Mountain spotted fever."

That didn't even sound like a real disease. "Is he going to di—"

"No." Señora Portalso turned to me and shook her head violently. "No *fiebre*."

"He should be fine with antibiotics." I watched the señora spread supplies on a clean towel. The doctor deftly inserted a needle into Tens's arm, and handed her mother an IV bag to hold up. The señora turned to me and shooed me toward the other bags she had brought. "*Comida*. Eat." She pointed.

"I think I'd do what she says." The doctor drew blood from Tens's other arm.

I dove into the food, not realizing how famished and drained I was. All the adrenaline left me wasted. Saffron rice, tortillas, and hard-boiled eggs. Chicken in three different sauces and strips of steak. I chewed and swallowed as fast as I could, barely able to take my eyes from Tens's furrowed brow.

"Meridian, Tens will be just fine. We'll stay with you tonight to make sure. The surrounding land is crawling with FBI agents and search teams scouting for you."

"Oh my God, I'm so sorry. You should leave—"

"Stop. This is nothing. Someday maybe I'll tell you about all the patients who come knocking on the back door in the middle of the night."

"Oh." I didn't know what to say to that. Illegal immigrants, maybe? "How did you find us?"

The señora answered in a rapid avalanche of Spanish that I couldn't follow.

Her daughter laughed. "Mama had a dream of you. Said the angels told her to drive to the rocks this way. To bring my supplies. So we got in the car and started driving here from home."

"Because of a dream?" I gasped.

"Mama will tell you dreams are the conduit between worlds and spirits. They're how God communicates with us."

"But how—"

"We reached the turnoff. We'd driven around all night, but we couldn't find you. We were ready to head home and try again after I'd fed the babies, when your wolf lay down in the middle of the road. She wouldn't move, and when I got out to see if she was okay, she spit out my business card. We followed her up here."

I grinned at Custos and watched the señora feed her half a chicken. Tens blinked his eyes and groaned. He drank half a glass of water.

"Are you sure he's going to be okay?"

"Yeah, his temp is normal, his heart rate steady. Even the rash seems to be disappearing."

"The medicine is working, then, isn't it?"

"It doesn't actually work this fast in most cases. I don't understand."

"Los ángeles de Dios." The señora patted my head and touched her heart.

"Angels of God? Maybe. Best explanation I can come up with."

I wondered if Josiah's light healed as well.

Tens woke up briefly in the night and drank water until I thought he'd explode, then fell back into a deeper sleep. I tossed and turned, finally giving up when the watch turned to four and our guests followed Custos back to their car. Tens was out of the proverbial woods, but we were now fugitives.

I drew out the thick journal. I kept reading the words of my ancestors, memorizing details and repeating dates and times. If I ever lost this book I, too, would be lost. I threw myself into the stories, listening for the unspoken, soaking up the wisdom shared.

"Meridian?" Tens's voice was scratchy and dry.

"Right here." I scuttled over. "How are you feeling?"

"Thirsty. Better." He tried to sit up and fell back with a groan.

"The doctor said to give you a few days of recovery, and by then the search for us should be called off. I was left with strict instructions to call on the satellite phone Perimo left behind anytime, if there was any change."

The phone number my brother had answered at was no longer in service.

"What happened?"

"I'll fill you in later. We have time."

We live next to you and with you. We are your friends and your neighbors. You may know us by our surnames: Porte, Tussen, Mittlere, Medio, Portello, Castor, Gannon, Lukus, Myer, Orly, Ailey, Wynn, among others. Our first names you might recognize from history or they might belong to a friend: Alison, Cassandra, Cynthia, Deirdre, Eleanor, Helena, Leann, Noamy, Lucy, Nellie, Ranessa, Leah, and more.

We are shining just beyond your sight. We will be there when you need us and you *will* rise.

—Meridian Fulbright, b. 1903–d. 2009

CHAPTER 35

I wrote Auntie's death date below one of her first entries in the journal. It didn't seem right to add my handwriting to that of the dozen or so other authors. I didn't feel as if I'd earned the privilege yet, not really. But perhaps I'd get used to it in time. I wanted to add my own story. My modern version of these lessons. In case. Just in case. Hopefully, I'd learn more and know more.

"Snazzy pen." Tens's voice smiled with his teasing.

I was writing with a rhinestone-encrusted pen that made me giggle every time I picked it up. "My birthday present from Sammy. Josiah left it in my pack when he made his appearance." I'd found it hours later. I'd saved the newspaper comics it had been wrapped in and the handwritten tag—the only pieces of Sammy I could carry with me.

Tens caught me scrutinizing him and smiled. "See something you like?" He felt good enough to flirt again. I missed the gentle teasing. The heat in his eyes. The kisses I dreamed about.

"Hmm." I grinned back, ready to open my mouth and ask for a kiss.

"So?" he asked. "Look at me." He turned me until we were flush against each other.

I kept my eyes closed, feeling like a coward, but hating to see in his the possibility of what might be.

"Look at me," he commanded again.

I raised my lashes and lost my hold on the fear long enough to fall just a little bit further in love with him.

"We are even. I nursed you. You nursed me. I protected you. You protected me. As of right now, right this minute, we are even."

"Oh." I didn't understand.

"No obligations. No commands from Auntie insisting I'm your Protector. If you want me, you have to tell me that you want me."

"Of course I want you." I threw my arms around his neck and felt a shudder rip through him. "I love you."

He buried his face in my hair. "Then we do this right. Side by side. We have each other's backs."

"No secrets?"

"No secrets. Together. You and me."

"Together," I repeated, finding his lips with my own. Soft and firm, the kiss pulled and tugged all over my body. We fit together like we'd done this a million times before. I tasted tomorrow on his lips.

We ended the kiss and held each other until we both said, "Let's get this show on the road." Almost in unison.

Custos yipped at us as we packed up the gear, cleaned up our garbage, and put the mats and blankets away. I knew that if we were ever here again we would find house sitters, as nature moved back to fill in the spaces. I hefted the journal and bank records, leaving most of my clothes and magazines behind for the squirrels and the spiders to enjoy.

"Got it all?" Tens left his wooden creatures, but tucked the brown sweater I'd worn the first night into his bag.

I contemplated the cave one last time. "I need to say goodbye to Auntie."

"I know. We'll be down there before sunset if we leave now." Tens gripped my hand and tugged me along.

The forest was full of animals enjoying the spring weather in winter. We saw deer and elk, lots of birds, and a few bunnies. Custos never went far from our sides, as if she knew our time in these woods was nearing an end.

I smelled the house long before we broke through the trees and saw its burnt skeleton collapsed, as if it'd heaved one last sigh and given up the fight. We picked through the debris, searching for anything that might be salvaged. I collected a few pieces of china, a melted and misshapen silver fork. Charles's paintings were gone and so were the photographs. It occurred to me that I didn't have a photo of Auntie, and my heart broke a little.

The rumble of tires had us ducking for cover behind the melted hulk of what used to be the Land Rover.

"That's Jasper's truck," Tens whispered in my ear.

I recognized Sarah, his granddaughter, as she turned off the ignition and slid out of the driver's seat. I moved out to greet her. "Sarah."

"Meridian, I'm so glad you're okay."

"How'd you know to find us?" Tens stepped out.

"You probably wouldn't believe me if I told you." Sarah shrugged. "I thought you might have a use for this truck. My granddaddy came to me last night in my sleep. He was reading the newspaper with a cigar and a cup of mud he called coffee."

Her expression grew wistful with recollection. "That was his routine, every day of my life, and I suspect most of his. He'd grab the paper before the cock crowed and see what he'd missed while he slept." She shook the memory from her eyes, "Anyway, he was reading today's *New York Times,* and he pointed at the date. He didn't speak, and for the longest time I just sat at the table with him while he read the paper and drank his coffee.

"Finally, he ended with the crossword. He was one of those rare people who did it in pen and always finished it. Only this time he just did one word, one line of it, and shoved it across the table at me. I read your name in the blocks. He nodded and then the dream evaporated. I figured you needed to see today's paper, that there's something in it for you." She held out a neatly folded copy of the *Times* along with a Colorado keychain.

"Here are the keys to his pickup truck. It's not pretty, but it's got a lot of life left in it, and after seeing the Rover, I figured maybe you could use the wheels. Lord knows, I don't need to haul hay in New York." Sarah laughed and we both smiled with her.

"You call me if you ever get up that way. You've got a place to stay and food to eat." She stuck out her hand to Tens, who shook it.

I hugged her. I knew in that moment there were more good people in the world than just the Portalsos. People who knew there was more to life than what they could easily explain and who were willing to trust their hearts and their instincts.

Without another word, Sarah started walking back down the road.

"Wait, don't you need a ride?" I called.

"Nah, the walking is good for me. It's only a couple of miles, give or take, if you know how the crows do it." She waved and went on her way.

Tens put his arms around me and I leaned back against him.

"What now?" I asked.

"I think you should read the paper. See what Jasper had in mind."

I spread out the pages, but it wasn't until the Across the Nation section that I saw it. "Look!"

I hauled Tens over. "Sheesh, that's a headline." He read it out loud. "Girl and cat—angels of death in nursing home."

"You think maybe?"

"I think it's the best place to start."

I nodded. "What do we do with Custos? Wouldn't she want to go with us? She can't stay here alone." My heart broke at the thought of leaving her behind.

"Turn around, Meridian. I don't think that's gonna be a problem."

Custos had already launched herself into the bed of the truck and settled down against the wheel well in the back.

"Road trip?"

"Where are we headed?"

"Says this nursing home is in Indianapolis."

"Then I guess that's where we're headed. How are you at reading a map?"

"Passable." I giggled, but sobered as the smell of charcoal and burnt plastic met my nose. I surveyed the house's corpse one more time. "You think we'll be back?"

"Maybe. Seems to me you have a house to rebuild someday."

"We. *We* have a house to rebuild." I linked my fingers with his.

"We."

The breeze blew through my hair as we headed down

the highway. The sun warmed my bare toes on the dashboard and my heart finally felt like it was the right size for my chest.

Glenn Miller's "Don't Sit Under the Apple Tree" played on the radio and I could almost see Auntie sitting between Tens and me, smiling and tapping her toes. The world went on, but it was changed. The sunset in the distance made me tear up a bit. "It's rising on someone else right now."

"Maybe another Fenestra?" Tens asked.

"Maybe another Protector," I answered.

Maybe another sister. Knowing I wouldn't see my family soon, my heart sang a sad song. Not while I knew the Nocti were capable of hunting them. I wouldn't put them in danger.

The most glorious colors unfolded in pinks and oranges across the sky as we drove east.

"What's the date?"

"Why?" Tens signaled and we drove onto the interstate, no sign of the FBI or the sheriff ahead of or behind us. "The sixth, I guess."

"Epiphany?" Not the new beginning Perimo envisioned for me, but one I'd do a hundred times over.

I extracted a jar of teal nail polish from the backpack at my feet and eyed my bare toes. "I've been meaning to do this for weeks now."

"Next you're going to dye your hair again."

"Maybe." I was thinking blond. "Aren't you hungry?" I asked.

"Aren't you?" he answered, teasing me. I was gaining inches and pounds. Starting to look like a healthy, well-fed sixteen-year-old.

"As a matter of fact . . ." His chuckles joined mine and he turned the music up, tapping along with it on the steering wheel. In the back of the cab Custos let out a glorified howl. I'd swear Auntie's and Charles's laughter tickled along the breeze with just a hint of rose.

March 2009

Each stitch was a heartbeat, a breath; each seam an experience, a lesson learned. Each piece of fabric was a feeling, a like, a dislike, pain, happiness. Combined, they build a life, a picture of a life anyway, in bits and pieces. Like memories, they have no linear logic, but they resonate. You can tell a lot about a person by the quilt Auntie made for them after they died.

Some had big blocks of bright colors, as if they marked the big moments but forgot to pay attention to the clock ticks in between. Some were a kaleidoscope of scraps, a riot of shapes and textures, as if those who inspired the quilts packed more life into each breath than most people do in a year.

My Auntie was a quiltmaker. I don't know what I am yet, or whom I'll find on my journey.

I do know this: the Hollywood idea of death as painless and quick is a complete and utter lie. Those are the lucky ones, the souls hit and transitioned before they are even aware of it. But mostly, it's a process. Long and drawn-out and difficult. It can be years, months, weeks, but rarely is death a light switch. I stand at the end of that process. If death were easy, the balance in the universe would mean birth was just as simple, and any mother will tell you pregnancy and birth are complicated, painful processes. Except for the lucky ones, those few.

I don't bring death, just as obstetricians don't bring life. We simply are around it a lot. Them life, me death.

You don't have any idea how scary it is to see that expression come over someone, to see their eyes widen fractionally, to see the echoes of lives on their faces. To know who their soul mate is, know their child's middle name. Each soul that passes through leaves a part of itself behind. I feel the emotions and the memories of each life I escort. I recognize the calls of certain tree frogs as friends and family. I know the howl of a sibling coyote. I recognize addresses and phone numbers. They're just bits and pieces of emotion, but I carry them.

With each day and each soul, I carry more. Someday soon I'll have to find a way to let them go, but I am not a quilter.

No living creature sees us as pure light until they are ready to transition their energy. Light, heat, life, and movement are all energy. When the body dies, the energy lives on. That energy must go somewhere. It's a universal law. We are conduits. We move that energy by being alive, by being near transitional energy. By walking down the street, or running a marathon, or going on a trip. We are living, breathing windows for heaven. To put it plainly, we are born so they—so you—can die well and be at peace.

My name is Meridian Sozu. I am a Fenestra. I have always shared my world with the dead, and the soon-to-be dead. But I really didn't understand what that meant until the first day of my sixteenth year, my sophomore year of high school. You see, while we may be born to human mothers, we are taught as well. To understand the gravity and the glory of our existence. I am still learning and still looking.

I wish you luck with your death, but just in case, I, or one of my sisters, will be on the lookout for you. I'll be your window. And you'll rise.

Meridian Sozu, b. 1992

1. 2 Samuel 12:21
2. Deuteronomy 27:25
3. Genesis 6:5
4. Leviticus 20:22
5. Leviticus 20:27
6. Exodus 22:18
7. 2 Samuel 12:5
8. Judges 5:3
9. Judges 7:18
10. Exodus 4:10–12
11. Exodus 23:21
12. Leviticus 24:16
13. Leviticus 26:3–4
14. Leviticus 26:21–22
15. Numbers 11:1
16. Deuteronomy 13:10
17. Deuteronomy 4:4
18. Exodus 32:26
19. Leviticus 16:30
20. Deuteronomy 5:24, 27
21. 2 Samuel 12:19
22. 1 John 2:18
23. Judges 10:13–14
24. Deuteronomy 28:45
25. Proverbs 15:26, 29

Amber Kizer is addicted to trashy reality television, sour candy, loud pop music, and the scent of fresh lilies. Like Auntie in *Meridian,* Amber finds inspiration in quilting and baking. She likes to write with book-specific scented candles burning and a book-specific playlist going in the background (for this book, pine- and fir-scented candles and Celtic folk and rock music). She lives on an island with a menagerie of animals and too many yet-to-be-read books.

Amber Kizer's debut novel, *One Butt Cheek at a Time,* was named a New York Public Library Best Book for the Teen Age. She loves to visit schools and book clubs, and she enjoys hearing from readers via her official Web site, www.AmberKizer.com. You can learn more about Meridian at www.MeridianSozu.com.